PR/

SILK ROAD

"Randy Holland's Silk Road is a brilliant first novel depicting outlaw characters during a time when smuggling hash was an alternative to going to an Ivy league college. The characters are tough, colorful and fascinating. Based on a true story, the exploits of these rich characters is a hell of a journey and I enjoyed every page. Can't wait for Holland's next book. Highly recommended"

— Gerald Chamales,
Producer of Scorsese's THE IRISHMAN

Tracy,
Enjoy the ride!
& thanks for making
my Saturday breakfast
so enjoyable.
Best,

James R

SILK ROAD

From the True-life Adventures of a Legendary Smuggler

Randy Holland

Story by James Respondek

Respondek Publishing
15308 W Sunset Blvd
Pacific Palisades, CA 90272

First trade paperback edition August 2020

Cover by Rick Holland
Interior Design by Evan Conover

Printed in the United States of America

Library of Congress Cataloging-in-Publication Data has been applied for.

ISBN 978-1-7355888-0-3 (paperback)
ISBN 978-1-7355888-1-0 (ebook)

1977 PHOTO OF
JAMES RESPONDEK,
LEGENDARY SMUGGLER
WHOSE ADVENTURES
INSPIRED THIS BOOK.

SILK ROAD

1

Some of us are dead now so it's time to tell the story. It was the summer of '77. We were deep into risky business on the Silk Road, hung up in the town of Peshawar in northern Pakistan, waiting for word from the connection that our deal was a go. Explosive times. Dangerous times. A military coup had tanks rumbling through tense streets. Next door, India was nuclear. Iran was about to erupt in a revolution. On the other side of the Khyber Pass where we were to make our buy, the Russians were maneuvering into Afghanistan. American "advisors" were countering in the shadows. We were in the middle of it all seeking gold-at-the-end-of-the-rainbow, trying to score 200 kilos of hash.

Our connection was a mystery man with the street name Tariq Rahim. We'd heard he was a black sheep member of the recently deposed Pakistani royal family. He'd been elusive, hung up the deal for weeks. He'd send a little message to us at our hotel, *Be patient, be patient.* I figured he was vetting us. Maybe he'd heard we'd been briefly detained and questioned by the CIA in Kabul. Just when it seemed we might be getting burned for our initial down payment, a message came from Tariq. Jack and I were in the bar when Grant was summoned by a bellboy to a meeting with a somewhat furtive Asian beauty who told him the deal was on and we were to meet Tariq at a museum. Grant was so stunned by this chick he talked about her for days, "Karina... Karina," he'd say, in the cadence of the song. I wondered if she was not sent by Tariq but some scammer. Her name sounded fake and it was weird she'd only speak with Grant alone. In any case I followed her instructions.

We were quite a sight, the three of us from Down Under, walking in the marketplace. I figured we should blend in with the locals, so I'd bought the full Peshawari outfit -- the white turban, ballooning Gunga Din jodhpurs and a Nehru shirt that draped from my neck to my knees.

My partner Jack, a retired history and classics professor, witty and well connected and sporting a white linen suit, Panama hat and cane, was way too proud to change his southern gentleman threads. Besides, he was a humpback, and how do you disguise that?

My other cohort in crime was Grant, a laconic, charismatic smack aficionado, and a volatile mix of Irish, Greek and Aborigine. It gave him a sort of swarthy ethnicity that allowed him to blend in wherever we went – Egypt, Turkey, India and now Pakistan.

It was not the best mix of outfits or personalities. Jack and Grant had gotten off to a contentious start at the gate and it had been a rocky road between them since. My bad in a way because I'd brought Grant into the deal. I'd known him from the time we were teenage groms surfing Dee Why Point. We'd sold a ton of weed together over the years and had many adventures before he went to prison. When he got out, he needed a break and I needed a buffer from Jack's unwanted advances, so I brought Grant into the enterprise. At the start the three of us had agreed to function as a democracy, but anarchy often reigned. Getting the mates to agree on anything was such a hassle that at times I felt like pulling the plug on the whole deal. An agonizing prospect since we'd come ten thousand miles through a dozen countries, getting caught up in wars, revolutions, and coups. We'd almost been busted numerous times and had the CIA all over our asses. We'd been detained and hassled by Iranian border guards, Turkish bandits and Bombay policemen. There really was no turning back.

I was relieved when Tariq Rahim made contact, and the deal was finally a go. It required that a down payment of half the money be delivered to a tobacconist at his store in the bazaar. But as we stood outside the smoke shop, I had second thoughts about fronting the fifty grand in cash. Jack was cavalier about the danger. "My boy, we'll either get ripped off, killed, or be rich. Are we mice or men?"

"You a man, Jack? Or maybe just one big gammon?" Grant said.

Gammon meant fake in the Abo tongue, but Jack took it as a slur on his sexuality. Though gay as a day in May, he was never one to take a dig to his manhood without a riposte. "My rugged friend suffers under the delusion of Hollywood masculinity – when all he really seeks is..."

Jack let it hang, Grant took the bait, "Okay, Professor tell me what I really seek."

"A loving father."

That hit Grant hard and he just stared at him a moment, then, "Gubba..." which was Abo slang for white dude. "...you don't know shit about me."

"And apparently you don't know shit about yourself."

And so it went at times. They were like opposing thumbs that sometimes got together to fuck things up. Mid-journey Jack had developed a goofy crush on an American photojournalist who turned out to be working for the CIA. Grant, still wearing prison stripes of the mind, hated cops and burgled the guy's car. This shit put us on the radar of the Bureau Station Chief in Kabul, Afghanistan, a woman by the name of Patricia Adams. I had no idea there were boss female spooks, and it turned out she was the first. Soon I would be sleeping with her, but I didn't know that at the moment either.

"Fuck it. Let's do this," I said, and we went into the smoke shop. The old tobacconist checked me out in my native garb. "Lawrence of Arabia," he said, with a grin, baring his beetle-nut-stained teeth. "Tariq Rahim?" I said.

"But of course, you are making a delivery."

I handed him the money belt and he slung it over his shoulder. He gave us the location in Landi Kotal where we were to meet with our guide.

So we were pot committed as the saying goes and as I walked out into the bustle of the bazaar I found myself at the intersection of trepidation and relief. The deal was going forward, but it was to happen in a place we'd already been - Landi Kotal at the top of the Khyber Pass. This was a dangerous No Man's Land to the north along the border between Pakistan and Afghanistan. But I was not in control of the game. Tariq Rahim was making the rules, and I was just happy we were doing business.

Jack came out of the tobacco shop, opened a pungent tin of Balkin Sobranie cigarettes. He looked like a hip-jutting Cuban gangster in his wide-brimmed hat and Zoot suit. "All right, gentlemen, let's get you two some fire power," he said. Landi Kotal was a tribal outpost home to many warring factions and almost everyone up there had been packing firearms - the old farts, young studs, even the waiters. I imagined the women also sported AK's under their burka beekeeper suits.

Jack said, "Get a .357..." The Balkin smoke was blue and curled out of his nostrils after a French inhale. He was in full Jean Paul Belmondo mode. I thought he was joking but he pulled his coat open displaying a .357 Magnum in his waistband.

We were in the middle of the bazaar dense with locals so we were objects of interest. "What the fuck are you doing?"

"Forewarned is forearmed."

"We're not going up there packing," I said.

"Let's not be pussies now," he said, gripping the handle, smiling at Grant.

"Watch out you don't blow your budoo off," Grant laughed.

"It'll be a shit show. No guns," I said.

Jack liked the drama. He was actually hoping something would explode so he could pretend he was a gangster. I'd had enough drama on this trip already, and I knew Tariq Rahim wouldn't want us going up there armed. Besides, we'd have a guide for protection.

Jack held a PhD in classical lit and was given to theatrics. Waving the pistol, he shouted, "*Into the breech... when the blast of war blows in our ears, imitate the action of the tiger!*"

He was on stage and had an audience. Within moments we had a cadre of Pakistani cops elbowing through the crowd toward us. It turned out they'd been watching us. It was, to say the least, yet another unexpected development. And there'd

been a Greek tragedy's worth of those on this trip. Mr. Big, my
drug smuggling kingpin mentor back in Sydney, had warned
me to "expect the unexpected" in any smuggling operation,
but especially one in this part of the world. A crowded dark
cell loomed in our future. There was probably a whole shitload
of guys like us – call us entrepreneurs – in Pakistani prisons
and it looked like we might be joining them.

Grant grabbed Jack's wrist, wrenched the gun from him
and moved swiftly away through the crowd. The cops shouted
for him to stop, pulling their weapons. I was corralled and held
and so was Jack. As we were being searched, the cops yelled at
Grant who kept walking away. They caught up to him, spun
him around.

What was Grant going to do with that gun? Possibilities
were few and not promising. Half the time it was a mystery
why he did the things he did and the other half the motive
could only be pure self-destruction. It hadn't always been that
way. He was never the kid your parents wanted you to play
with and after he got out of prison he was a troubled soul at
times. I got the feeling he'd like nothing more than to stand in a
bullring blindfolded and see if he could take the rush of horns.

The police had Jack and me muscled into an alcove. They
searched us and were pissed when they didn't find the gun or
any drugs. They were sharp-faced, young, and wanted a bust
bad. I couldn't understand a word they were saying. Pashto,
Urdu? But I got the message as they shouted in my ear, slamming the rifle butt into my shoulder. I felt like a goldfish in a
piranha tank with all the people watching. One raised his rifle
butt to my nose threateningly, "Gun!?" Grant was ten yards
away in the crowded bazaar being searched. I knew he had

the .357 and we were all going down. Jack was giving his usual semi-true rap about being associated with the Aussie embassy. They pulled him by the hair, spun him around and slammed his face into a wall. He groaned, then laughed. They slapped him upside the head. One yanked my ponytail back so hard I was eyeballing the thatch of the overhang. Then just when I had surrendered to the prospect of spending a few years in a Pakistan jail, the nightmare ended. The soldiers searching Grant came back. They'd found no gun, no drugs and were grumbling. One last shove, they let us go and split.

When we were back out on the street Grant got in Jack's face. "That's twice you almost got us busted with your yabba mouth!"

"Sorry but you were the cause of the first one when you broke into Tim's car."

"Your budoo fix on the Brit press boy is what caused that shit in Kabul."

"No. I think it was you stealing his photographs."

I stepped in before Grant did some real damage. "The truth is you both put us in that CIA holding cell in Kabul."

Jack waved me off, "For God's sake we were in there all of ten minutes."

Actually, it was two days. The station chief, Patricia Adams, had sweated us hard and then abruptly cut us loose, which was a mystery in itself. I mean, she knew we were smugglers travelling on forged passports and could have turned us over to Interpol, but she'd let us go. A benevolent act of mercy from the spook? Naaa.

I asked Grant what he'd done with the gun. "Tossed it in a bloody trash can."

Jack was impressed, "And how is it they didn't see that?"

"Because I'm not a budoo loving pussy showoff waving it around, am I?"

"Au contraire. We all have our latent passions, don't we?"

Grant stared at him. Since he'd gotten out of prison he'd had an icy side I hadn't seen in all our years together. He'd always been unpredictable, but now he seemed truly scary at times. I could see Jack was unnerved to the point of silence, which was unusual for him.

"Hey come on," I said. "We're partners, right? We've all fucked up a time or two. Remember back in Istanbul when I blew it and let that hooker steal the money belt?"

Grant laughed. "Yeah. Classic, mate."

"Jack got it back for us, remember? And Jack saved your ass in London when you overdosed, didn't he?"

Grant conceded the point, crouched into a boxer's stance, threw a few mock punches at Jack, then patted him softly on the cheek. "Don't worry, Professor. I love ya." And suddenly we were all right again.

2

Sydney, Australia – my early days

Why someone becomes a dealer seems a less interesting question than how. I was thirteen. Just transplanted to Australia from Texas. My dad had died in a San Antonio hospital after a long and painful illness. My mom had four boys to raise on her own and so she moved us all back to her hometown of Sydney where she had family. It was 1967, the world was going through some big changes and so was I. A cataclysmic upheaval inside and out that I didn't understand. But it sure was exciting. My Bobby Darrin and Beach Boys albums went sailing over a fence while I rocked to the Beatles, the Stones, and the Who smashing their way into revolution. The Vietnam War had turned society on its ear, throwing raw guts and death onto living room TVs. Kids not much older than me were in the streets carrying signs protesting the war. Hippies were in the parks smoking weed, taking acid, finding God.

I fell into the waves and found religion and solace there. On the beach I discovered pot, smoking doobies with surf buds. I realized early on that if I wanted something like a matchbox of weed, or a surfboard, a new album or a bike, I couldn't hit on my poor mum for the dough. She was working two jobs to support our family. So I found jobs after school and in summer. I was a kid with an entrepreneurial spirit who fate sort of nudged into the drug trade. My first job was a harbinger of my future dealing career. I worked for a pharmacy delivering prescription meds. So I worked hard and in the summer before my senior year, moved up the employment ladder to a job working construction.

The blue-collar world had its benefits and its drawbacks. On the downside, laborers started work at the crack of dawn. Which meant I had to forego my usual morning surf. I noticed there was one guy on the job who had the luxury of arriving several hours after the rest of us. Hair still wet from the waves, this guy would roll up in his new cherry pickup truck with a surfboard in the back along with his plumber's tools, welding tanks and copper pipes. He unrolled a mosaic of building plans, did a few calculations and I was intrigued. "You surfed this morning?"

"That's right, mate," he said.

"How is it you can show up late like this?"

"I'm a plumber," he said as he put on a pair of road warrior goggles. He flicked on his acetylene oxy torch and began welding. His crisscrossing sculpture of copper beauty running along the studs took about two hours and then he packed up his tools.

"Done for the day? You must have a cool boss," I said.

"I'm me own boss, mate."

He was his own boss? I asked him how much a plumber makes.

"Oh, about a thousand a week."

I told my mum I was dropping out of school in the fall to be a plumber. She stayed calm but I could see she was thinking I'd lost my mind. "You're a straight A student, James. You could be a doctor or lawyer, an engineer or a businessman."

But I didn't see myself in a suit behind a desk like my dad. I thought of him working all those years and then dying young. Maybe I'd be dying young too. Maybe I had the same sickness coursing through my blood and bones as him. So carpe diem, baby.

By the age of seventeen I was doing pretty well as an apprentice plumber. I had a car, surfboards, girlfriends, and plenty of pot. I bought mostly from Grant, who'd grown up with surf wax on his soles. He was a couple years older and kind of a legend as a really good, fearless, badass rider of waves. And to tell the truth, we were all a little scared of him because he'd throw down in a hot second, especially if anyone gave him shit about being part Abo. That prejudice against Aborigines wasn't new. By his looks you couldn't really tell for sure what his ethnicity was, but the word was out.

I'd buy a matchbox full of primo weed from him for five bucks, which was good for five pencil thin joints. One glorious day of surf and sun I'd had the ride of my life and was rolling up a congratulatory doobie when one of my surf-buds asked to buy one. Okay, I said, two bucks. Then another mate came out of the lineup and wanted to buy one. Cool, two bucks. And then another grom did the same. So I had sold three joints for six bucks. I had made a buck and had two joints for myself and then came the Ah Ha moment. I went back to Grant and bought another matchbox. Grant gave me the stink eye and said, "Hey, bunji, you're cutting in on my turf."

His lean, broad-shouldered frame leaned in on me, tough and edgy. But he had a funny side and it came out, cracking a joke about me being a natural born salesman. He sold me the matchbox, I rolled up five joints and sold them all before dusk. I caught some waves and had my friends asking to buy more. I was now officially a dealer.

My little matchbox pot biz took off. Sales were so good I moved up to buying an ounce for thirty bucks, cutting it up into ten matchboxes, making twenty dollars each. And then I figured if I bought a pound for $200 and sold sixteen ounces for thirty bucks each, I could make $280 bucks a shot. Buy wholesale, sell retail. I realized Grant was right – I was a natural.

Before long I convinced Grant that we should partner up. We were a good team because he had connections to quantity but the Abo side of him hated to hustle, preferring to stroll his own road at his own pace. He stood out in a crowd and he'd been snagged off the beach to act in a couple of movies, but quit because he didn't like all the ass-kissing that went with being an actor. His big loves were surfing and his dog - a royal blue Afghan hound that waited for him on the beach, usually sitting right next to his classic '54 XK 120 Jag. He also had a mean old mare he'd rescued that was pals with the hound. This horse was unpredictable and might bite your fingers if you tried to give her a carrot. Like his horse, Grant didn't play by the rules. Red lights weren't for him. A ticket? Fuck it. A few nights in jail? So what. There was something magnetic about his unpredictability. One day he might be all cool and laid back, and the next day it was cut, slash, rip, burn and tear through life. "Leave vital, jagged edges, mate," he once said, I think because his view of things was that the world was going crazy. Even the rock world was all wacked out according to Grant. Woodstock had given way to the Hells Angels at Altamont. The Sixties had produced the night of the living dead. Charlie Manson and his psycho cheerleaders had proven there was a dark underbelly to the counter-culture vision of a social paradise. People were all divided up by race and class. The Russians and Americans were threatening each other with nuclear war. A megaton conflagration would wipe out the rest of us anyway so what the fuck, why not make a few bucks and surf while you could? Or so Grant said. This only augmented thoughts about the possibly precarious blood I had running through my veins like my dear old dad.

I hadn't thought a whole lot about this stuff since I was too busy hustling. We'd smoke a couple joints, get to talking and I could see we had certain similar philosophies. Work hard, get paid, surf, go out with pretty girls, smoke pot and ride motorcycles. Freedom! I had no idea that this path of freedom was heading toward a stretch behind bars.

3

The Buy – Peshawar, '77

Pakistan was right up there with Turkey on my list of least desirable places to be in jail. This was in the days of *Midnight Express* so the horrors of these places were graphic and fresh in the minds of smugglers plying the trade along the Silk Road. Even before our close call in the marketplace, I was looking over my shoulder for lawmen be they CIA, local police or the Pakistan army. Nervous as I was, we'd come too far to back out now, so the show carried on. We went back to our hotel in Peshawar to get a solid night's sleep before our journey up to Landi Kotal. My plan was to get up there, meet our contact, buy our load, and return to Peshawar all in one day. Spending the night in risky territory didn't seem like such a smart idea.

The next morning we hit the road at dawn. It was only a fifty-kilometer trip, but what a long and intense drive through the Khyber Pass it was. Two lanes of rutted dirt winding up over precipitous crags and plunging canyons through clouds of dust and gravel that covered everything in brown. Occasionally there was the lone tree, or the scavenging bush trying to survive in what seemed like the most inhospitable terrain outside of

Death Valley. The cars, the mules, the grasshoppers all had a sepia coating. We bounced past broken down trucks, and then had to careen around a psychedelic bus out of Peshawar that looked like it had been painted by the Merry Pranksters. There were dare-devil bicyclists hanging on to the back being towed as they fish-tailed around a bend just inches from the cliff edge. Overheated cars were stopped here and there. Men with dust covered canvas water bags tried to calm angry radiators and deal with finger-scorching caps.

There were soldiers everywhere, driving, walking, standing, watching, through the whole trip and up to the top of the pass where a mile-long line of cars awaited inspection and suddenly we were at rest, waiting with them. "Oh, my aching back, I need a couch," Jack said.

Grant growled, "Some painkillers. That's what you need."

"And I know what you need, my boy."

"Yeah? And don't tell me it's a daddy."

"Love."

"Love..." Grant fell silent, as though the word was a shadow with a will of its own. "Wonder what happened to that chick Karina."

"Love," Jack went on, knowing once again he'd hit the mark. "As Romeo says, *A preserving sweet. A choking gall. A madness most discrete.*"

"Madness, yeah," Grant said.

"You ever been mad about anyone, Grant? Heart in a cheese grater mad?"

Grant was silent. I had never known him to be wildly in love. He usually just jumped from chick to chick. But it seemed like there was someone from the past scratching their way to the surface. And it wasn't Karina.

"Like James and his girl Andi. He's mad about her but then he'll fuck the next little tart he sees. Even the CIA bitch. You would have fucked her, wouldn't you?"

"Shut up," I said, even though it was true. Take one for the team with a hot older chick? Sure. Maybe I was just edgy from the precarious drive and I couldn't get the tape player to work. "It's the goddamn dust," I complained. The windows were down and the air conditioner was on strike.

"The dust that buried the bones," Jack said.

"Now what bloody bones would those be?" Grant asked. Most times he would feign disinterest in Jack's great wellspring of knowledge, but in truth he soaked it up.

"The bleak bones buried in the dirt and in the crags and the caves of this treacherous land that so many have come to conquer and so many have died trying. Alexander the Great, the British twice in the 19th century, the Americans and Russians of today..."

"This place is bloody purgatory. Why would they want it?" Grant asked.

"Because it's here. For adventure. For power, for money. And we're the same, mates. Seeking our fortune in this beautiful wasteland."

"You just said it was treacherous."

"Treacherous can be beautiful, no? Like you my fine friend."

Grant laughed. You never knew what the fuck he was going to laugh at. We rolled up to an inspection station. The guards seemed quite amused by us and I have no idea why. But better an amused guard than a suspicious one, and we passed right on through. I hoped the return crossing would be as trouble free.

We finally made it into Landi Kotal which, even with all the burkas and turbans, had the look and feel of an El Paso or Tombstone of the old Wild West. We went to an open-air saloon/coffee joint for our rendezvous with the guide known as Azziz. We three Aussies stuck out like a dog's balls. Picture Truman Capote, Brando, and me the pony-tailed blond faux Peshawari. We sat down at a roughhewn table, ordered coffee and zarda, a Pakistani dessert that looks like a plate of worms but is actually delicious. We waited for Azziz. We were by this time very good at waiting because we'd had a lot of practice with Tariq Rahim. Couple hours later a hulking, bearded local came up to our table, covered in brown dust. "The drive from Peshawar is like a curse from God."

"Hellish indeed," Jack said.

Azziz coughed, and remnants of his journey fell from his pajamas onto our table.

"Azziz?" I asked.

"Al-salaam alaikum." Azziz was large like a linebacker gone to donuts and Spam, bald, missing more than a few teeth. A huge waffle of a hand that you didn't want to see clenched into a fist waved at me. "And you are James," he said, his Paki accent obscuring some further words that left him grinning, most likely at my localized getup.

"At your service, cowboys." We followed him outside to a beat-up Toyota sedan, white underneath a speckled veneer of road dirt and bugs. We climbed into our Range Rover and fell in behind him as he led us out of Landi Kotal about three miles up the highway to an overgrown mountain path that was barely wide enough for a motorcycle. Behind us, way off in the distant valley, we could see Peshawar through a brownish haze. But it soon disappeared as we wound up into the dun colored hills on a rocky switchback trail.

We bounced along for an hour winding deeper into nowhere until eventually all signs of civilization disappeared. Finally rolling up to a few huts with a herd of goats and a couple of kids running around, they swarmed our vehicles with their palms outstretched, begging for money and cigarettes. We paid the toll and kept on bumping along.

Beyond the huts, cradled in a valley surrounded by hills, we came to a sprawling brick and wood fort with walls thirty-feet high and thick wooden gates cross-buttressed with iron. Ahmed stopped when we were confronted by turbaned guards with bandoliers crossing their chests and AK 47s at the ready. A few stepped up to Ahmed's sedan and others came to us staring, rifles poised.

We were like interlopers from another universe getting the full inspection. A whole platoon of turbaned bandits on the parapets had weapons trained on us. Hounds were barking. I heard Dylan in my head, *"All along the watchtower, princess kept the view..."*

This was the showdown moment of our whole adventure. Azziz was out of his jalopy talking with an armed sentry while other guards encircled our Rover.

"Outside in the distance a wildcat did growl, two riders were approaching, the wind began to howl..."

The sentry questioning Ahmed stepped over to his brother-in-arms who was watching us. They conferred in Pashto then pulled out a walkie-talkie. We waited ten tense minutes, not knowing what the fuck was going to happen. Then two more Afghans toting Kalashnikovs came out of the fort through a door in the gate. One leaned in the window inches from my face. He smelled of tobacco and onions. He was absolutely a mountain man, the kind who could barefoot it over rocks. "You... out of car," he said in English blurred by a thick accent, his meaning clear as the sky that seemed so much more friendly and peaceful than this scene we'd found ourselves in. We did as we were told. He said, "You carry weapons?"

"Us? No, never!" I said, shooting Jack a look like how dumb and useless a .357 pistol would be right now. The massive wooden gates creaked open on burly hinges that craved oil. We drove into the courtyard and saw groups of bandits hanging around, guns slung over their shoulders. "Welcome to Xanadu," Jack mused. "The ghost of Coleridge awaits us."

"Whatever the fuck that means," I said. "Please do not be talking shit to them."

He recited a few lines to the guard, "*In Xanadu did Kubla Khan a stately pleasure dome decree...*" The guard had no idea what he was talking about. "You're right. They'll understand Shangri-La." sweeping his hand toward the walls of the fort. "Shangri-La!"

The guard nodded "Yes. Shangri-La!" Apparently, this was an Urdu word meaning pass through the mountains. It didn't look that idyllic to me. The moment we got out of our car we were going to know in ten seconds if we'd be scoring or if they'd put a bullet in the back of our heads and throw us down one of their shit holes.

4

"Be careful what you wish for because you might get it." When I first heard that platitude it made about as much sense to me as a desk job in an office without windows. I mean who wouldn't want what they wished for? I wished for an adventure with a pot of gold reward. Only when the road ended at the fort in a life-threatening situation did I grasp the truth of that sage adage. In my previous career as a dealer there had been warnings and situations to foreshadow the coming disaster. Naturally I ignored them. Youth thinks it knows everything, can survive anything. A fatherless kid sometimes learns quickly he might have a lucky gift for handling unexpected predicaments.

Grant and I had moved up the food chain. We'd hop-scotched over our various middlemen and were dealing weed by the bushel-full, scoring direct from Sweepo, the underworld crime boss at the top of the Sydney drug ladder. This mobster had it all, beach pad, penthouse in town, a fleet of cars, a boat, a trophy wife, and a goombah entourage. I wanted all those things except the crowd of gangsters and the notoriety. I preferred doing biz on the down low. I floored it occasionally in the fast lane, but I also knew that a dealer needed stealth to avoid the law. Which was why I continued my plumbing biz as a front. I thought I was way too slick and smart for the cops. The truth is I was incredibly lucky. But even Lady Luck can get trumped by hubris and greed and it's the rare teen who understands that. Lessons like those come from Greek tragedy or from sitting on a wise daddy's knee.

The intrigue and the money had us taking chances. "No guts, no glory. In it to win it, right, mate?" Grant would laugh. He was known for his critical late takeoffs over sharp shallow reefs and he had a road map of laceration scars to prove it. He was one of the few mates I ever knew who truly didn't give a shit what anyone thought. Unless it was something disparaging about his heritage. Then he could launch and get high profile all the way. His motto was never a thought for the future. He'd draw me in along his wild side, pry bar me out of the security-encased vision of the "Good Life" that I had all mapped out: to build up a sizeable bank account then retire from the pot biz and buy a plumbing outfit or get into real estate. The truth being I was living the dream with blinders on. Arrogantly oblivious that we were being watched by the cops. We were in business with a major underworld figure. How did I not see that he was on law enforcement radar and therefore so were we?

We were doing such lucrative deals with this crime boss that we rented a three-story manor house in an upscale neighborhood called Killarney Heights. We had the full-on department store of drugs going. First floor was weed, second floor hash, third floor Buddha Sticks and hash oil.

Business was going so great if we sold stock options they

would have gone through the roof. We had quite a lively scene going and were a bit more notorious than we should have been. It was a night like any other. Party till the red birds sing, a few joints left on the table, some coke spilled on the rug, a lude in the cushions, me on the third floor curled up in dreamland with my sweet thing sleeping au natural by my side. Grant in his room on the second floor in pretty much the same scenario. And suddenly the world exploded. Front and back doors crashed in, the cops yelling "Police! We have a warrant!"

I ran to the stairs, looked down, saw Grant on the floor in the entryway in his skivvies being handcuffed, his girlfriend looking terrified. Cops and detectives swarming all over. I told myself, *Never mind the little shit, get to the Big Stash*! My girl was by my side freaked out. I said, "Go down there."

"What??"

"Go down there naked. Buy me five minutes. Faint, do something. Five minutes."

I ran off to the bathroom, locked the door, and pulled twenty pounds of weed in a gym bag from the bottom of a towel hamper. But even a plumber can't flush a load that size. I looked around for a place to stash it. A cop wanted in, "Open up! Police!"

I prayed for a stash place. I looked to heaven. God bless the architect who designed that house. There was a high-pitched ceiling built in the open style, lower part sealed, but the upper area had exposed rafters. I climbed up on the sink, shoved the gym bag packed with grass down through the exposed part into the sealed section by the eaves. The cop slammed against the door shouting for me to come out. I pulled my shorts down, sat on the toilet, and the door crashed open. A couple cops stood there looking at me, an officer came in, identified himself as Detective Marx, held up a warrant. I flushed the toilet.

Marx looked around the bathroom, gingerly sniffed, "Apparently you're one of the precious few in this world whose shit doesn't stink." Then he had his guys tear the room apart. God, or the Higher Power, the Big Amigo or whatever you call him had answered my foxhole prayer and the cops didn't find the weed. Marx, the lead detective, chewed on a toothpick, looking at me for an unnervingly long time. It was almost a look of appreciation. "It's here," he said. "We'll revisit this." The cops searched the rest of the house and found the roaches and a few ludes, some scales. In the garage they found ten ounces of Buddha sticks in my van. In my room they found two pickle jars full of cash. "So... what do we have here?" Marx asked.

"Plumbing money. My savings." He counted it: six grand. He handed me the dough to count before he held it as evidence. I wondered if he was an honest cop and decided to try some enticement. "Six grand? What do you know. I thought I only had five." I peeled off a thousand, put it in his shirt pocket, "This extra thousand must be for the policeman's fund."

Marx smiled, removed the money and put it with the rest of the cash he had now confiscated, "We can add bribery to the possession and dealing charges."

They let the girls go and they ran Grant and me in, booked us and locked us up in separate cells. After letting us sweat for a while, Marx came in and cut right to want he wanted from me. He offered me a "deal." I set up Sweepo the big underworld boss I was buying from and he would drop the possession charge, and the bribery, give me a pass on the dealing.

"I'm a plumber. Not a dealer. That money came from good

honest hard work."

"I don't call burglary honest work."

"Burglary?" I said.

He looked at me, "Come on now. We've got you dead to rights. You're the cat-burglar." He pulled a sketch out of a folder. "We have this artist's rendering of the cat burglar from an eyewitness. That's you, mate." It did look more than a bit like me. "The burglaries were done around the area where you hang out at Newport Beach. So you play ball with me and I'll do what I can to squash the burglary case."

I was almost disappointed I couldn't do it. Number one, I wasn't the cat burglar. Second, if I set Sweepo up I'd be dead, or, if they couldn't find me, he'd take revenge on my mum and my brothers.

"I am a plumber, sir."

"Plumber, huh?"

"Right you are, sir."

"And all the drugs and paraphernalia we found... just recreational."

"Exactly."

"Plumber? What brand of solder do you use?"

"Worthington. Acid flux."

He asked me another trick question about plumbing, which I answered. He stared at me, then stared at the sketch, thinking. A cop came in and told him his wife had called again. "Fuck," he said. He slid the sketch back into the folder and left.

Grant and I were arraigned in court the next day on a slate of charges that would have us behind bars for years to come. Bail was set was set at some enormous amount. I whispered to Grant, "Can you come up with anything?"

"Just what we have stashed," he said. "Don't worry, I'll bust us out when we get to the big house."

"What about your dad? Could he come up with something?"

"Yeah. A letter recommending they send me away for life."

His dad was a hard ass old sunburned Irish rancher, a bitter alcoholic who hated him for some crazy reason related to Grant's mum. My mum didn't have any money so all Grant and I had was our dough that was either confiscated or tied up in weed. And we couldn't sell the weed now for obvious reasons. "Maybe your mum could sell my Jag. But as for my dad? Forget it. He wouldn't even take care of my dog." Luckily Mum came through for us and sold the Jag. She met us on the street. She was in tears, holding a newspaper with a front-page story about us being busted and how I was suspected of being the Newport Cat Burglar.

"My son," she said, "I know you're not this cat burglar. You're much better looking. And I know you're not a thief. We'll get the authorities to see the truth. Don't worry."

Mum had to return to work and Grant and I went to a pub, ate fish and chips and examined our options. They didn't really have anything big on Grant and would eventually have to drop his case. Meanwhile, I was looking at no less than a few years behind bars if the cops tried to pin the cat burglar rap on me.

"You could split," Grant said. "I'll go with you. We'll head to the States."

I was touched at the show of brotherhood, "You'd chuck everything?"

"New adventure, mate. Move to Oahu. Plenty of surf, chicks and pakalolo. Mob brothers to the end."

Our moment of grim solidarity was interrupted when we glanced at the door and saw Detective Marx walk in. He came over and sat at the table with us. "How's things going, boys?" he asked.

"What the fuck, gangie?" Grant said.

"Shut up, punk," Marx said. "We're going to have a talk."

"Yabba someplace else," Grant said and rose but I put a hand on his shoulder and sat him back down.

I figured Marx was there for another attempt at selling me on the plea bargain. "I can't do what you want," I said.

"Oh, you're going to do what I want, all right."

I looked at Grant, and we both thought the same thing – they found the weed stashed in the bathroom rafters.

"No," he said like he was reading our minds, "we didn't find it yet, but we will. If I don't get what I want."

I resolved then to take Grant's advice and get out of Dodge.

"I've got Sweepo all wrapped up on tax evasion." Sweepo was the dealer he wanted. "I don't need you to nab him." Hmmmm, I thought, you never know when opportunity knocks.

"So what are you doing here fucking yabbin' with us, then?" Grant asked.

"Got a very pressing problem. And you're going to help me fix it. And then I'm going to make all your troubles go away."

If he wasn't referring to Sweepo, then what the fuck "problem" was he talking about? There was a moment where it all just settled. Marx looked around as though to see if anyone was listening, then he leaned in across the table and spoke softly. "I want my daughter to have a beautiful wedding."

We didn't know what to say to that – yeah, fine, cool, hope

it happens? He looked at us serious as could be, "You know
what it's like to come home and have your wife hysterical? Your
daughter freaking out? Caterers calling, planners waiting to
hear when the fucking room addition will be finished. I need
to get my bloody room addition finished because the reception
will be in there." Grant and I exchanged a look. "You blokes
really are plumbers, right?"

"I'm the plumber. Grant's the business manager."

"Damn plumbers I hired disappeared on me. Nuptials are
in two weeks. The floor slab needs to be poured and we can't
do it until the pipes are in. So you are going to set the pipes."

Grant was about to tell Marx to fuck off, but I put my
hand on his shoulder again which usually worked when it was
time to calm him down. He bit his lip staring at the detective
and let me handle it because if there was a fast-talking bullshit
artist between the two of us it was me. "Uhhh, so... Detective
Marx. You're saying..."

"I'm saying, lay the pipes and...you'll walk. I know you're
not the cat burglar. You understand what I'm saying."

I got the pipes laid and the slab was poured. The wedding
was on and Marx was a happy man. A few days later Grant and
I went to the courthouse with our attorney and we saw Marx
having a casual talk with the Crown Prosecutor. The judge gave
me probation for the ounces. The bribery charge was stricken
from the record. The suspicion that I was the cat burglar was
a thing of the past. All charges against Grant were dropped.
The gavel banged and we were out of there free men.

Grant patted me on the back, "Remember everything I
said about you wasting your time in the plumbing biz? Forget
I yabbered all that. I'm buying you new pipe-wrenches and a

blow torch!"

Ambitious and practical as I was, the plumbing trade was staying a part of my future. But then so was dealing. I figured luck and pluck would always get me through whatever dicey situations I might face as Grant and I ramped up our business. We gave nary a thought to Detective Marx's sage advice to tread the straight and narrow. Of course, at that time I had no idea that a few years down the line we'd be staring at 200 kilos of pure hash on the winding Silk Road.

5

The Bad Lands of Afghanistan, '77

A thousand hash and weed deals after our close shave with Detective Marx – whose warning to keep our noses clean went ignored – we were risking our freedom, if not our lives, to make the Big Score. A rotund Afghan pirate brandishing a machine gun came up and checked us out. A vicious-looking hound at his side eyed us as well.

Grant eased his long frame out of the car and rearranged his package. He looked at the dog, "Reminds me of Bunji," he said referring to his hound back home. Bunji meant best friend in the Abo tongue. He put his hand out to pet the beast, which I thought was asking for a chomp, but the hound liked him, enjoyed his muzzle scratch. Grant had a special way with animals. It surprised the steely pirate. By his confidence and the deference paid to him I figured this was the Chief of the hash operation. He looked at us like he was inspecting a tray of spoiled meats. He called Azziz over and had an old buddy chat in Pashto or maybe it was Urdu. Grant, looking around at the men and artillery, "Don't look like no Shangri-La to me, Jacko." Jack stood by the car mopping the dirt and dust from his face with a handkerchief. "Maybe it's Hades. And that's the hound from hell."

Jack had dogs of his own, but this beast did not like him and growled, straining at the leash. The Chief pointed to Jack and said something derogatory about him that made Azziz laugh. Jack knew they were making fun of him. I didn't give a shit what they thought. We were finally here, and the hash was here. Make the fucking deal and split. But Jack was not one to take prejudice lightly. "Excuse me. You have some comment about my attire or my person? Is there a problem?"

"No. No," Azziz assured him, "You are friends of Tariq. You are welcome here." He bowed to Jack. Jack just stared at the Chief. To diffuse the tension, I shook the Chief's hand in the old hearty American way jacking it up and down like it was a pump in the desert. Definitely an awkward but encouraging cultural exchange. The Chief spit a trailing brown glob into the dirt and walked over to a carpet. Azziz led us over to him and we all plopped down. "Tea and cupcakes?" the Chief asked as though we were sitting in Piccadilly.

"You have a real drink?" Jack asked. "Alcohol? Vodka, beer? It's been a bloody long drive."

The Chief was not happy. "Alcohol haram. The Qur'an forbids it."

"What kind of pirate doesn't drink? Never trust a man who doesn't drink," Jack said.

"They're Muslims, Professor," Grant explained. "Booze is bung with them." Bung was the Abo word for no good.

It was tense again. I said, "Oh hell yeah, we love tea and cupcakes, thank you very much."

Some feathers were ruffled, but a couple of the hash men brought out a silver tray with a beautiful teapot and little cups and cupcakes. The cupcakes had sprinkles on them. Made by Sarah Lee. American cupcakes in the wilds of the Kush. They'd had an even longer journey than we did getting here and seemed less in line for disappearance than us at that moment.

Another silver platter arrived. This one with little fingers of various types of hash. The Chief said, "Decide what you like."

"What we'd like," Jack said, making a show of wiping his face with his lace kerchief, "is some goddamn shade. Might we reconvene out of the sun?" I knew what he was doing now. Showing off for Grant, subtext being, *You're not the only badass among us.*

The Chief issued orders and soon four of his men were holding a large purple batik over us, offering shade as we scored a hundred grand worth of hash.

I nudged Jack, "You trying to blow this deal?"

"He's a homophobic asshole. Fuck him and his dog." He hissed it under his breath but the Chief's eyes narrowed and moved to the machine gun at his feet. It felt as if only our association with Tariq Rahim was keeping us alive just then.

Grant was looking around, maybe counting how many guys there were on the parapets with AK's. "Opium?" Grant said to the Chief.

"Opium?"

"Yeah, mate. You have some deadly for sale?"

"Deadly?" the chief asked.

"Just means awesome, that's all." I explained. Scoring O was a weird twist that normally I would have squashed immediately, but maybe it was just the diversion we needed.

"You come for hash and now you want opium?"

"Both," Grant said. "No worries, mate. No sorry business."

"We have opium," the Chief said. "Stand up." Grant eased to his feet, seeming even here to own the space he was in. The Chief checked him out. He'd made his assessments of Jack and me and now it was Grant's turn. I thought, this could go really good or really sideways. Grant was cool as the hound nuzzled his hand. The Chief seemed to appreciate that and had one of his men lead him to a storage room nearby.

I was all smiles thinking one of us had to play politics. I looked at the slabs of hash we had to choose from like I was deciding which nugget to grab out of a box of chocolates. They were all slightly different colors, textures, smells, and each one looked like it packed a wallop.

Jack said, "Smoke a pipe-load of each."

"A *toke*, okay. One toke." If we smoked some of each we'd get so high that we couldn't conduct business or defend ourselves. It had always been my policy not to get stoned while doing business.

I cut a small pinch off a slab, put it on the end of a stick, and spot burned it. It flamed, and I blew it out, then sniffed it just a bit. I passed it to Jack. We did that with all the samples and decided we'd go with the blonde.

"We'll buy two hundred kilos," I said.

"Six hundred American dollars each," the Chief said. I tried to haggle but the price was firm.

"Now about transport? How do we stash this in our Range Rover?"

"Since you are friends of Tariq Rahim, we will help you." The Chief had two mechanics come out and inspect our car. We had plywood roof racks and I said we were thinking about hollowing those out to stash the hash.

"Amateur. We have better method," he said. "False-bottom petrol tank." He explained, "We take gas tank out, weld in a secret chamber inside."

"Okay, that's good. Hermetically sealed? Dogs can't smell through it?"

"Safe. Even from x-rays."

I said, "Okay, great. Let's do it. We want to be back in Peshawar by nightfall." Suddenly it was all going swimmingly.

But the Chief shook his head. "Impossible. Tomorrow is the start of Ramadan. There is no work done during the holy days by the faithful. Only fast and pray."

I couldn't believe it. "What about the unfaithful? Could they do the work?"

He didn't like the joke. "There are no unfaithful here."

"So when is Ramadan over?"

"A few weeks."

"Are you bloody kidding?" Jack said.

"You will leave your car here."

"No fucking way."

"You must leave the vehicle and the work will be done when you return." He gave us a my-way-or-the-highway shrug.

"We're not bloody leaving our Rover," Jack said, afraid it could get ripped off. That Rover was the mack-daddy vehicle for their terrain. You can pack a lot of AKs in that baby, some surface-to-airs, bazookas.

"If we leave the Rover, how do we get back down to Peshawar?" I asked.

"With Azziz." He indicated our guide who was arm wrestling with some muscle men nearby.

"Great, the four of us piling in that little rattletrap excuse of an automobile?" Jack said. "Not going to happen."

"As you wish," the Chief said.

I tried to reason with Jack, but he was adamant about not leaving our $50,000 vehicle and waiting weeks to complete the deal. "We'll drive back down to Peshawar and when all the fasting and praying is done, and the chanting from the bell towers 4am to midnight, when all that's done, and if we haven't found another deal, maybe we'll come back up and make the buy. And *wait* here for the Rover."

Grant came back to us holding a baseball-sized lump of opium. "This is all they have." He picked up on what was going down, "Whoa. Tense. Thought we had a nice little mob going here."

Apparently, the Chief had seen American gangster films and didn't like the connotation. "Mob? You say we are a mob?"

"It's an Abo word for family," I explained. He still didn't quite know what was up. "Aborigine. His tribe. Family. Like you mates here." The Chief laughed as Grant scratched the hound's ear. Once again I thought all was well, but then Jack stirred the shit up again.

"You want us to leave the car here for a month," Jack said. "A fucking bloody *month*??"

"Why don't you calm down gubba," Grant said. "It's Ramadan. If we don't do it his way, we take a loss on the fifty grand."

"*We* take a loss? You mean James and I take a loss." The truth was clear as Grant, though an equal partner, wasn't invested. "We'll get the money back from Tariq," Jack said.

Grant laughed, "Sorry, Professor, that ain't the way it works in this game. No moola refunds."

It was obvious we weren't going to get our investment back.

This was their world, their rules. But while Jack could charm the pants off a kangaroo, he could also be a fucking hardhead. "I say we return to Peshawar and try for the money. If we don't get it then we come back and do it his way."

The Chief dismissed him with a wave of his hand, "We make deal now or not happen. No *coming back*. That is security risk Tariq does not permit."

"Tariq should have told us it was Ramadan. So fuck it," Jack said.

I chimed in quickly, "Sorry. No disrespect intended. It's just that the delay wasn't in our plans."

"Inshallah. God has his own plan, eh."

Jack snorted, "Sounds like Tariq is God around here."

I had always known that Jack had a self-destruct button. He had fantasies about going out in some gloriously heroic way that would have all the students who had ridiculed him over the years for his hunchback and his fey demeanor take back their put-downs and genuflect. I just never figured I'd be part of his death myth. But there it was being created before my eyes. The Chief reached for the machine gun lying at his feet. As his hand went to the stock, I put my hand on the stock too. "Easy, take it easy," I said. We were in a bubble for about a second, then rifles were pointed at us from all over. No joke was going to fix this situation. No pleasant handshake. And no amount of money.

Grant shoved his hand down his pants and came out with a snub-nose .38. A sentry sprang up behind Jack and I saw a flash of silver as he unsheathed his pulwar dagger and brought that long curved blade to Jack's throat. The steel pressed into Jack's Adam's apple, blood trickled. My partner in crime was about to get beheaded, and Grant and I had machine guns encircling us. One little itchy trigger finger - and maybe Grant's was the itchiest – and we'd all be dead.

6

Time lurched to a stop and I saw the future. Grant would aim his little peashooter at the Chief. He'd be cut down like he was in a spaghetti western. Jack would crumple to the dirt with his neck severed like a sacrificial cow. And I'd die in a fusillade thinking about how much more desirable a desk job would be. Back home there would be a little obit about the young adventurer who died seeking his fortune on the Silk Road.

People can react in strange ways in situations of great danger. I tend to stay calm. I looked at Grant who sported a firm smile that was not so much calm as determined. I saw his hand rise up – the hand holding the .38 - and I thought okay, this is it. That gun raised, but then it turned toward Jack, the butt slamming into his face square between the eyes. Jack sprawled backwards onto the dirt, knocked out cold.

The Chief was stunned. The fort compound was pregnant with silence. Then the Chief nodded to Grant – "Dirty Harry. Okay." Everybody laughed. Except Jack, of course, who was unconscious. He lay there like a dead soldier while I finalized the deal with our Afghan hosts. We'd leave the Rover and return for it at the end of Ramadan. A couple Afghan women came out of the fort and dabbed Jack's bloody dirty face with wet cloths. He woke up sputtering, trying to figure out what had happened. "That sonofabitch Grant broke my nose! Where is that bloody primate?"

I took him off to the side, "Look, mate, I made the deal and we are leaving the Rover."

He wiped blood off his face onto the fine white linen of his sleeve. "Never! Not doing business with those..."

"Jack, shut the fuck up," I said.

"Grant hit me!"

"Goddamn right. That's why you're still alive. It's done. We've come all this way. And we've forked out fifty grand. We have to do it Tariq's way."

"Fuckin' A," Grant muttered, wandering over, blowing a pretty blue puff of opium smoke out his nose. He looked like some mad Bedouin prince, eyes scanning the courtyard through half closed lids, chillum in hand.

Jack seethed, "Little doth he know what he hath done."

"You need a righteous charge-up, mate." Which meant have some drinks and chill out. "Shotgun on the ride back," Grant said, strolling over to Azziz and his miserable Toyota.

Jack sighed heavily, "My boy, I'll be honest with you. The real issue for me is riding back down to Landi Kotal and then all the way from that desolate backwater hovel to Peshawar in a goddamn jalopy with no suspension. My back won't take the pressure. I just can't do it."

"Tough it out mate. When we're in Peshawar we'll find ourselves a cushy limousine. We'll find a sloe-eyed chauffer to drive us around. He'll open the doors and put you in a hot tub and give you a massage. I promise. I'll take care of you when we get down there."

I went back to the Chief and said, " Sorry about all this craziness. It's his hunchback. He's in constant pain."

The Chief pointed to Grant smoking the opium/hash, "Dirty Harry has what he needs. The hunchback will smoke that and he will have no pain." I went to Grant and he had that ball of black hash with a big white marble going through it. He stuffed a pebble of it into his chillum bowl, asking casually, "What about sending the Professor back home?"

"He's not going home and you know it. Just try not to piss him off."

"Hard to do when he's trying to get us killed."

"And that .38 of yours could have got us killed, too."

"But it didn't, did it, mate? I should have asked you a long time ago – why are you hooked up with the Professor?"

"He's smart."

"Smart enough to land us in a fuckin' holding cell in Kabul. He fucked up getting us on the wrong side of that station chief."

"She'll forget about us. We're long gone from her zone. Meanwhile, I'll find Jack a little boyfriend and he'll be happy."

"Yeah, he loves his doori. You want to do some doori with the professor?" He was joking. Sex with Jack was the last thing I wanted. "Hey, but watch out now. He's little but he could have one big budoo. Maybe it's crooked like his back." Finally, we had some levity going on. "Seriously, bunji, he'd be happy if it was you. You got a thing going with him?"

"Yeah, right."

"So send him back to Oz. We can pull this off better on our own. Mob till the end, right mate?"

"Ride it out, Grant. We're close to the end now." I took the chillum over to Jack. A big purple bruise was emerging under both his eyes. He dabbed drops of blood from his nose with his handkerchief. "I should have let you send Grant home back in London after he OD'd."

"Give it a rest, Jack. And trust me..." I lit the chillum for him, "... a little of this and you won't feel a thing on the drive back." He took a few tokes and mellowed out. Then we climbed in the Toyota and our big bruiser of a guide Azziz ferried us back down to Landi Kotal where we stopped for a moment to buy cold drinks. Jack was drifting in and out of a nod. Grant was blissfully riding shotgun. The town didn't seem quite so ominous now. The brown crust over everything seemed not quite so dirty, the obstacles in our plan not quite so daunting. Azziz was actually a comforting presence now. And the rattletrap Toyota even had a radio. Azizz found some American music on a G.I. station. I kicked back sipping my Coke. And on we went down the Khyber Pass, through the Land of the Bones to Peshawar, ready to take our Ramadan vacation, waiting for the Afghani connection to get back in business. One more bullet dodged. We were safe at the moment. Cream was on the radio singing "I feel free..."

Sometimes you think you're free and you wind up more boxed in than ever.

7

Moving to Byron Bay – '72

Up until the bust on Killarney Street I had taken my freedom for granted. Never appreciated it until I was confined in a cell. I looked at the names scratched in the gray paint with each day they'd been there carved in neat rows. So many days! Plenty of time to artistically scroll *Just tryin' to be free* as well. I had been blindly cavalier about my freedom and vowed never to risk it again. But of course as soon as Grant and I were released, I did. My confinement receded into the past like a righteous scare left behind in the dark funhouse when you roller coaster out into the sun.

The old feeling of invincibility was back. But Grant and I knew our days of dealing around Sydney were at an end. We were under heavy scrutiny, like butterflies pinned to a board by Detective Marx. I felt safest in the water. Spent a lot of time surfing. We had a secret spot and one peaceful morning I was bobbing on my board with Grant. Pelicans swooped the wave crests. Gulls cawed over urchins on the rocks. It was sunny though fog was slowly creeping in, giving everything an eerie vibe. Sharkey. You get the feeling like Jaws might be headed your way. I got out, Grant took a few more waves in the mist, then we smoked a joint by a palm-frond fire.

"Hey mate, we almost got bit," Grant said. I thought maybe he'd actually seen a great white out there stalking us. But he was talking about doing time in the slammer.

"That's right, mate. The gangies are watching us."

"Yeah, the cops are all over our asses. No going back to our old routine."

"Nope. We're too bloody famous now."

The bust had hit the news and weeks afterwards we were still in the Sydney papers. A move out of Sydney to greener pastures was the answer. The criteria for the right place was a small town with great surf and an abundant supply of stoners we could sell to. So over the next month we searched up and down the coast for a cool town to set up shop and decided on Byron Bay.

I always travelled light with a surfboard and a suitcase, but Grant had his dog and his horse and a girlfriend. He lived in an Airstream on a bluff overlooking the sea. The trailer belonged to his doori chick, as he called his girlfriends. She was pissed he was leaving without her and wouldn't babysit the horse. We took the tired mare over to his father's ranch a couple hours drive into the outback to see if he could leave her there till he got settled. His old man, a red-faced Irishman, was leaning against a tractor drinking a Fosters, barely making eye contact, gruff, sunburned, and more inclined to relate to his hounds than his son. I was standing apart, giving them their moment. I wondered if this is the way it would have turned out had my dad lived. Maybe what I had was better. A void where dad should have been, a kind of vaporous longing seeping through the hole like some mist off the Irish moors that carries with it

some indistinct murmur. I didn't even realize it. I just figured
it for a weird mood.

My dad died when I was seven and what does a seven year
old know about death? A caterpillar squashed on the sidewalk,
a dog run over in the road, sure, but a father, grey, unmoving,
strange smells coming off him, cold to the touch. I had a few
blurry memories like him tossing my youngest brother up in
the air and catching him and putting him on his shoulders.
Or being at the dinner table with only rice and milk to eat
because according to him that's what all the starving people
in the world had to eat so we should do the same. These little
whittled chips of the past added up to my history before we got
to Oz. It was a void, a nothing since we weren't all that close
before he died. He was pretty much an OCD workaholic, and
apparently so manic-depressive he was given shock treatments.
While he was hospitalized he'd contracted encephalitis and
was comatose for a year. I'd stare at him silent and unmoving
in the iron bed connected up to tubes and restraints.

To me, the past was nothing but a swamp and I had a wall
around it. Painted nice bright colors. The hues of the sea and
sky and the golden ponytails of pretty girls. When all that
was working for me, I didn't feel so different from my mates
who all had fathers. And in a way being on my own was a
blessing because I might have missed out on many a wild and
sometimes illegal adventure if a dad had been teaching me
right from wrong.

Grant and his old man were now in a heated argument that
looked like it might come to blows. "You want your Mum?
You want your mum?! You're just like her! So go fucking find
her then!" Grant shoved him in the chest and waited for the

old man to come back at him, but he just sneered and limped off. Grant came over to me. "God damn gubba ocker," he said. Gubba meant crusty white person or racist. "All the time all charged up. I know why my mum left us." He watched his dad walk over to a teenage ranch hand who worked for him. Grant stared at the white kid like he was the son the old man wished for. "I'll catch up with you later, bunji," he said and walked off into the scorching backcountry, to where I didn't know. His dog followed and then so did his swaybacked horse.

I went to tell Mum I was leaving town. I was anticipating a tearful goodbye, but she surprised me. She was on board with my plans. "Well, it's good you boys are getting away from what you were doing here. You can go up the coast, concentrate on your plumbing business and do some surfing." Then she had me sit down to a cup of tea. Whenever the teapot came out, I knew it was gonna get heavy. "Son," she said, dropping a sugar cube into my cup, "You need to give up selling drugs."

I patted her hand to reassure her, but she had me fixed in her no bullshit stare. "You could be killed."

"Mum, I'm done with dealing and that's a fact." Okay, I lied, but it was for the greater good. And therefore justifiable. Right? A question of ethics and loyalty, putting me on the horns of a dilemma. I bought peace of mind for Mum and thus I could split Sydney in good conscience.

But first I had to find Grant. I had a feeling where he might be. There was a billabong – a lake – in the outback a day's walk through the desert from the old man's ranch. He had done his Abo walkabout there when he was a kid and he'd taken me out on occasion. He didn't look much like an Abo. He didn't look like his Irish father either. His mother was half Abo and half Greek and my guess was he pretty much resembled her. He didn't talk much about her. She was a mystery to me, maybe to him, too. I don't think he'd seen much of her over the years. He had no extended family that I knew of except an Abo uncle he would visit on a regular basis who schooled him in the Abo ways and lingo.

I drove out to the billabong and there was his old horse grazing on some shrubs and his dog cooling down in the shade of an acacia tree. Grant was naked and squatting on a boulder in the middle of the billabong. He'd used mud and ash to paint himself in the Abo way, tracing the lines of his ribs, masking his face. I took off my clothes and dove into the powder blue water, then climbed up on the rock with him. "Bunji," he said, using the Abo word for friend.

"Bunji," I said.

We had nothing else to do so we hung out there for a few days. He was in total Abo mode, made himself a woomera, a spear thrower and a javelin, nailed a wallaby, rubbed sticks together to make a fire, said basically nothing for forty-eight hours, and by then enough body paint had rubbed off to give him the look of a zebra and he was ready to get on with things. He would walk his horse to his uncle's Abo settlement and leave the animal and I was to meet him there.

A couple days later I went out to the village in the outback. It was like a small mining camp with a few corrugated iron roofed sheds. The Abos were working over buckets of plaster making little statues of kangaroos and koalas that they'd sell to tourists. There were a lot of flies in the plaster goo and they sort of added to the speckled look of the trinkets which they were trying to sell me. Grant came out of a shed with his uncle who was half Greek and ran the place for the Greeks who owned it. We had a few beers, said our goodbyes and hit the road. I was ready to head for Byron Bay, but he had us drive to a town about fifty miles back toward Sydney. I parked on a side street in a quiet little neighborhood and we just sat there in the car for a time. Finally I said, "So what are we doing here mate?"

"Seeing my mum." She lived in a house in sight of where we were parked. It was one of those times when it's best to just go with the flow so I sat there with him playing private eye. A couple hours went by and he said, "Forget it. Let's go."

I said, "Look, you've come this far and you want to see her so let's stick it out. Better yet, let's go knock and see if she's home."

"Naaa," he said.

"I know you want to see her, mate. So let's do it. I'm with you, okay?"

We rang the bell and a man answered. He looked like some over the hill Greek guy but without the twinkle you see in most Mediterraneans. He had that smell of disease about him. He asked what we wanted and I told him. He said, "She left. Like a hawk."

"Where? Grant asked.

His shrug said it was no concern of his. "So you're her son."

"Is she coming back?" I asked.

"Maybe. Don't know for sure. Never know what that woman will do." He was staring at Grant like he was looking for a certain town on a roadmap. "Yeah. I see her in you, boy. Try the Blue Mountain settlement or some dance studio in Sydney."

We walked to the car and I said we should go to Sydney

next. He said, "Leave the history where it is." He had questions. Lots of unanswered questions like I did about my dad. What do you do with them? Store them in some mind closet until they start rapping to get out again.

We hit the road for Byron Bay. Back in those days it was a sleepy little paradise with subtropical weather, rich volcanic soil, verdant mountains, rainforests, and best of all... perfect surf. Break after break with uncrowded pristine waves. The other major concern was who controlled the weed and hash trade. Investigation revealed there were a few small-time dealers around but no major players. We settled into the good life up in Mullumbimby, a country village overlooking the coast. We rented a little farmhouse with a creek running through and the grass was high, the soil rich and red. After a rain we'd have magic mushrooms growing out of the cow pies in our front yard.

We continued our front as plumbers while we set up the dealing business. Our first dope customers were some hippy chicks we met while dirt biking. They were part of a family of freaks who lived in banana shacks and loved beads, dobro jams and hash. Hash was in short supply and they were so hungry for it they'd come down out of their hippy haven and hang around our place waiting to score, looking in the windows with that psilocybin stare, tapping on the glass with seashell rings.

Our clientele soon expanded to include surfers and blue-collar guys, more like our clientele back in Sydney. From there we branched out into the hip scene with more cultured dope smokers. In the early seventies, Byron Bay was filled with a spiritual, mystic vibe that attracted unique and interesting people doing some wild ass partying.

Soon we were swimming in a melting pot of art openings, movie premieres, theater extravaganzas and raucous pubs full of writers, artists and musicians. The Cheeky Monkey was such a place. One of my regular customers was a drummer in a band who rocked out there. His group played extended half hour jams with an artist who slapped paint onto a giant canvas capturing the spirit of the music. People would come from hundreds of miles around when he did this thing. Grant and I were there one night watching the show and I noticed a face out of the past. Jack Shannon. He'd been one of my teachers in high school. He was infamous back then, a hunchback strolling the campus in his black cloak, hood always pulled up, and the students called him "Richard the Third." He was a history master and probably the smartest teacher at the school. It was rumored he was gay. But nobody dared give him shit about his sexual orientation because you didn't want to get sliced up by his razor wit.

Jack had changed his look. No longer dressed all in black, he was now sporting hat to shoes in white, like Colonel Sanders. He had come to see the mad painter who was tossing colors on a ten-foot high canvas to create Don Quixote tilting at a windmill. The band was deep into a screechy, wild riff, then merged into some exotic flamingo concerto, drawing even more passion from the painter. Jack was mesmerized, but then got jostled by two cowboys bumping through the crowd beers in hand.

These Aussie rednecks, known as ockers, were looking to wet their whistle, but had stumbled into a foreign world. They were amused and confused and heckled the scene. Jack was at a table of queers and fag hags and he stood up and faced them. He was way shorter than them but still managed to look down his nose as he said, "Perhaps you need me to help you understand the nuances of this fine performance."

"Fuck you, ya pufter."

The cowboy spit at Jack, who threw a drink in his face and then it was on. Crazy, but there was Jack going toe-to-toe with the redneck. A wild brawl broke out and the band kept playing, the painter continued undaunted, and I made my way through the melee to Jack. By the time I got to him, he'd had a beer bottle broken on his forehead and was streaming blood and still swinging. I got him away, but he was pulled back into it and then Grant decked one of the ockers and we managed to get out of there just as cop cars, sirens blasting, pulled up. The last thing we needed was more police trouble.

Jack was dazed and it was dark. He got his wits about him and said, "That was exciting. Let's go back in there."

"Not such a good idea, Jack."

He focused on me and nodded in recognition. "A face from the past. James! Now this is surely good fortune at work."

"You know this guy?" Grant said.

"You sir, have a firm grasp on the obvious. Know me? Of course he knows me. I taught him history. I watched his grand exploits on the rugby field! An Adonis in short shorts he was. Now let's go back in there and give as good as we got!"

Grant laughed, told him he needed stitches in his forehead. Jack called it a scratch and nothing to worry about. His friends came out of the pub and we handed him over.

"James! I've followed your exploits in the papers." He was sincerely impressed by the bust in Sydney. He fancied me as some sort of gangster. He gave Grant an appreciative once over.

"Your partner in crime. You were at Waverly Academy as well?"

"No, Dee Why Public," Grant said.

"Well, we won't hold it against you. Very glamorous, these two, eh?" he said to his pals. "Your clandestine operations no doubt would make a riveting tale. And we would love to hear it. Wouldn't we, boys and girls?"

They all nodded and smiled like we were a couple of gladiators up for auction. One elegant woman stroked my ponytail, said, "Oh do come with us you gorgeous thing." I looked at Grant to see if he was into hanging with them, but cougars weren't his scene. "Next time," he said.

"Well, call me when you're in Sydney. Either at the embassy or at home." Jack handed me his card that had some official government logo on it. The police came out with the two ockers in tow and asked Jack if he wanted to press charges, but he declined. He smiled at the cowboy he'd been fighting with, "You are saved by the colossal magnitude of your ignorance." His mates and their hags got into a limo and off they went.

The months went by and Grant and I were selling so much hash that I was flying down to Sydney to score a couple pounds almost every other week. I called Jack and we had lunch and a few schooners. He was coming on to me strong but I managed to fend him off with a promise to call whenever I was in town. And actually I meant it because I did realize I could learn a lot from the man.

He called me his "Criminal mastermind" and asked if I was still in the drug trade. I was vague, which peaked his interest. Jack let me know that he fancied himself a networker supreme and a broker of many things both esoteric and intoxicating. One of his skills, and part of his job as Chief of Protocol to the

Minister of Culture, was putting people together. "I happen to have some acquaintances in your line of business," he said. "Do some acquisitions and distribution as well. The top of the heap. Gentlemen of impeccable pedigrees. Keep that in mind."

Jack, my former classics professor, as a connection? This made me laugh and I didn't give that idea a second thought. But then some months later a drought hit. I don't mean rain. For some strange reason there was absolutely no weed or hash around. The worst dry spell ever to hit, not only Byron Bay, but Sydney as well. And this went on for months. It went on so long and we were so desperate to score, I actually called Jack. But he was out of the country. What's a dealer to do in such a dry time? Diversify. I came up with the bright idea of making a big heroin deal. I pitched the plan to Grant. "No way, mate," he said. "Nothing but trouble in the junk trade." Our golden rule had always been don't sell heroin or cocaine. Weed, hash and psychedelics only. Start selling powders and you got problems. Still, I tried to convince him, but he wasn't having it. Ironic that he later became a junkie himself. But back then he was so against doing any deals with heroin that we actually split up the partnership over it. I moved back to Sydney where I had found a heroin connection and set up the deal. Just about the worst decision I've ever made in my life.

8

*"Oh mama can this really be the end? To be stuck inside
Peshawar with the Ramadan blues again..."*

Desperate times call for desperate measures. We had three
weeks to kill until the end of Ramadan when we could go
retrieve our Rover, which we hoped by then would be loaded
with hash. We had no weed, Thai Sticks or ludes. Hadn't run
into a coke dealer in months.

So we were looking at the ominous prospect of complete
sobriety for the next few weeks. I hadn't been sober that long
since the third grade. There was only one prudent course of
action. Get drugs from a pharmacy. We called in the hotel
doctor who was a Paki Muslim educated in London. He said,
"I'd like to help you, but the current political situation has put
everyone under a tremendous amount of scrutiny."

"What the fuck does that mean?" Grant said.

"It means no drugs, gentlemen."

"Because of the coup," Jack said.

"Exactly."

"There was a right-wing military coup," Jack said, showing
off. "Prime Minister Ali Bhutto is out and General Al Haq is
in." Then he started pumping the doc for his political take on

the new dictator.

"Jack, never mind the coup. We need some medicine here."
I put the case again to the doctor, pulling out a few hundred
to entice him.

"Impossible. To prescribe any narcotics would be a danger
to us all."

"Okay. Then how about a couple of Quaaludes?"

"Suicide. Government agents scrutinize every prescription.
Especially to foreigners."

"Dangerous times," Jack said.

"Indeed. India has the bomb. Everything is changed. I fear
we will never have peace again," the doc said and left.

Even our alcohol supplies dwindled to nothing. That's
not good because let's face it, we're alcoholics. We quizzed the
bartender about where we could get some booze.

"Oh, no." he said. "Can't do it during Ramadan. A major
offense. If we get caught, the police will torture us."

Ramadan was really cramping my style. I pulled out
a few hundred-dollar bills to see if he was more malleable
than the doctor. "Come on, really. Where do we get some
booze?" Finally, we convinced him to facilitate a backdoor
deal. There was more stealth involved than a George Smiley
plot. He said we should come back in a few hours and he'd
have an answer for us. The time dragged by, we went back
and he had us order dinner. He was filling our tea cups and
said, "You make the buy at midnight on the golf course."

"Okay. Where?"

"Shhh. A hole."

"Which hole?" I asked.

"I do not know. You put the money in the cup on the

green. There will be a note telling which hole the alcohol is at."

"So which hole do we drop the money?"

"I do not know. In one hour wait at the phone booth."

"Which phone booth?" I asked and if he said, "I don't know" again I was going to fling my mashed potatoes at him.

"On the side of the golf shop."

Okay. We went there and hung around. Who hangs around a golf shop at midnight? We were conspicuous but fuck it. Finally we got the call. A muffled voice told us to go to a golf cart parked on the side of the hotel and look in the battery compartment. Scrawled on a grease-stained note was the number "14." We drove the cart onto the deserted course, found the 14th hole with a note saying, "What you seek buried in sand trap of 13." We careened over there in the dark of night, started digging with our hands. The stash was buried so deep it was like we were grave robbers. But there it was - two bottles of whiskey and about fifty bottles of beer.

We laid in the sand, got good and buzzed and then went streaking over the golf course back to our hotel - three crazy white guys with all those bottles clanking in the dark so loud you could hear them in the bar. I said, "Let's get some hand towels off the tees and silence the bottles." No hand towels so the racket continued.

We were on the service elevator smuggling the booze up to our rooms when the elevator stopped. But it wasn't our floor. The doors opened and two suits confronted us. They flashed Paki Secret Service credentials and ordered us off the car. We were standing there with all the booze. We figured this is it, torture time. One suit pushed me back on the elevator, got in, the doors closed and down we went to the garage. The doors opened and there was a long black limo waiting. The agent opened the back door, pushed me in. I found myself sitting next to Patricia Adams, the CIA Station Chief who had detained us in Kabul.

9

The Big Burn – Sydney, '73

When I made the heroin deal back in Sydney, a little voice on my shoulder warned me, "James, this is a really dodgy idea. Don't fucking do it." But another voice was saying, "James, you're a businessman. A businessman has to adapt to a changing market." So against my better judgment I set up a buy for a pound of smack. My connection was a sketchy guy named Airport Stan who knew someone flying in from Thailand with pounds of China White. I wasn't going to front Stan the money so the deal was he'd get the dope fronted to him and bring it to me. I had the bright idea that Mum's house was a good place to do this because it was way off police radar. Mum would be at work, Airport Stan would bring the smack, I'd give him the cash, we'd cut up the pound and Stan would take care of sales.

Saturday morning as agreed there was a knock at the door right on time and I expected to see Airport Stan. Lo and behold it wasn't Stan but two creepy looking guys I'd never seen before pointing .38s. Each put his gun on one side of my cheek and pushed me back into the house, kicking the door closed. "You're under arrest," one of them growled.

"What??" I knew these fuckers weren't cops. They were fucking junkies, sweating, pupils dilated like saucers, every pore craving a fix. "If you're cops, then let's see your badges," I said.

"This is my badge, motherfucker!" and he pistol-whipped me across the face. "Bring out the money or I'm going to blow you away."

I laughed. "Sure. You can shoot me right here in suburban DY. By the way, since when do cops shoot people for no reason?"

That was good for another pistol whipping. I hit Mum's nice floor which was a bloody mess now and needed mopping. I was hoping she still kept the mop and bucket on the back porch. Mum, I prayed to myself, whatever you do don't leave work early today.

The junkies tied and gagged me so I couldn't give them any more shit. Meanwhile, my brother walked in. He hadn't seen me in a while, so imagine his surprise walking in on a scene like that. They soon had him tied and gagged, too. The junkies were searching the house for money when a couple of my surf buds came by to say hello. They were soon tied up and gagged, too. To get all of us bound up, the junkies cut the cords off Mum's custom venetian blinds. I had bought those special for her. I wasn't happy about that.

They finally found the ten grand in cash and with visions of needles in their arms, they were about to split. Suddenly one of them began to search a box on the bookshelf and found my dad's graduation ring from Notre Dame. Without a word, he took it. A healing had recently begun taking place where I'd look at that ring sometimes feeling him, remembering bits and pieces of our history. That ring was really all that I had that was his. And now these fuckers were stealing it. I was gagged and couldn't stop them. I didn't care that they were strolling out with my cash, but the ring... don't take the ring! And I couldn't even say that. The junkies left and a while later some more mates came by and untied us all.

I said, "Who's got a gun?" feeling royally pissed. I was going to find those fuckers and shoot them in the kneecaps. Make them suffer and get my dad's ring back.

One of my buddies said he could get a .45. From a junky, no less.

"Great. Let's go."

I got the gun, then bought a bottle of bourbon and fueled up. My first stop was Airport Stan's place. But he had bolted. I drove around looking for the junkies. I went by the big smack dealer in Sydney and waited but they didn't show up. I never did find them.

In the aftermath of the rip off I was freaking out. Lost my money, lost my cool. I called Grant and said I was coming back to Byron Bay because the smack deal went haywire. He said, "I got it all together mate. I'm dealing smack up here."

"What?? Don't do that, Grant! You were right. It went bat-shit bad." And I told him what had happened.

"No, this deal is cool, dialed in. Come on back and we'll partner up."

Sometimes I'm just too hardheaded to learn. A month later against my better judgment, I got my gear together and was about to leave for Byron Bay. But I had a weird feeling and called him. A girl answered who sounded nervous and scared. She hung up on me and I called her back and made her understand who I was. "His friend, James. His best friend.

Okay? Now tell me what happened, because I can help."

"Okay," she said, loosening up a little. "They have him in the jail in Byron Bay."

"And you are?"

"Tuesday."

"I mean what's your name?"

"Tuesday. My name is Tuesday."

"Okay. Tuesday. What did he do?"

"I better not say on the phone."

"All right. Hang tight. I'm coming up there."

I found Tuesday at our old place in Mullumbimby. She looked barely out of her teens but there was a tired, almost used look about her that made me wonder if she wasn't a working girl. Not so much a streetwalker but more of an upscale hotel "employee."

She told me Grant's smack deal had gone sideways. He'd gotten ripped off and then went after the junkie who did it. He busted up the guy, took his heroin back, then got pulled over for a taillight and the cops found the smack. Now he was in jail. My first thought was how much is the bail on that going to be? I went to the jail to find out and learned Grant was on a prison bus headed to Sydney.

I couldn't believe we'd had parallel experiences dealing smack. What a fucking sign to chill. All I wanted was a safe haven, somewhere way far off the radar of cops and junkies. I felt very exposed, wondering if the fuckers who had ripped me off were connected to the cops or if they'd given me up for a lighter sentence like junkies often do.

It occurred to me to call Jack. He was back from his travels and was all ears to hear about what happened. I explained I did the smack deal because of a drought in the smoking dope world.

"Well, I know some suppliers who never run out of... *cannabis sativa*." He said with a lilting flair as he loved the turn of a Latin phrase. "Too bad I was travelling in your time of need. Could have saved you a pistol whipping. Thank god they didn't mar that pretty face of yours."

He wanted to be a dealer. An upscale dealer. Selling to doctors, lawyers, architects, business people. Even politicians. Jack had entre into this world. "And we'll expand from there, my boy," he said, eyes all aglow like a wild visionary.

"And where do we get all the pot and hash?"

"Leave that to me," he said. "I have excellent sources."

Turns out Jack had never actually done a drug deal. But why not play this out and see what would happen? Besides, I figured it might be a way of helping Grant. I talked Jack into using his connections to intercede on Grant's behalf. He looked into it and came back with the news that Grant had escaped during the ride on the prison bus from Byron Bay to Sydney. He was now a fugitive at large.

I decided to bunk up in Jack's mansion. He lived in his mother's palatial enclave in Double Bay, an eastern suburb of Sydney. This was a safe, guarded patrician area way off the radar of cops and junkies, which was just what I was seeking. I knew I was going to have to deal with him coming on to me, since I was like catnip to him. But what the heck, I could handle him. I moved into the guest wing to hide for a couple of weeks and it was Jack, his mother and me in a fifteen thousand square foot home. Kinda strange. A whole new paradigm from the cool scene Grant and I had going up in Byron Bay. I missed my surf bud and somehow I knew things would never be the same.

10

I was sitting on plush leather but I was a prisoner. In the back seat of a limo in a darkened garage in Peshawar with Patricia Adams staring at me, I was thinking – how did I get here? There had been a ton of crazy mistakes the whole trip that led to this imminent bust. But I could trace the present dangerous moment to one fiasco – that stupid heroin deal I set up back in Sydney. If I hadn't done that, Grant might not have got into heroin and gone to prison, I wouldn't have partnered up with Jack, the Silk Road deal would never have happened.

Patricia Adams held me in her gaze. At that moment I dared to really look at her. Couldn't decide if she looked angelic or hard as porcelain. Maybe both at the same time. Kind of like Faye Dunaway in *Chinatown*. Or Mary Queen of Scots. Her eyes - were they grey or blue? - wide set on a sculpted face. When I'd been her prisoner back in Kabul her hair was dull and grey at the roots. Now it was gold and lush like the flame you just have to touch. She was so cold she was hot. Dry ice steamy in her black suit jacket, ice blue silk blouse, three buttons undone revealing the lace edge of a white bra, a thin black strand around her neck from which hung a creamy pearl. Quite a change from the unadorned woman who had previously interrogated me.

When she'd let us go in Kabul I had a feeling I'd be seeing her again. Maybe it was because I wanted to see her. Crazy thing for a smuggler to say about a spook. Especially one close to twenty years older than me. But I'm ahead of myself. Best I digress here to explain how it came to be that I was within the sphere of Patricia Adams.

Three months previous – a hotel in Tabriz, Iran

She sat on the far side of a horseshoe bar alone in the mellow light nursing a highball. A cigarette burned in an ashtray. She took no notice of anyone and yet seemed to see everything. My eyes kept returning to her as Jack, Grant and I sat in the art deco elegance of the lounge in the Tabriz International. We had just crossed the border from Turkey into Persia. Road weary, we needed some good food, a few drinks, a hot shower and a plush bed. The International, a stately old place that catered to western businessmen and journalists, was just what the doctor ordered. We sat at our booth and I wondered about this mysterious woman across the room. Before long a group of suits came in. With them was a rugged dude with dirty blond hair and wispy beard, way hip in his white silk scarf and motorcycle jacket. Jack elbowed me, "Now isn't he a magnificent sight!" I noticed the guy glance at the woman at the bar as he and his group took the booth next to us. With Jack spinning tales it didn't take long before we were drinking and talking together. They were reporters for western news and the rugged dude was a photojournalist named Flannery. All were on their way to Tehran to follow a brewing story.

It wasn't long before Flannery left the group, went over to the bar and bellied up next to the woman. He slid a manila envelope across to her as they talked intimately. For some reason Grant took note of them, even as tired and high as he was. He glanced at them a few times then went over to the bar and stood nearby, coolly eavesdropping as he ordered a drink. When he came back I asked him, what's up?

"Just got a feeling about them. Her really." His instincts were telling him she was law and order. Carrying the envelope, she left the bar, and walked past us. She was more confident than sexy. Poised. Self-controlled even when all eyes were on her. She said nothing to any of us, didn't even glance in our direction. She went through the lobby to the elevators.

Flannery came over to his friends at the table next to us. He looked to be about 30. He could have been hanging with the Stones in London or been a star of stage and screen. By the sound of it he had a penchant for chasing rebellions because he had a twinkle in his eye when he said "Tehran's about to explode. The Shah is under fire."

A British journalist winked to an American reporter, "Now where would he have gotten such clandestine information?"

The American raised an eyebrow, glancing at the blond getting on the elevator, "Hmmm... he does appear to have the inside track."

I knew next to nothing about the Shah of Iran except that he had a beautiful wife and lots of stallions. Flannery described the tensions that were brewing in Tehran, and the political unrest, a "populist revolution" caused by the oppressive regime of the Shah.

"So, hey mate, why you going there?" Grant asked. It was a question that he'd already answered in his head.

"Taking pictures," Flannery said. "Why you going there?"

"Who says we are?" Grant said.

"It's the place to be. Unless you're headed somewhere else. Like Afghanistan, maybe?"

He was essentially saying he had us pinned as smugglers.

"Marvelous guess," Jack blurted.

Grant waved him off, "But wrong. We're headed west."

Grant walked away and hung with some hippy trekkers at another table. Meanwhile Jack wanted all the details from Tim Flannery about the situation in Tehran. And so did the journalists. "The Shah is a puppet of the West, "he explained. "He has 22 billion bucks. That's 22 BILLION. All from oil. All of it going into the bank accounts of the Shah. He passed a law mandating he alone has absolute and total control over the nation's assets." There was dissension and upheaval percolating. Primarily with the younger people, the students. They were being fueled and fired up by their religious leaders, the Mullahs.

Jack knew about this. "Right," he said, "What's his name, Khomeini?"

"AKA the Ayatollah. He's been exiled for fifteen years to France and is now sending messages home exhorting the people to overthrow the Shah and his regime."

"How is it you know all this?" Grant asked.

"I read the papers, mate."

"What else? Come on, give us the inside dope about the revolution."

"There is no revolution. Yet. It's in the air but the Shah has a massive army trained and funded by the U.S. and a brutal secret police force called SAVAK that disappears any dissenters." It was almost midnight and that was it for Tim. He said "Goodnight, gentlemen. Maybe see you in Tehran," and went off toward the hotel elevators.

After more drinks and conversation Jack found a "friend" among the Brit journalists, and the two of them strolled outside together to smoke some hash. I figured Jack would then ply the fellow with ludes and that would be the last I'd see of him for the night. I looked around for Grant. He and two hippy chicks he had been sitting with were now gone. I called it a night and went up to my room and crashed.

In the morning I couldn't find anybody. Jack wasn't in his room, nor was Grant. I asked around about Tim Flannery and learned he had checked out. I asked the desk clerk about the woman I'd seen Flannery with and he said he didn't recall any woman of that description in the hotel. I was having breakfast when Jack walked in. "Let's go, my boy!" he said, on fire to hit the road for Tehran.

"Look, Jack, I'm not so anxious to drive into a revolution."

"Well we don't have much choice now, do we?"

He was right. To circumvent Tehran we'd have to go up into Russia, around the Caspian Sea, into Kazakhstan, down into Turkmenistan, then into Uzbekistan. It was too costly in time and money. Plus we had a date with Tariq Rahim in Peshawar to score our 200 kilos.

"So the sooner we get into Tehran the better, before things explode there," he argued.

I finished up breakfast and finally found Grant in a room with the two girls, all three still up tripping on acid from the night before. He was a fucking mess, but I managed to get him out of there and into a shower.

"Going to Tehran is nothing but trouble," he said. "And that chick in the bar last night – government issue all the way. I guarantee she knows exactly what we're up to by now."

"And how would she know that?"

"Her bunji with the silk scarf."

But I thought that was the crazy long night of drugs talking. So I made an executive decision and decided on Tehran.

The Beginning of the Big Score on the Silk Road – Sydney '76

Jack wasn't kidding about having a waiting market of high echelon buyers. His Rolodex was bubbling with entertainment people, business tycoons, politicians, doctors and a few lowlifes. Many of them interconnected through a kind of gay mafia. Now it remained to be seen if he had a connection to a high-level supplier. He set up a meeting with an American guy he knew named Garrett Jones, aka Mr. Big, and because everything happens in the pub, we converged in the King's Head. Jones was a tall, rowdy, formidable-looking beach bum who had been a soap opera actor in America. He had played a badass cop on the wrong side of things in "The Young and The Restless." He'd also had a little side operation going. Actually a *big* side operation - smuggling major amounts of hash into L.A. He'd gotten too big, hired a sketchy mule who set him up for a bust. His connections in the LAPD told him the Feds were about to pounce and he split the U.S. and escaped to Oz. He soon returned to the smuggling trade and within a few years he'd become one of the biggest importers of weed and hash in Sydney.

We had a few beers and started talking about surfing and

life in the states, since I was a Yankee transplant too. Feeling each other out you might say. Then we got to the real deal and he brought out a little hash, passed it to me under the table for inspection. "Like to try it?" he said. "I certainly would," I said.

So we left the pub, went over to his house that was on a bucolic tree lined street in the eastern suburbs. Not exactly a beach bum type pad, it was a huge, old, beautiful, colonial brick townhouse with filigree iron fencing and a terraced lawn. The interior was super buffed out, total luxury, elegant couches, hip paintings, antiques reeking of history, one-of-a-kind rugs made by tribal hands. So obviously he was doing quite well in the smuggling trade. He got his chillum out and we smoked up the hash. It was primo quality stuff. Smoke got thick in that room fast, my head started to spin into a good stone. We kicked back listening to Steely Dan... and out of the haze Natalie Wood leaned over me and with an angelic smile asked if I'd like a Mimosa.

"Babylon sisters shake it
So fine so young..."

I blinked, the haze cleared a bit. It wasn't Natalie Wood before me but a chick who had the same girl-of-your-dreams sloe-eyed beauty. I could have gazed at that vision forever, but then she was gone. A Mimosa brimming with promise sat on the coffee table, a bright orange slice glowing at the rim of the glass, the chilled curve of the body sweating crystal drops. And over in front of the fireplace the girl was now dancing with another chick...

"The kid will live and learn
As he watches his bridges burn
From the point of no return

Babylon sisters shake it..."

Oh, they were sisters there all right. Maggie and Andi. Maggie was Mr. Big's wife. She was a scrumptious Italian from New York and Andi was her younger sister who'd come to visit. From the moment Andi appeared with the Mimosa, I was hooked like I'd never been. Before her, my thing had been raven-haired city girls who smelled of lilac and lavender, or strawberry blond beach chicks who surfed, loved adventure, and carried the scent of lemons and Sex Wax. Andi embodied both.

The sisters danced while we smoked. And oh, how they could dance, these two beauties. Jewels amidst the opulence. This was the life I wanted. Andi included. My mind was on her, but I was there to make the deal. As the stone started to settle down a little bit, I said to Mr. Big, "I'm down. Let's do it."

And he said, "No problem, get you all you want next week."

"All I want?" I set up a buy for a couple of pounds. I told him my philosophy of not putting the dope together with the money and he said okay he'd front it and I could pay later since he knew where to find me. I think he played a bad cop on the soap because he was very adept at the Dirty Harry squint. As I was leaving, I told Andi I liked the way she danced and would she like to go dancing with me sometime. "Why not?" she said, an Aphrodite smile spreading across her angel face.

So the enterprise began. With Andi and with Mr. Big. The next week I waited for him at a crossroads in Waverly. He pulled up in a van, handed off the packaged hash and said off you go.

I thought to myself, that was easy. I like this. I went back to Jack's place in Double Bay and started to cut the brick up into ounces. I had scales there to make sure I had the weight right, but soon I got really good at just eyeballing an ounce. Cut, cut, cut. Loved it when I could hit it right on the button. The world was abuzz with possibility.

I paid Mr. Big and we began dealing on a regular basis. Each time getting more weight. After a while we'd get slabs of hash weighing ten, fifteen pounds. We'd cut those into pounds and I could guesstimate those cuts too. Meanwhile Andi and I grew closer and closer, spending sun-filled days together on the white sands of a private cove near Lennox Head. And nights rolling in each other's arms at her hilltop pad. I couldn't bring her back to Jack's mansion because, quite frankly, he hated girls. He would have said something derogatory about her, pissed me off, and that would have been the end of our partnership.

Business was growing. We'd started out selling ounces and now were dealing in kilos. Then Jack pitched the idea of ramping up the operation and becoming importers like Mr. Big. The importers were the ones making the real dough.

Importing made me very nervous. The thought of being incarcerated overseas in some Midnight Express slammer for ten years, or even ending up dead, wasn't romantic. Jack was undaunted by those dire possibilities. In fact, the danger and intrigue excited him. He was drawn to the excitement of being an international drug smuggler, and like me, to the money. Andi thought I should be doing something legit. But I was going for the fast, big bucks with the idea that later I'd play by the rules.

I was happy to continue with the operation we had. We had a great network. Our market was cornered. If we kept a level of security and cool, it could work for another couple of years, we'd make bank and then I could get out. My plan had switched from being a plumber to being a real estate titan. The dope business definitely had a limited life span, but it was a great springboard to the land business which would always be there. I promised Andi that in two years I'd quit dealing and we'd buy property in Lennox Head above the sea.

And then Grant showed up. He'd just gotten released from prison and looked like himself again. He'd been lifting weights and spending time out on a road crew. He'd made "connections," he said, in prison. He'd "come up with a plan." Strangely, it was a similar idea to Jack's. A Big Score from the source in Afghanistan. He had a wealth of information about how the importing side of things worked and a contact in Bombay to get it going. Jack looked at Grant as kind of "rough trade" but if Grant being in meant I was in, too, then Jack was down for it. Grant thought Jack was a joke as a partner in crime, but he agreed because that joke had sixty grand seed money.

Andi knew all about the consequences of a score like this, her sister being married to Mr. Big. He'd taken over from Sweepo and was now one of the all-star importers in the Sydney drug trade. Andi had seen her sister agonize over the close calls he had. "James, I've seen my sister live in fear something will happen to the man she loves. I don't want to live with those same fears."

I said, "Baby, it's only going to be a one time thing. One big score, we'll take the money and buy that big piece of land in Lennox Head, subdivide, build and I'll be set up as a real estate developer."

"I'm happy with the way we live now, James. You don't need to do this." She had been dead set against me doing the deal from the first mention of it. And she had warned me not

to get involved with Jack. Ten minutes with him and she knew
he hated women. True. But the allure of the big score was so
strong I had to go for it and we set it up. First stop – Bombay.

12

Tehran, the revolution - '77

Grant wanted to circumvent Tehran, go south to the Gulf of Oman and then cross the border into Pakistan. He grumbled about "heading into fucking chaos." I understood. I mean, waltzing into a revolution? I liked a party in the street as much as the next guy, but not with close to a hundred grand worth of In God We Trust bills strapped around my waist.

"I'll carry the money," Jack said.

"It doesn't matter who carries the money. It's about asking for trouble. Right, Grant?"

"What the fuck, mate, you already cast anchor so why ask me?" I'd never seen him look so saturnine. He was still hung over from his all-night trip with the hippie chicks in Tabriz. I knew he was craving opiates but we had no drugs at all, not even any hash, so he was trying to drink himself into oblivion, flush out the darkness that had been on him ever since he went to prison. He was in the back seat and he leaned over to the front, grousing in Jack's ear, "I know why you're so hot on Tehran. You think you'll get Flannery to fuck you."

Jack knew better than to come back at him, and besides it

was true. He went into his "eyewitness to history" rap about how we'd feel derelict having missed world-shaking events and if nothing else it had the effect of putting Grant to sleep. We rolled into Tehran and it seemed like any other city in the Mid-East. Certainly, there were no battles erupting in the streets.

Nevertheless, we could see why the Ayatollah was gaining influence. Iran was suffering an economic recession and it was bringing the people out of the countryside, the small rural areas and towns, into the big cities to try and find jobs. The roads were potholed, the buses decrepit, stores boarded up. Foreign laborers, mostly displaced Africans and Iraqis, were working construction sites. But then we got to the Hilton and everything was elegant, prosperous and Americanized. Jack, cynic that he was said, "Look behind the curtain, boys and you'll see the whole thing crumbling."

Politics aside, the three of us each had our own more immediate concerns. Jack, despite all his eyewitness to history talk, had one thing on his mind – finding the photojournalist Tim Flannery. He grilled the hotel staff to find out if Flannery was staying there. He wasn't. "Well, where do the newsboys reside?" Who knows? Off he went on foot into the streets on a mad search. My main concern was keeping my erratic partners from committing mayhem or getting jailed. And when I had that together, I wanted a chick to hang with.

But Andi and I had had a heart-to-heart before I left and promises were made. "Honey, while I'm gone, you look up at the moon, and know that I'll be looking up at that same moon. Thinking of you and only you." And I meant it when I said it. But now it turned out, being here thousands of miles away, adjustments had to be made. I had needs, as they say.

So we were all trying to score in our own way. I knew Grant's mission was to get drugs. Some hash, some coke, some booze, some more ludes, but especially some narcotics. He was as dark as a coal mine, seething with toxic fumes, no telling what he might do. So I put in a call to the hotel doctor. Lovely the way that works. A doctor comes to your room and writes a prescription. The Hotel sent an elderly Persian physician. Very dignified. Trim little mustache, a gold studded cane, a black leather doctor's bag that had made more house calls than the Avon Lady.

He didn't even blink when Grant told him what he wanted. Although he did draw the line at the request for cocaine. "Why would you need such a medicine?" he asked.

"A topical anesthetic for a lesion on my ass," Grant explained.

"Oh? Such an injury happened how... ?"

"Who the fuck cares?" Grant said.

I felt the need to be diplomatic and explain, "Climbing a palm tree in Libya." The doc hoisted a questioning eyebrow. "He was rescuing a cat," I said.

The doc nodded. "Of course. But cocaine is out of the question."

"No problem. Skip it then," I said.

The doc then wrote for some Demerol, ludes and tranquilizers and we went to a nearby pharmacy. The pharmacist was young, clean-shaven, tall for a Persian. A serious looking sort underneath his boiled cabbage hair. He gave those prescriptions a long look. Without moving, his eyes lifted. It was the kind of look you give to someone sitting naked on a bus bench. He asked for Grant's passport.

"Why?" Grant wanted to know.

"It's the law."

"I left my fucking passport back in the hotel room okay. Do I need to go back and get it? Or do I need to come over the counter?"

The poor guy froze. I jumped in, "Uh, sorry, he's in a lot of pain. We're at the Hilton. If you need the passport, I'll be happy to go get it. We're with the Australian Embassy. Delivering some horses to the Shah. I can call the Shah's Chief of Protocol..."

He waved his hand for me to stop. "This will take a few minutes. Perhaps you'd like to go next door for a coffee while I fill them?"

"I'll wait," Grant said. I stayed, too, since I was concerned the pharmacist was going to call the SAVAK, but if the secret police had crossed his mind, he kept it under wraps. The guy just wanted us out of there so he filled the prescriptions quickly and we split. I needed a little buzz and we settled into chairs in front of a coffee house.

Grant dug into his sack full of drugs and came out with the Demerol. He poured out a half dozen and swallowed them then chased it with coffee. Just knowing the narcotics were in him and would be working shortly took a decade off his hardened troubled face. I flashed on how he looked so young over the years until he got sucked into the heroin trade. He sank into a chair next to me, sighing deeply. For weeks now he'd had no drugs to quiet his demons. He smiled for the first time in days. "Thanks for what you did in there, mate. I fucked up, huh? It just all seems like sorry business to me sometimes, you know." Sorry business was Abo for death.

"Why is that? What's eating at you, man? Ever since you got out of prison something is tearing you up. What?"

He drank some tepid coffee. Some seconds went by as he seemed to be deciding whether or not to get into it. He leaned over the table, rubbed his eyes. "Ah, youries have holed up inside me." Youries were hairy demons to the Abos.

"Come on mate, that's crazy talk."

He took out the Demerol and popped one more. "We had it good up in Byron Bay, before all the gammon shit happened. Mullumbimby. Hippies. That whole art scene. That was cool. Surf." He leaned over and held my gaze, "I should have listened to you after you got ripped off. Not done that smack deal."

"It's all in the past, bunji. We're cool now. Right?"

He paused, staring down into his coffee like it was an abyss. "Yeah, bunji. Except Tuesday's dead."

"Tuesday?"

"You met her in Mullumbimby when you were going to bail me out." He shrugged, "See, it's all timing. If I'd known, I wouldn't have escaped. And then I probably would have got off with a slap on the wrist and not done any time. And Tuesday would be alive."

He was on the verge of telling me more when Jack scuttled up to us, out of breath and excited. "Come on! It's happening. Just like Tim said. A revolution. To see that happen..."

Grant leaned back, laughed, "A revolution. Bring it on."

"A movement! A world-shaking event. The world runs on oil, boys! Oil!"

"Too bad it's not hash oil."

"Black Gold, mates! It runs the fucking world!"

"Calm down, will you." People passing by were looking

at us. Bicycles, cars, trucks, moms pushing strollers, moving by in peaceful perfect order. Revolution? What revolution? This could have been a street in Melbourne, or London, or Tallahassee, Florida. Still Jack kept hammering on about "The Movement" and Flannery, and how what was happening here was going to rock the world and topple governments, and not just in Iran. Repercussions would be felt for years to come and that it warranted our closer look and involvement.

"Involvement? What the fuck do you mean?" I said. People were suddenly running past us. The pharmacist hurried out, locked his iron gates. Other shops were closing as well, boarding up. "What's happening?" I said.

"Let's go. Tim is going to be there. You'll see the world change!"

Some young people hurried by handing out flyers. I took one. "Come to the march. Join us."

Off they went. Jack wanted to follow them and I decided to tag along. Grant leaned back with the drugs kicking in. "I'm staying here. Have a blast changing the world. Sorry business."

Jack and I started walking and suddenly it was no longer a normal day on a downtown street. The energy was changing. People began appearing from side streets, students in groups of twos and threes, and working people carrying signs in English and Farsi. Masses of them blocking traffic, horns blared with people yelling and there was a surge from behind and suddenly the street was packed. Before we knew it, we were being swept up into this massive protest against the Shah. I wanted to get out of there, but it was too late. Government police in riot gear were everywhere. They had shields and clubs and formed a line to block the protesters. Army trucks moved in and shots were fired. A bullhorn voice screamed repeatedly in Farsi and though I didn't understand a word, I knew what the message was.

Behind us I could see clashes as the army arrested protesters and loaded them into trucks. When the tear gas exploded, it was utter chaos. In the middle of all this Jack was standing stock still, like he was wide eyed at the gates of heaven looking up at Saint Peter. We were in a churning mass of people getting shoved about and I tried to pull him away, but we were so hemmed in there was really no place to go. And then there was Flannery before us, with his camera, snapping away. He moved past us in a cloud of smoke like a ghost and Jack reached for him trying to trail in his wake, but I pulled him back. Flannery was swallowed by the crowd. I grabbed Jack by the shoulders and yelled in his ear, "We have to get out of this! Come on!" He seemed confused, very unlike himself, oddly hunched and questioning, like one of his heroes, Richard III, unhorsed in the midst of battle at Bosworth Field, smoke and weapons and bodies in turmoil around him as his kingship slipped away. "Jack! Jack! Come on!"

Soldiers in gas masks were moving through, corralling the marchers, carting them away. There was a mass of people surging against us. Jack was pushed to the ground. People trampled over him. I was trying to help him up, but I kept getting knocked back. Grant elbowed through and we got Jack to his feet and out to the fringes where we ducked into an alcove and found our way into an alley. The smoke and the gas and the screams of "Revolution!" gradually receded.

We made it back to the hotel. Later that evening, I went down to dinner and found Grant alone at a table. He was cruising on Demerol and brandy. I sat down with him and he pushed the brandy over to me, tapped a pocket and I could see the bulge of some pill bottles. "You want anything?"

I said no. I had to keep it together. "Where's Jack?"

"Probably chasing down that gangie with the camera."

"He's no cop, come on."

"You think the blond chick back in Tabriz isn't CIA? Let's get the fuck out of here. Get on the road. Quit fucking around."

"All right. Tomorrow." I thought about being nosey and then just went for it. "What were you going to tell me back at the coffee place?"

"Forget about that. Yeah. Fucking forget about that." He lit a cigarette, thinking, his brow furrowed, "You ever think about your dad?"

"What?"

"Your dad."

"Think about him?"

"Yeah, mate, memory lane with ol' pops."

I was confused, had no idea where he was coming from. A picture floated up from the past. Watching through a glass window, dad in a hospital bed. Electric shock treatment blitzing into him, jerking him like a skewered fish. "Uh... yeah. Sometimes."

"Good memories?"

"Some, maybe. I don't know. Why?"

He put the cigarette out on the back of his wrist. Didn't flinch at the burn, smiled as the smoke rose up.

"What are you doing, Grant?"

"A payback."

"For what?"

"When I was a kid my dad used to slap me around. Then when I was about fifteen, he went to hit me and I grabbed his wrist and told him, You ever do that again, I'll kick your ass. I was so close to him I could smell the booze. He made his own brew and it had a moldy odor. His nose was all red and veiny, his eyes full of hate. He head butted me. I broke his wrist. Came within a heartbeat of doing more damage. Old Pops said, 'You look like your mother.'"

"Yeah, okay. That's not a bad thing to look like your mum. So what's with the human ashtray?"

"You don't believe in paybacks?"

"Sometimes you gotta let it go."

"I did some bad things, bunji."

"Who hasn't?"

"I killed Tuesday."

"Bullshit." The mate I'd surfed with, done drug deals with, lived with, scored chicks with, known for years? He was not a killer.

We heard a marching band right outside the hotel. And then Jack was standing at our table shouting, "Come on! Come on outside! Look!"

Everybody in the place went out to the street. There was a huge parade in front of the hotel. A sea of marching people, absolutely filling the street with a very organized, almost choreographed demonstration. "This is a *pro*-Shah demonstration!" Jack yelled. The marchers carried ten-foot tall photos of a regal looking Shah and his wife. A thousand of them, dressed in blue with yellow hats, singing the praises of the Shah and the royal family. This was a counter demonstration and the powers-that-be had wasted no time making it happen. The effect was chilling because it was so *effective*. Young and old, workers and students, marching together in solidarity with the forward-thinking humanitarian genius Shah Mohammad Reza Pahlavi who was bringing them all the beauty and bounties of the West. The Great Civilization as he called it.

Jack was in a daze. "I'm riding with Tim tomorrow. We'll caravan to Mashad." Before I could question that, he went off down the street following the parade. I looked around for Grant. He was gone. I knew I had to keep focused. The whole scene was crazy. The partnership coming apart at the seams. Jack was out of his mind over his new fantasy Tim Flannery. Grant was ripped up by his past. I had to keep him together because he was not only my best bud, but also the contact to Tariq Rahim. The whole deal really hinged on us being in the right place at the right time and only Grant would know where and when that was.

13

When I saw Patricia Adams that first time in the smoky light of the bar at the Tabriz International, I figured her for a businesswoman, a boss probably from the way she carried herself with ease and confidence in a world of men. The next time I saw her when she detained us in Kabul, she looked steely and a bit weary under the harsh fluorescence in her CIA bunker. Now under the soft glow of the panel lights of her limo in the garage of the hotel in Peshawar she looked cryptic as always but younger, even accessible.

She leaned toward me. I noticed for the first time that her eyes were not grey or blue, but dark green. The opaque green of a wave on a stormy day. It was an *I've-got-you* look coming at me from her. I'd felt safer in shark-infested waters.

"James, you've put yourself in a very precarious position."

"The booze. Yeah. Bad move."

"I'm talking about you being a smuggler."

"Me? No. Rugs. That's my gig."

"Right now your Range Rover is in the Kush near Landi Kotal waiting to be loaded up with hash once Ramadan ends."

I thought, oh fuck, she knows everything. This is it. "I want to talk to the Australian consulate. I want a lawyer present for this."

"James, if I wanted you in prison, no lawyer could help you. No consul could help you. They'd toss you to the wolves. Wolves bite hard in Pakistan prisons."

She was, I sensed, capable of anything, which made me feel like I was capable of nothing. But then a shift in the tide happened. A softening in her gaze. With a tilt of her head, a slight smile. A reassurance. "Relax," she said.

"Hard to do, wondering if I'll be in a jail cell tonight."

"We're just going to have a little chat is all. You're in trouble, James. But I'm going to offer you a way out."

"A way out?" I knew what was coming. Same thing Detective Marx wanted. And it wasn't plumbing.

"Let's talk about your connection," she said.

"Don't know what you mean."

"Tariq Rahim says a call girl who works for him came to Grant, told you where to deliver the money. The Bazaar." I was silent, frozen. She leaned over and put her hand on my thigh. Her fingers were long, elegant, with short clear lacquered nails. "Trust me. Right now I'm the best friend you have."

"Look, we're just three guys from Oz. Travelling..."

She hit a button on a console. A tape began playing. It was unmistakably Jack's voice. He was in conversation with the photojournalist Tim Flannery. Jack had wormed his way into Flannery's car on the ride from Tehran to Mashad. He was talking about the deal we were heading to Afghanistan to make. Tim Flannery was drawing him out. Jack kept rattling on revealing way too much about our operation as Flannery reeled him in. She'd had this tape when she detained us in Kabul. She turned the tape off, "Let's get to the truth."

My anger at Jack boiled up. For such a smart man how could he have been so stupid? And Grant had predicted it all. He had pinned the photojournalist for what he really was - a front working for the CIA.

"Jack was just trying to impress Flannery," I said to her. "He made all that craziness up. Jack's gay. You know that. He's got some goofy fantasy about Flannery. There's no *deal*."

"Let's get real, James." She produced some photos of Jack, Grant and me in Landi Kotal meeting with Azziz. I told her we were buying rugs from him.

I knew what she wanted from me. Information about Tariq Rahim. She produced photos of me talking with Tariq in Peshawar. "It's a bad move lying to me, James. Especially about things I already know." The dark glass partition separating the front seat slid back. An agent told her there was a situation. They were having a problem with Grant. Her presence was needed. She got out of the limo. The partition slid back. The doors were locked. I was sealed in, couldn't see a thing outside the confines of the rear seat as all the windows were opaque. She would get nothing out of Grant, that much I knew. He'd become such a cop hating hard ass.

As I sat there a moment, the years peeled away and I recalled how he had looked in prison when the guards brought him to the steel chair on the other side of the glass. He looked like Death was his shadow, like Willy Deville in his worst days. Those days when the singer was all physically broken up, shattered knees and hips, the disease ravaging him. Beyond gaunt. One thing Grant had never been was gaunt. Now there he was, almost a cadaver.

"Hello, bunji," he'd said.

"You need anything?" I asked.

"No."

"I'll get you a lawyer."

"I got a lawyer."

"A shitty lawyer."

"Fuck it. I like it here."

"You like it here?"

It went like that until the guards took him away and he just disappeared into the fathomless depths. His prison blue denims merging into the cerulean walls. He was like a brother. But there was nothing I could do for him. I put some money on the books for him so he could buy cigarettes and candy but for two years after that I didn't hear from him.

The limo door opened bringing me back to the present and Patricia Adams slid in beside me again. "Grant is not showing a very strong sense of self preservation. Nor is Jack. Let's see if you can do better."

"I'd like to help you but..."

"Obviously we know your contact is someone you call Tariq Rahim. Do you have any idea who he really is?"

"I don't know that person," I said.

"Sure you do." She was all hard business but there was a cat and mouse thing going on, too, that she seemed to enjoy. "You heard about the coup here? The president, Bhutto, out. The army is now in power."

"Yeah. Volatile times. Since India has the bomb," I said, trying to sound hip to the politics. "What side is the CIA on?"

"The good guys, of course. And we could use your help."

"My help?"

"Your help."

"How?"

"We'll get to that later at my hotel." She gave me the name and room number and said, "See you at 9." She pressed a button on a control panel and the door swung open. I got out into an empty garage, and the limo pulled away.

I tried to find Jack and Grant but they weren't around. Nobody had seen them. It didn't take a genius to figure out they were still in custody. And I could easily be joining them soon if I didn't play this exactly right. And how do you play things right with someone so much smarter than you?

Make up some serpentine fiction? She was too hip for that ruse and besides she probably already knew everything. But if she knew everything, what did she want from me? I knew I had to skirt the subject of Tariq Rahim. Say anything about him and I'd be dead. But if I clammed up, my partners would stay in jail and I'd be joining them. Having to come up with something, I settled on how the Silk Road enterprise began including some of the crazy things that had happened to get us to this point.

It was a good bet Patricia Adams knew about all this. She probably had bank records. She probably knew where I bought the forged passports. She knew how Grant had flown to India to set up the deal. Jack was supposed to travel later on a separate flight, but he jumped the gun and boarded with Grant. I got a hundred and twenty grand cash together and followed a week later. My idea had been to keep the money and the Carnet de passagess document separate because if you get caught with a huge amount of cash together with vehicle transport papers, it's not hard for even the dumbest cop to connect the dots.

I was ever-conscious of Interpol because they were hyper

vigilant on the hash smuggling trade back then, especially in Bombay. We didn't need to create any flamboyance to pique their interest. Jack was flamboyant enough on the natch. He said, "Sure, my boy. It will all be fine. I shall take care and be an innocuous little mouse. Don't you worry."

I landed in Bombay on a moonlit night and got a cab to the hotel. The Taj Mahal Palace Hotel was a beautiful, old, elegant establishment. It was straight out of the days of the British Raj, like you'd see colonels in jodhpurs strolling through with a host of red-capped Hindu bellboys murmuring "Sahib, sahib" behind them.

I went up to their room which turned out to be the penthouse. There was a full kitchen, two giant bedrooms, an office, and expansive decks all around looking out on the city. I took all this in, wondering how much it fucking cost. More importantly, making a note that this was not low profile.

Jack was on a silk-covered divan smoking a hookah, looking like the Caterpillar in "Alice in Wonderland." Meanwhile over in the corner, Grant was injecting himself with smack. "What the fuck?"

I discovered that for the entire seven days they'd been there Jack was spinning on speed, booze and opium. Grant had been doing smack and I found a syringe in the potted palm. It was a miracle they hadn't been busted by hotel security.

Of paramount importance though was a problem of a different kind. The middleman Grant was supposed to connect with was unavailable. Permanently unavailable. He'd been murdered. His body was found in the Dharavi slums with a bullet to the head and the tongue cut out. Then I remembered what Mr. Big, my mentor back in Sydney, had warned me about, "Plans change. On an international operation things are going to go sideways on occasion. You're going to have to roll with it." I thought, all right, this is it. Let's keep on going.

We had to find another connection and we went to the Dharavi slums. Why? Because that's where it all goes down. It's lawless. A million people living in the worst conditions imaginable. The garbage, the stench, the children playing in trash heaps was heartbreaking. You can only stand and wonder at the tragedy, the degradation of humans in these conditions. I wished I had the money to fix it, but of course it was unfixable. So I gave rupees to the kids, some without limbs because their parents amputated them so they could be more effective beggars. I got numb and needed to leave. They stay in their world and you go trekking on in yours carrying their market goods that you can't say no to. The beggars and prostitutes trailing behind you like you were the Prince of Siam tossing coins. This is the way of life there. Some of the prostitutes in cages. Penned up like crazy little animals. For a moment our operation seemed so trivial. But... then it was back to the business of finding a connection. Grant said he could do a better job of it on his own so we split up. Days later, he returned to the hotel and said he'd found someone even better than his murdered predecessor – a British ex-pat named Mick. And the next day our new connection showed up at the penthouse.

Mick now lived in Bombay but knew the sources in Afghanistan. He was a well-dressed, hip-looking guy with his handcrafted leather satchel slung over an elegant native shirt but there was no disguising that he was still a practicing smack head. I got Grant and Jack in the other room and said,

"We've had bad experiences dealing with junkies and you know it. There must be somebody else we can talk to."

"He's together. I say we go with him," Grant said.

Jack's rare moment of solidarity with Grant meant the meeting would take place. Mick brought out some coke, but I had him put it away. Coke and business are a guaranteed bad combo. I quizzed Mick about his background and it turned out he was a former British Special Forces operative who got sick of the killing, deserted and went native. He had married an Afghan chick in Peshawar and that's how he knew Tariq Rahim.

My biggest concern was Tariq's reliability. Mick said he was connected at the highest levels.

"What does that mean?" I asked skeptically.

"It means he's *affiliated*."

Jack perked up, "You're saying he's well connected above and beyond the drug trade. Into the corridors of power, let's assume?"

"Whatever you want he can get. Heroin, hash, AKs, guns, missiles..."

"Missiles?"

"He's a merchant of opportunity, and let's leave it at that."

I liked the phrase, "merchant of opportunity." Like a wide open door.

Jack said, "Hmmm, we could use a .45 Magnum. And an AK."

I said, "No. We definitely don't want guns."

"But what if someone tries to rip us off?"

Mick laughed, "Nobody fucks with Tariq or his clients."

I paid Mick half his fee of ten grand. He'd get the other half when we met up in Peshawar and he made the intro for us.

Thinking about all that, I had to wonder how much Patricia really knew. All of it, I guessed. Maybe she'd busted Mick and he'd told her everything. So what did she want from me? Remembering the commodities Tariq Rahim had available helped me get a clue that it was him she wanted and probably not because of the drugs he was selling. More likely it was the guns and missiles. She was going to grill me hard and put me in a squeeze. In her hotel room, no less.

14

After dark I took a cab to Patricia's hotel and went up to her door. I knew it was her door because two American agents stood outside it. I was told to wait on a love seat by the elevator. A few minutes later I was summoned and shown into a comfy suite and she came out of an adjacent room. Cool jazz followed her in. This was a different woman than I'd seen previously. She wore a dark blue silk dress so thin I could see the contour of her breasts and nipples, and her hair was down now and across her shoulders. This was not the severe hard-as-nails businesswoman who grilled us in Kabul, or the somewhat softened fox in the limo.

Behind her was a long balcony with the lights of Peshawar glittering in the background. She closed the curtains but kept the veranda doors open so the breeze could blow in. "You boys are very adventurous being in this part of the world right now. A coup last month in Pakistan. One coming in Afghanistan. The Iron Curtain extending right down the Khyber Pass. Countries building nuclear bombs possibly on the verge of attacking each other. And you are right in the thick of it. Buying hash."

It was useless to deny it, but I tried anyway. "Look, I'm just a surfer... a plumber..."

"You are one of the biggest marijuana dealers in Sydney.

And before that you and Grant had quite an operation going in Byron Bay."

"Why ask me questions when you have all the answers?" I tried to keep my voice level.

"You're so tense, James. I'm here to help you."

"Ok. Tell me where Grant and Jack are. You have them in custody I guess?"

"I'm doing what I can to keep them safe."

"Safe from who? You?"

"Pakistan authorities. Grant could be headed to Interpol. He's violated parole. He has a five to ten-year sentence over his head. Jack is gay and an infidel who broke the rules of Ramadan. You're all on forged passports. You're looking at serious time."

"Everybody's fate now rests in your hands?"

I felt like I was tiptoeing through a minefield. She was offering me a deal. But what kind of deal? And she was seducing me? "Why am I here?"

"Sit down and relax." It was an order and I obeyed. "What are you drinking?"

There was a bottle of VSOP on the table and I said I'd have some of that. She poured a tumbler for me and sat nearby. I could smell her perfume and it was like wispy fingers motioning me closer.

"The Soviets are moving into Afghanistan and that will upset a very delicate balance of power." She gazed at me quietly like I was supposed to tumble to something, but I couldn't figure it out. "You are involved, James."

"I'm involved? How?"

"By virtue of your association with Tariq Rahim. Let's stop the dumb show right now. You hear me? Your contact's true name is Khan. He went to Harvard and Oxford. He has a doctorate in political science. He's the son of Majid Khan, one of the leaders of the Afghan resistance to the Soviet incursion. We want to talk to him. We want you to set up a meeting."

I stood there frozen and she came to me and took the glass from my hands. I noticed that the big silver Rolex which had been on her wrist was now replaced by a small delicate gold bracelet. "You know what it's like being a female in a man's world. You were sensitive to that when we talked in Kabul. Rare in my world, James. I'm the first woman Station Chief. Eyes are on me. I'm tired. I'm sick of being stuck in this desert. I want out. But I have to go out with a win to pave the way for the women coming up behind me. There's resistance. A lot of old boy resistance. So we're going to help each other."

Her fingers went to a button on her dress, "Help a girl out, James," she said. I held back like you would from a delicious looking but potentially poisonous cookie. "Uhhh..."

"Oh come on, I'm not that scary."

I tentatively released two pearl buttons from their loops. I was going for number three and she put her hands over mine stopping me. She moved away, sipped her cognac, looking at me. "Turn out the lights." I flicked a switch and now it was a candle-lit room. The long blue silk of her dress rustled in the breeze and I could see her shape, her graceful shoulders, schoolgirl waist, gently curving hips as she stepped toward me smelling of that come hither perfume. She took my hand and led me into the bedroom. And it was all perfect – the lights, the jazz, the jasmine, her dress falling to the floor. I have to say that usually I was the seducer, but not on this night with this woman.

She unbuttoned my shirt, slipping it off my shoulders, and floated me over to the bed. Lying very still, she ran her hand over my chest. She purred and kept stroking me, her soft palm moving down across my navel. She unbuttoned my pants, slid her palm below my waist, brushing my cock. All of a sudden, I was spinning and felt like I had to get out of there or be swallowed by a wave I couldn't control.

She pushed me down, smoothing me into the sheets like I was some rough blanket that needed de-wrinkling. It was like I was drugged and had to give in to it. She was kneeling over me sucking my cock. And when that was good, hard and wet, she straddled me and lowered herself, deeper and deeper. Goddamn it, she was beautiful the way her hair fell down over both of us like a golden waterfall. With a fierce moan, she came and I followed, hardly knowing what had hit me. We lay there, her head cradled on my shoulder. I couldn't reconcile the girl next to me with the woman who just hours ago had been. grilling me in the limo. She had to be in her early forties, but in that moment in my arms she looked much younger. Soft, vulnerable, prom queen sweet.

I said, "Wow, we should have done this back in Kabul instead of that interrogation."

"I wasn't ready to take a chance on you then."

"Why now? Why me?"

"Maybe someday I'll tell you. But for now, let's talk a bit of business. I need you to introduce me to Khan. You do that and I will get your friends released and you three can carry on with your enterprise uninterrupted."

"Even if I knew this guy Tariq, he'd shoot me if I told him I was working with the CIA."

"So dramatic. Look, Tariq will be grateful you set up the introduction."

"Why is that?"

"He wants what we're offering."

"Which is?"

"The less you know the better."

"You fucked me and now I want to know why."

She paused, choosing her words carefully. "There was a communist backed coup in Afghanistan. Tariq is a capitalist. He's also a freedom fighter. We sanction his cause and his cause needs... support."

"Guns and money, huh."

"Material," she said. "Be a patriot. And if that's not enough of a reason, do it in your own self-interest."

"Otherwise you unleash the Pakistan police?"

"Think positively. You do what I say and you have my protection all the way to Bombay."

"The problem is – assuming I knew this person Tariq - I don't have a clue how to get hold of him."

"The guide who met you in Landi Kotal, Azziz. Send a message through him."

I was edgy and feeling like a puppet. "How the fuck am I supposed to find him?"

"You'll think of something. And maybe we can help you."

"Does anyone ever say no to you?"

"Not often." She laughed, "Just set up the meet. All will be well."

She got up, went into the bathroom, turned on the shower, calling to me. "We'll be in touch."

The one up-side to the whole business was that I had just

had a mind-blowing experience with a sexy, complex, scary, powerful woman who was apparently unencumbered by ethical constraints in the pursuit of what she wanted. Our values seemed equally matched. Witness me cheating on Andi. But I was twenty-four and besides, this was a matter of national security. I had to do it. And now what? I was just trying to stay free, but I was boxed into a corner with one apparent option. When you're surfing there are times when you're sitting out there on your board and the waves cease. You bob on the water, you look at the horizon, you daydream, you pray, you sing to the ocean to send a wave. But you are in a lull. It happens. You wait. Hopefully, you're paying attention when the next big one arrives so you don't take a few on the head. I was in a lull. My partners were in custody. I didn't know where or even who was holding them. CIA? Interpol? The Pakistan Army? All because Grant and Jack had fucked up. Jack had opened his big mouth and Flannery fucking recorded him. I should have listened to Grant. He had known what Flannery was all about. Despite his foresight, he then made things worse, breaking into Flannery's car and stealing the photos he had taken for the CIA.

15

Three months previous – on the road with Tim Flannery

The troubles with the CIA started when I let Jack get in Flannery's car back in Tehran for the drive to Afghanistan. Flannery was going to "escort" us. Sort of a "Charon," Jack said.

"Sharon?" I said, thinking he meant the Israeli General.

"No, my boy. Charon the Ferryman of Greek mythology who guided souls across the River Styx into the Underworld."

"Uh, that would imply we're dead, Jack."

"No, no. Certain heroes, like Odysseus, crossed over as well and lived to tell the tale. Tim has things to teach us."

I reminded him that the mission was to score the hash and not get sidetracked with a classics lesson.

"James, this whole business is about the *journey*. Think Virgil guiding Dante through Hell and Purgatory. The great challenge then becomes – how does one escape from Purgatory and be Heaven bound?"

"What?"

"Acceptance," Grant said.

Jack was surprised at Grant's response. "Acceptance? Of..."

"Sorry business."

"Meaning?"

"Death," I explained.

Jack raised an eyebrow, "I didn't know you were such a philosopher, Grant."

"Fuck you, Professor. You yabber too much."

We hooked up with Flannery on the outskirts of Tehran and Jack rode with him in his Citroen 2CV while Grant and I followed. We drove in silence for a long time. I wanted to ask him about what he'd revealed to me in the bar about killing a girl. Not an easy subject to get into. I finally asked him what he meant when he said that line about accepting death.

He was edgy. "You have a conscience, bunji?"

"Sometimes."

We rode in silence again with him sort of grinding his teeth. Then he asked me, "What kind of shit is in your head, mate? What kind of nightmare voices rattle you so bad even drugs won't shut 'em up?"

Did I have anything that heavy? I didn't think so. My conscience bothered me about cheating on Andi. Or when I used my mum's house for that heroin deal and exposed her to danger. But I wasn't in the black hole of Calcutta about it. I waited for him to open up some more but that was it. He was done talking.

Six hours later Flannery turned off Highway 44 onto a dirt road and we followed him into a little village that had the look of a medieval hamlet. Dirt and rocks and deep ruts cut through some ramshackle dwellings, mostly thatched roof huts with crude stucco walls. Fire-scorched trees jutted behind the corrugated tin overhang of a half-finished dwelling. And there were a number of those, abandoned in mid-construction, about to collapse with the next breath of wind. The whole area felt like some sudden mass exodus had just taken place.

Ducks chased emaciated rabbits away from the few edible plants around what was once a small pasture. The shepherd fence made out of rusting barbed wire hung on crooked tree limbs. Grant took it all in, "The yowies are here." He meant the evil spirits. "This is the landscape in my head, mate."

Flannery stopped and we pulled up behind him. He got out and rummaged around in the little 2CV, came out with some cameras. Jack was proudly at his heels. Flannery said he was going to take some photos. Jack trailed along with him. Grant told me to go for it if I wanted to check things out and he'd stay to watch the Rover.

I followed Flannery and Jack over a rickety bridge made of branches. A stream gurgled below, two men with backpacks stood with fishing poles, not having much luck. They looked at us like we were aliens, and of course we were from another world.

Flannery took photos as we traipsed along a little side road for a few hundred yards to a mud brick shack of a house. There were a couple of skinny ducks vying with some chickens over a corncob. Some puppies shook off their fleas and romped over to us. Flannery called out in Farsi to a man, apparently asking him if it was okay to take his picture. The man was deeply weathered and could have been thirty or he could have been sixty. A thick cigarette held between thumb and forefinger sent curls of smoke up into the greyness of the afternoon. Flannery gave him a couple packs of Marlboros and he was happy. Some lively kids came over, gathered around Flannery, who pulled some presents out of his backpack. Candy, a Rubik's Cube, candles, a carton of Marlboros, some chocolate. Everybody was happy to see Santa Claus.

Nearby, a toothless woman sat on the floor of an open shed playing patty cake with cow dung.She had a fire going and was cooking some bread. She added some more fuel on the fire, and the fuel was not wood but cow pie. The thin man pointed to her and talked with Flannery in Farsi.

Flannery translated, "The Shah is pumping $22 billion worth of oil out of this country, and these people do not have any fuel here. They use cow pies to heat their houses, to cook with. No oil. No gas. No electricity."

Jack said, "So this is the Shah's Great Civilization at work here. Viva la revolution!"

"But then what?" Flannery said.

"Can't be any worse," Jack said.

"Oh, it could be worse. It will be worse. It'll be a whole lot worse if the mullahs take power."

I gave some money to the thin man. His jaw dropped. He didn't want to take it. Flannery had to talk him into it. Foreign aid. From the Great Civilization of drug smugglers.

We left our Iranian friend and walked back across the bridge to the vehicles. Grant was leaning up against our Rover, dark Ray Bans on, arms crossed, stony looking, waiting. He was vibing Flannery in a hard ass way. Flannery went to unlock his Citroen and saw that the back window was broken. The car was unlocked. He said nothing, just put his cameras in the back seat, rummaged around, searching for something. When he emerged, he was pissed but contained, "I want those photos back."

"I don't know what you're talking about," Grant said, but of course he did.

Jack and I were wondering what the fuck was going down. Jack was more embarrassed than anything. "Now, Grant, you... you didn't break that window, did you? And take something of Tim's?"

"Would I do that, Professor?"

"Give me the photos and I'll forget about it."

"Who was the blonde in the hotel bar?" Grant asked like he already had the answer.

"You have no idea who you're fucking with."

"You're a fucking stooge for the Yanks. All these pics you're taking – it's for them huh."

Flannery went up right in Grant's face. It was tense. Neither one was a pushover. If there was a fight, it would be ugly.

"Fuck you gubba," Grant said.

Jack put a hand on Flannery's shoulder to stop him. They looked like Mutt and Jeff. He tilted his nose up at Grant, "My boy, you've got our friend here all wrong. He deserves an apology."

"Professor, you're dumber than you look. You can't see past your little budoo."

Flannery grabbed Grant by the shirt. Grant broke the hold and hit him in the jaw knocking Flannery back a few steps. Grant was going to hit him again but Flannery was too fast for him, got hold of his wrist, put him in an arm bar and forced him to the ground.

"You've got your head up your ass man," Flannery said. "The photos!"

He applied pressure but Grant wouldn't give. "Let him go," I said. "We'll get it straightened out." Flannery let go, stepped back. Grant rushed at him and I stepped into the middle of it, put my arm around Grant's shoulder, "Hold it, hold it, mate. Can we talk for a second?"

He had come to think of me as a brother over the years and he let me lead him away. "Grant... What the fuck, mate? You broke into his car? You took his photos? Why?"

"Because he's a lying dickhead gangie motherfucker."

"We don't need this bullshit. Give him back the photos."

"Not a chance. I'm leaving. Get in the car if you're coming." He got behind the wheel. Fortunately, I had the keys. I went over to Flannery not knowing what to say. I asked where he was staying in Mashhad and I promised him that whatever Grant had of his I would return to him at his hotel as soon as we arrived. There was nothing more to say. I told Jack to get in the Rover.

But Jack moved to Flannery. "Tim, can I ride with you again?"

Flannery laughed. "Sure. Why not."

Jack patted Flannery's shoulder. "All will be well, Tim, I promise you. And I apologize for the despicable behavior of my countryman there."

I climbed in the Rover with Grant, gave him the keys and he floored it. We jammed down the dirt road for a few clicks and when he finally calmed down, I asked him about the photos. "What's the big battle for, mate? He's taking some pics of scrawny chickens."

"Yeah. And a few other things."

He reached up under the dash as he drove and pulled out some 8 X 10 black and whites. I went through them and saw a convoy of British Army trucks. "Yeah, trucks. So what?"

"Check out what's in the trucks."

A photo showed a long flatbed trailer covered with camo tarps. In the next photo the tarps were pulled back revealing a row of missiles. Stamped on the side of the weapons was "U.S. Air Force."

16

In the wake of my strange interlude with Patricia Adams, I walked out of her hotel room spinning like an off-kilter top. If I'd encountered government agents before I didn't know it. Now they seemed everywhere and inescapable. As I hit the streets of Peshawar, I glanced around thinking G Men and the Paki police were coming for me. Basically, me and my partners were fucked. It was an impossible situation. I was in the middle of it, being drafted to tell Tariq the CIA wanted to meet with him. Jack would have said something like, "Oh it happens all the time, my boy!" and launched into an expose of the CIA's use of criminals. His advice would have been appreciated but he wasn't around. As to where he and Grant were being held, I still had no idea. I considered going to the Australian embassy for help but that was problematic. We had forged passports and had been detained and branded smugglers by the CIA. There were pictures of us meeting with international criminals. My options were few. But I'm a glass-half-full kind of guy and I saw a flicker of hope. Maybe what Patricia wanted of me wasn't so impossible. Grant and I had been in many dire situations and swam through every time. Handle this one right and my partners would be released, we'd get our Rover, and go on our merry way. Maybe.

I went into the hotel bar to think over a beer. The situation boiled down to a familiar concept I could relate to – a Deal. Tariq was an arms broker. Patricia wanted to give him arms and make him an asset. She wanted him to work for America against the Soviets. He was against the Russians invading his country. I perked up seeing how it just might all work out. But how to arrange the meeting when I didn't know where to find Tariq?

I needed more information from Patricia. Some clue as to how to contact Tariq or Azziz. The next day I went back up to her hotel room. This time there were no suits guarding her door. When I knocked some Iranian businessman answered. I asked for Patricia Adams at the front desk. Of course, no one by that name had ever even registered.

I went back to the tobacco shop where we'd made the down payment to the old man thinking he could get a message to Tariq. But the shop was closed and looked like it had been for a while. I walked back out of the bazaar to the street and that same hearse of a limo pulled up. The door opened and I got in with Patricia.

"Well, James, you don't appear to be making much progress."

"It might help if you let my friends go."

"How would that help?"

"Grant might know how to get in touch with the person who set us up with Tariq."

"Grant's not talking. Jack's talking too much. So it's on you. Time is critical." She had the silver Rolex back on her wrist. "You have forty-eight hours before I turn you over to Interpol."

"Assuming I do this, how do I find you?"

"As I said, we'll find you."

"Can I ask why you slept with me?"

"Maybe it's the ponytail." She leaned over me, brushing herself against my lap. I could smell her perfume, feel the bulge of her breasts, her hair across my arm. She opened the door. "Azziz," she said. "He can help you. You'll find him at the Qasim Ali Khan Mosque."

I got out into the teeming street. The limo was a crowd pleaser and had drawn a circle of fans. I felt like I was in a cage at the zoo. But at least I had a possibility. Azziz. Our guide to the hash dealers in the Kush and now my best hope to keep three bunjis from Oz out of the Pakistani slammer.

17

Back in Sydney when we were still in the planning stage of our enterprise I knew there would be complications. You don't go halfway around the world to score two hundred kilos of hash without a complication or two. I also figured there would be some oil and water problems between Jack and Grant. But never did I anticipate what actually happened out there on the road between Tehran and the Afghan border. Both of my partners had succumbed to madness. I'd been dealing with it since I found them crazy high in Bombay.

As Grant and I drove away from the little village where he'd broken into Flannery's Citroen, heading east back on Highway 44 to the Iran/Afghan border, I wondered what fallout was to come from these stolen photos of American missiles. He was gnawing on old bones, in the blackest of moods because he had gotten his ass handed to him. In his mind, by a cop. To a bloke who'd recently spent time in prison anyone associating with law enforcement was the enemy. He was certain that Flannery was in bed with American Intelligence. And as it turned out, Flannery was the one who put us on the radar of Patricia Adams by getting Jack to blab about our agenda. But I'm ahead of myself.

I looked through the stolen photos and there were many

of the uprising in Tehran showing faces in the crowd, especially of mullahs and student leaders exhorting the masses to overthrow the Shah. I didn't need Jack to tell me what was going on. The U.S. had propped up the Shah and the CIA wanted to know who the rebel leaders were. I wanted to get rid of these pictures because I knew they would be trouble. The best thing to do would be to get them back to Flannery. Grant was too hot now to listen to reason so I tried to keep it light until he was in a better mood. "Just like the old days, mate. On our way to score," I joked.

His mind was elsewhere. "I'm going to drop that gammon the next time I see him."

"Listen to me, mate. If you're right about him, and it looks like you are – we don't need him pissed off at us."

"Too late. The Professor is back there riding with him sucking his dick, telling him everything he wants to know about how to fuck us."

I couldn't deal with his dark mood anymore and had to do something. I had a guidebook and began reading out loud to him about how this two-lane rutted blacktop we were on, looking like a deserted road in the Aussie outback, had been a pathway through Asia Minor for thousands of years. "*Buried here in the valley and beneath the hills are the skeletons of many armies who had marched through since ancient times. Alexander the Great came through on his failed expedition to conquer Afghanistan.*"

"Yeah," Grant said with disinterest.

"*The Greeks thundered by on their way to conquer Persia, and the Persians on their way to conquer Greece. The English rode through on their way to conquer India and Afghanistan.*"

We were coming up on the border soon and I had to chill him out and get myself in a better frame of mind before the cross. Meanwhile the photos could be a problem. What would the guards think if they found us in possession of those?

I saw ancient ruins emerging out of the harsh high desert landscape and stopped for a break. We got out and I took the photos with me as we walked into the crumbling remains of a stone temple which had survived from antiquity. Part of it had been carved out of the sandstone and lime by unknown hands. *"Buddhist stupas,"* I read in the guidebook. The relentless desert had swallowed them up centuries ago and now they were being excavated. But it was weird because, while the archeological project was obviously in progress, no one, absolutely not one soul, was around. The place seemed suspended in time with the historic dig unguarded and only half finished.

We strolled around the walls of the ruins which were carved stones stacked twenty feet high surrounding the rust colored temple. It was like some dystopian city, half dead, half alive, existing in the middle of a moon-cratered landscape that spread out way up into the snow-covered mountains beyond.

I put my lighter to the photos. By the time Grant saw what I was doing it was too late. They were ashes in the dirt. He bored into me with those wide dark eyes, coal black, not a trace of mirth, and there hadn't been a smile wrinkle for days ever since we'd run into Flannery. "What the fuck did you do that for, man?"

I told him we were about to cross the border and we didn't need the guards questioning us about why we had pictures of Redeye and Stinger missiles. "What do you want them for anyway?"

"Proof, mate! Fucking proof that I'm right about him!"

"Grant, buddy, you're losing it. You're as obsessed with Flannery as Jack is."

"What the fuck are you talking about?"

"Jack loves him, you hate him. I need us to pull it together, mate!"

"I'm together. I'm totally together. Don't you fucking worry about me, mate."

"I'm worried about *me*! We're going to cross a goddamn border. I don't want to be detained because you go off on some soldier. We gotta look cool. You do not look cool, bunji. You look like you have piranhas inside you eating away. What is eating at you, man? What the hell is it?"

He was shaking with anger. I plucked a pack of smokes from his shirt pocket and lit one for each of us. He dragged on his and blew a grey cloud toward the ground. I had a flask with some brandy in it and gave it to him. We stood beside a two-thousand-year-old rock wall. He ran his hand over the stone and it seemed to calm him. "Okay. I hear you, man."

Some birds that looked like partridges nesting in the crumbling citadel swooped up into an azure sky. There were three men on a distant rise wearing white robes, walking in a line carrying hay bales on their backs. Grant watched them, "That's us, huh."

"How's that, mate?"

"Trudging along, carrying shit."

"What are you carrying?"

He inspected the glowing ash of his cigarette, "When you went to do the smack deal, I got word from my uncle that Sprinkles was lying down and wouldn't get up. So I went out there and sat with her while she passed away. Sweet horse. Then my uncle told me he knew where mum was. Working at an escort service in Sydney. I went there, didn't find her. I found Tuesday instead. Now because of me she's dead."

"How's that, Grant?"

"Forget it. Maybe she'll come back."

"What?"

"Her spirit."

We heard the rumble of trucks and out on the road we saw a caravan of British military vehicles passing by. They had camo-covered flatbeds like Flannery had photographed. "Wonder if there's missiles under those tarps," Grant said. He crushed his cigarette into the ancient dirt. He picked the butt up and put it in his pocket. "We don't want to desecrate the ruins, right? Come on, let's do this. I'm with you, mate. It's all cool." And he walked back toward the Rover.

I looked at the map and saw we were close to the border. I wanted to look straight as possible for the crossing, so I got into my blue blazer and tan trousers, tied my hair back in a nice, neat ponytail. Grant spruced up a bit, too, and just like that we were gentleman rolling up to the guard station on the Iranian side. Beyond the gate was a short no man's land and then the Afghan station. "We have no drugs with us, right, mate? You're not holding out on me right? Because we don't want to take any chances crossing through here."

"All clean, mate," he said.

I had my money belt neatly stashed under my nice clean white shirt. And I had a couple of hundred-dollar-bills to change at the border, so we'd have some local currency. There was a line of cars and trucks ahead of us. Up at the front was the convoy of British military vehicles. They rolled right through without an inspection.

When it was our turn, I went into the border station and presented our passports. That went okay and I figured we were home free. I went over to the Iranian soldiers who manned the currency exchange and handed them some hundred-dollar bills. The soldier changed one bill and then he looked at the other one. He scrutinized it closely and said something in Farsi to his cohort and they conferred together, checking the bill out. They did not like what they saw. They called a couple more soldiers over and next thing I knew I was under guard with American made M-16 rifles pointing at me. They sent for their commander.

Meanwhile, outside, I saw guards order Grant out of the Rover and then search him and the car. I wondered what the fuck was wrong here. I mean, there couldn't be anything sketchy with that money. I'd gotten the bills straight from Barclays Bank in London. The station chief came over and talked with his guards in Farsi. They scrutinized the bill, held it up to the light, checked it against pictures of American money they had. Then the station chief said, "Where Inshallah?"

What the fuck did that mean? "Ah, excuse me?" I said.

"Where In God We Trust?" he said.

"What do you mean?"

"No 'In God We Trust.' Counterfeit bill. You are being detained for this counterfeit money."

I looked at the bill. He was right. There was no "In God We Trust" printed on it. Had Barclays bank laid a counterfeit bill on me? I remembered Mr. Big's words about how you can go down because something stupid, something totally out of left field, something completely random blindsides you. I figured the next thing they'd do was search us and find my money belt with a hundred grand in it. A hundred grand smuggling money in counterfeit bills. They were going to fucking go through everything and they'd find the ludes in the shaving can. And we were going to fucking end up like Billy Hayes in a dark hole of a prison.

I looked at that bill, trying to fathom what was up. There had to be some explanation. "I got the bill from the Barclays Bank," I told the Iranians. Finally, I grabbed the bill and they about shot me, and I yelled, "Wait, wait, just let me see something here." I looked closely. Really closely. The date on the bill was 1934. 1934? This was 1977. The bill was an antique. I had a wild thought and just went with it. "Look, it's simple," I said, the story flowing like water right out of me. "In the old days, America didn't put "In God We Trust" on the money. They added it in the early '50s after they dropped bombs on Hiroshima and Nagasaki. They wanted the world to know they had God on their side."

The chief nodded. It seemed to make sense to him, so I kept rolling. "This bill is rare," I said and scratched my head for emphasis. "Worth a lot of money. More than $100. I'll keep it." The station chief was processing what I said. He looked at one bill, then the other. "I'll keep it, get you another one."

He waved me off, "No, no, no, we take it. We take it."

"I don't know..." I let the hook work its way in. "So, can we be on our way then? Release the car and my friend?"

He sent a soldier outside to his guards who had Grant detained. There was some dialogue out there and the soldier came back. The car and Grant were clean.

"You can go," the chief said. He kept the bills, I got some Iranian money in exchange and got out of that fucking guard station. Once we were out of Iran and into Afghanistan, I breathed a sigh of relief. I put some Stones on the tape player, and told Grant I wished we had a joint to celebrate. He said, "Pull over." Lifting up the hood of the Rover, he unscrewed the air cleaner top. He came back with a cube of hash and we lit up. As we toked, a little red Citroen 2CV sped past us. Jack was in the passenger seat waving.

"I wonder how Flannery will take it when I tell him I burnt the photos," I said.

"No worries, mate. We'll just print some more." He laughed, pulling two rolls of film from his shirt pocket.

18

Peshawar was a city with half a million people. I had for-ty-eight hours to locate one of them. Tariq Rahim or Khan or whatever his name was, the hash and arms dealing Afghan freedom fighter that even the CIA couldn't find. My best hope was to track down his gofer Azziz. I followed the tip Patricia Adams had given me and went to the mosque where he worshiped. It was Ramadan and the faithful gathered there five times a day to kneel on their prayer rugs, hundreds deep, under hanging fans. It was a massive stag meeting of old men and young acolytes, feverish committed believers with their beards, gaunt eyes, sanctity, swearing surrender and sacrifice. Was the bulky black-bearded one I sought somewhere in that throng? Hard to tell because all I saw were backsides. And not a female to be seen anywhere. Why no women allowed? How did that start? Who said cover them up and leave them at home? You start wondering about these things spending six hours watching from across the street. I waited till the service ended and wandered among them but if Azziz was there, I missed him.

It occurred to me to try a different course of action - plead my case to the Australian embassy. I mean, what crimes had we actually committed, really? All Patricia was holding over our heads was travelling under forged passports. I figured that's an Australian issue, not a Pakistani one. So I thought maybe I'd just tackle this head on, find a lawyer, see what our rights were. There had to be some habeas corpus regs in the Paki law canon. What better place to find an attorney than a courthouse, so I went to the Peshawar High Court and hung around outside. The lawyers are the ones with the briefcases, I figured and picked a jaunty-looking younger guy, offering a hundred American and a coffee for a bit of his time. I could have saved my money. I learned we had no legal rights. It was a time of martial law. People, suspected foreign criminals, could be held indefinitely without even being charged. It was his view the CIA had helped overthrow President Bhutto because of his embrace of the Russians. Bhutto had gotten friendly with the Soviets because the U.S. helped India with its nuclear pro-liferation. So the CIA was in bed with the Pakistani military and either way, whoever had my two partners were, according to the lawyer, fucked.

The day was almost gone. Dusk was settling over the smoky city. I took a cab to the hotel. As it pulled up, I was surprised to see Flannery's Citroen 2CV with the broken window parked nearby. I waited for him and was leaning against his car when he came out of a print shop clutching a leather satchel, moving fast like he was on a mission. And weren't we all. One thing we all had in common – Jack, Grant, me, Flannery and Patricia – was the inability to walk away from certain challenges that grabbed us. In my case, it was the challenge of getting the whole crazy enterprise that was now off the rails back on track and successful. Grant's challenge, I was discovering, was some sort of redemption or obliteration of guilt. Jack's issue was being respected, admired and sought after. Patricia was all about winning one for the girls. And Flannery? The challenge he couldn't walk away from was... what? I wasn't sure. I asked him straight up: "Why are you even fucking with us?"

"Your mate fucked with me."

"Before that even happened, though, you pumped Jack for information. Why?"

"Just looking for a story."

"You're going to write about three smugglers on the Silk Road? Or maybe it includes missiles?"

He shrugged, "You guys ain't the story. Missiles? Forget you ever saw those. The story is... the world at war. Or haven't you noticed?"

"Yeah, we're in a war zone. You traded what you found out about us to Patricia. I don't give a shit what it was, but it got me in a cross and my mates in jail. Now I've got to find Tariq to get them out. You can help me with that."

"Tariq who?"

"Come on mate, you know who he is. My partners and I could go away for a long time if I don't find him."

He laughed, "You're playing the sympathy card. It's weak, man. You got yourselves into this and you'll get yourselves out."

Military vehicles rolled by. Soldiers stationed at the intersection saluted the implementation of martial law. Still, the city just rolled on, business as usual, cars and buses honked, bicyclists yelled at cabs, trucks blocking the street. Muslim women walking three abreast with their heads covered hurried by. The orthodox men giving them the stink-eye because they were unescorted.

"You slept with Patricia. She's got the power stick. She

can do things for you."

"You seem to know everything. At least tell me where my friends are being held."

"Some black site somewhere. Do what Trish says and everything will be cool, then get your royal asses back to the kangaroos. You're out of your league here."

"Look, Flannery, you set us up. Now do the fucking right thing and help us out."

"Maybe if it was just you and Jack. But that asshole Grant can rot in a hole for all I care." He got behind the wheel, the 2CV fired up with a big puff of black smoke. Off he pulled into traffic, the cacophony of the city ringing, banging hard into me. I was fried and hogtied and not one bit closer to Tariq Rahim.

19

Grant's hatred of authority had gotten us into trouble before. There was that time in those rollicking early days in Byron Bay when we were racing our Montessas through the hills. We blew up over a rise, came down on the highway doing about seventy and saw a police car heading our way. They passed by, turned around and the flashing lights and sirens were on us. We gunned our bikes off-road over hill and dale and lost the heat. We found a dirt track that led to a little fire road, then followed that down into town where we pulled into a petrol station and parked the bikes behind the pumps.

We were congratulating ourselves on a great escape when we noticed we were across the street from the police station. Cop cars surrounded us and we were handcuffed and prodded into the jail. Grant wasn't one to be intimidated by cops. In fact, he liked pissing the pigs off. "Gubba gangie, how's that?" he said when they asked his name.

"Abo talk? You got some black in you, don't you," a cop said.

"You've got some white Irish shit in you, don't you," Grant said.

That put us behind bars for three days until finally I had to call Detective Marx and he got the hick cops to cut us loose. But now in Peshawar there was no one to call for help.

I was pissed at my partners. Things had been on track for a big win before each in his own way lost his cool over Flannery. I thought I had solved the problem when I burned the missile photos, but then Grant revealed he had also stolen the negatives. We had just made it through the border crossing from Iran into Afghanistan. Jack was in Flannery's car somewhere up the road ahead of us. We rumbled along the potholed highway heading toward a rendezvous with Flannery in Herat where I planned to give him his negs back. Grant was high on hash and had the negs in his pocket and I was going to get him to hand them over. We had the Eagles cranked up on the tape deck and passed a flask of brandy back and forth as I drove. I almost asked him why he was feeling guilt over the death of Tuesday, but he was finally in a decent mood and I didn't want to have him go dark again. Highway 1 through Afghanistan is a potholed, desolation row of a road. Two lanes, a thousand trucks. There was no passing anyone, because they absolutely wouldn't let us by. We just got in line and bumped along with the windows up tight to avoid the fumes and dust, passing rusting shells of abandoned vehicles and cows that calmly watched us from behind their barbed wire enclaves.

As we came up on a truck stop, we saw the British Army convoy on the roadside. Parked nearby was Flannery's little red Citroen. It was an attention getter for Grant that tweaked him out of his happy mood. He scowled, looking out the window. Flannery was talking to the British Army commander. I told Grant to give me the negatives. "Fuck that. Stop. I'm going to talk to that fucker." We did not need yet another crazy fight, especially one in front of the Brits. Grant grabbed my arm and tried to get the wheel. I pushed him off and kept going.

"You gotta get control of yourself, mate!" I saw Jack coming out of the truck stop. He waved, high on life, hanging with his new hero Flannery.

Grant breathed hard, "I'll get his ass in Herat." He had the two rolls of film in his hand and squeezed them.

"I mean it, Grant. I'm done babysitting. Now you're a fucking liability."

"Don't get your nut huggers in a twist, bunji. I'll be cool."

"Give me the film."

"Listen mate, you're not seeing the big picture. Flannery is playing everybody, okay? He's going to use those photos he took..."

"I don't give a shit! What I give a shit about is the score, man."

"Trust me on this – by now, Jack has told that fucker everything we're doing. Names, dates and places. Flannery will use that against us somehow and you'll be glad I have this film. It's gonna save our asses. I'm not the liability you think I am. The Professor back there trying to prove how cool he is to Flannery – *that* is the liability."

I admired Jack and didn't want to hear that about him, but part of me suspected that what Grant was saying could be true. As it turned out, he was right.

A couple hours later we pulled into the Arg Hotel in Herat, the appointed meeting place with Flannery and Jack. The big question was how to avoid a confrontation between Grant and Flannery. After we checked in, I took Grant down to the pool and we swam a couple laps. Then I got him in the steam room and we had the place to ourselves as we sat on the benches. I said, "Look mate, you've got something heavy weighing on

you. And maybe you need to get that shit out and let it go."
He sat there in silence for a while, sweat beading on a troubled
face, then poured water on the scalding rocks and the steam
hissed and coiled. "I pulled Tuesday out of that escort service.
She was afraid this guy, like her pimp, would track her if she
left. But I convinced her to come with me to Mullumbimby.
I really fell for her, bunji."

"She melted your walls mate, huh."

"Like no chick ever had." I had never known him to go
that deep with a chick. He usually bounced around from one
to the other. He had changed so much from the devil-may-
care beach master he was just a few years back. The "old days"
seemed long ago even though I was only twenty-four and he
was twenty-seven. Right then in the steam room he was heavy
with regret. This was from loving his dream girl? It started me
wondering if this was what really loving a chick did to you.

He poured more water on the rocks and breathed the
steam in. Internal brine spread across his brow and the drops
boiled into his chest. "She looked kinda like Lolita. She even
had those heart shaped sunglasses. Sweet, sexy, funny. She was
It, mate. The one."

"You knew she was the one right off?" I was thinking of
Andi the first time I saw her leaning over me with the Mimosa.

"Oh yeah. I'd just been told my mum had been there and
gone. I guess I was looking a little ragged. She was standing
around waiting for her date. I saw her and asked if she wanted
to get out of there for a minute. Just to talk. She said okay and
I took her around the corner for a coffee and we talked and
she forgot all about the date. And it was weird because she
was hot and I wanted to be with her but it wasn't really about

getting my budoo wet. It wasn't the doori, no. It was about knowing her. Really seeing who she was."

"That's the way I felt about Andi. Though I did want to fuck her. So, what happened?"

"We talked. Or she talked. I listened." He shook his head, like he really didn't understand it yet. "It was a story you hear about. Nineteen-year-old girl from the outback. Bad home life. Escaped to Sydney. Wanted to be a dancer. Young, pretty chick hits the city and the vultures are waiting. She got hung up with some bad people. Started using junk. Ended up turning tricks for a thousand a night."

"So you brought her up to Mullumbimby?"

"Yeah. Drove right to the beach and took some shrooms. We spent the day talking and finally making love. Best day of my life."

The parallels were weird. I had done the same with Andi, taken shrooms with her up on the headlands, making it, talking. Listening to Grant I couldn't help but think how lucky I was. My adventure into the matrix of true love hadn't ended like his. And if I could just keep our operation from exploding, I'd get back with a big load of cash and start the good life with her. Maybe.

It was too hot for me in that steam room but I kept him talking. "She moved in with me. But Romeo and Juliet don't have a happy ending, right mate? She was afraid her pimp would find her, track her to Byron somehow. I thought, *no fucking way*. But she was so freaked I decided to make a big score and move us to Hawaii or someplace. There was no weed or hash in Byron Bay at the time, remember. I figured you were doing a smack deal, so why not get one going here.

Yours turned cruel man but I still kept going with mine. I had to go over to Adelaide to make the buy."

The rest I knew: he got busted, escaped, they caught him and he went to prison. I asked him why he felt responsible for Tuesday dying. "While I was doing time, the pimp tracked her down, cut her face. Mouth to ear. She was in the hospital and jumped from a fifth story window."

I put my hand on his shoulder. The silence echoed in that small room and I felt like I needed to say something. "We need to surf. Since we're in the middle of Afghanistan, probably not going to happen. Let's get a drink instead." The door opened, steam rushed out and some guys walked in. We gave the room over to them and went to the showers.

When we were up in the bar with our beers I said, "Hey man... that's a bloody awful tragedy that went down. But it's not your fault."

"I should have been there when her pimp showed up."

"Look mate, you want to kill yourself over this? That's what you're doing. Just get it over with. Jump off the roof. Or overdose." I saw some fire come back into his eyes. Even if it was anger directed at me, it was better than the dead look he'd had before. "Get yourself together, bunji. You didn't tell her to jump. You were trying to save her. And my guess is you avenged her."

"I looked for the pimp when I got out, but I couldn't find him."

"Ok, you tried. Are you going to self-destruct? Or are you going on with me to make this deal happen?"

"Fuck the deal." He meant it. I let him brood for a while then his eyes wrinkled at the corners. "I remember when you first showed up on the beach selling joints. Cocky little motherfucker. I said to myself, am I going to kick his butt or partner up with him? I chose right. All the fun, all the girls, all the wild shit and the deals we've done, huh, mate."

"Right. In it to win it. Oh, but I forgot – you're bailing."

"Asshole."

"You want to quit on the big one, okay."

"All right... I'm in."

"All right then, let's do it without any more fucking calamity."

He slapped me on the shoulder, came close to my face looking at me with the eyes of Job, holding my gaze. There was vulnerability there, a softness, "James, you've been a bro to me. I know I'm not easy. You've had a rough time keeping this thing together. You're the glue. I'm grateful, I'm in all the way and you can count on me." We shook on it and ordered another brew.

"Now where's that sonofabitch Flannery?" he said with such malice that it belied the progress we'd just made.

"Come on now, mate. I need you to give me the film."

He thought it over a beat and shook his head. "I'll give it to him personally. As an apology, right." What would happen when Flannery appeared was still a worry. But it didn't come to that, because Jack walked in alone. He was in a jaunty mood, strutting like he did when he was pontificating about some arcane historical event. He ignored Grant and spoke to me. "My boy, I have had myself a grand adventure. And there's more to come."

"More to come?"

"We're meeting Tim in Kabul."

That set Grant off. "The fucker's not coming in here? He chickened out?"

Jack rolled his eyes almost out of their sockets, "Oh my God, you are so butch. He doesn't want to engage with you, Grant. That kind of macho craziness is boring to him. He doesn't even care about the film. He's friends with the Brits and he's got plenty of pictures."

I had to stop this in its tracks, "Jack, what the fuck are you doing? You don't go setting things up on your own."

"Tim is a chum. We get along famously."

"What did you tell him, Professor?"

"Now, Grant, I don't believe that's any of your business. No offense."

"You told him all about yourself of course, right?"

"Yes, and he told me about himself."

"And then you told him all about what we're doing."

Jack said nothing. He'd spilled the beans for sure. I knew now that Grant was right. But it bothered me that he kept berating Jack like he was the enemy, "He's playing you, Professor. What exactly did you tell him?"

"The history of the Land of the Bones." He launched into a lecture about Alexander the Great entering Afghanistan in 400 B.C. "It was called Bactria then and he invaded after conquering Persia. Chasing a warlord called Spitamenes..."

Grant got in his face, "I don't give a flying fuck about 400 B.C!"

"Well you should because it bears heavily on our business," Jack said, not backing down. There was seldom any fear in him even though he was barely five feet tall and had all manner of physical ailments. In a crisis he could be very cool, though unpredictable which sometimes saved our asses and others, got us in trouble. He stayed calm and continued his lesson, "Listen and learn my friend. Alexander the Great found a harsher land than he bargained for. Packs of wild dogs gnawed on the bones of the dead. Hence the Greek nickname for this inhospitable country - Land of the Bones..."

For the most part, I loved Jack's history lessons. I had a thirst for knowledge and one of the benefits of hanging with him was hearing all his tall tales of truth from the legendary past. He was twenty years older than me and had become essentially my mentor. Plus, he was funny as hell and in a way kind of filled the role of the father I had lost. I didn't like to see him dissed. I didn't like to see Grant laying into him so I stepped between them and draped my arm over his hunchback. I also needed to know what he had said to Flannery. "What did you tell him, Jack?"

"The history. How Alexander failed in his attempt to conquer Bactria. How all the other invaders that had come over the centuries to subdue this feral land with its fierce tribes also crashed and burned. Like the British who tried twice in the 1800s and failed miserably both times. And they'll fail again."

This was curious to me. "You're saying the Brits are invading Afghanistan again? With American missiles?"

"Let's say the Brits are a carrier service."

"So why is Flannery taking pictures?"

"Why shouldn't he? It's news. He's a photojournalist. With, I might add, a very sophisticated world political view. He knows the Afghans have defeated all invaders. And he said the Russians will fail, too. He knows what's happening with the Soviet buildup of arms and materials. Civil war is about to break out, assassinations and coups are coming soon. Desperate times." He eyed Grant mischievously. "*Sorry business*, you might say. A severe drought killing hundreds of thousands of people. The only crop they have is opium. The Russians are coming to save the day. The Americans and Brits don't like that. The missiles will be front page news."

"The west wants the public to know there's an arms buildup?"

"Of course. Making the world safe for democracy. Now that's a comfort."

Grant pressed him, "Forget about the missiles. What did he say about me grabbing the photos from him?"

"He said that you are an angry, paranoid, misguided individual."

Grant chuckled, nodding ruefully like that was true. "Angry? Misguided? Sure. Paranoid? Occasionally. But not when it comes to what he's up to and what you told him. I'd be dumb as a kangaroo if I didn't know what's up with that."

I felt the shades closing on a sunny window. "Is it true, Jack? Does he know... what we're doing and who we're buying from?"

There was a beat that said I was spot on, but he shrugged it off. "Methinks you boys do protest too much. Now let's have drinks and dinner and a grand party. Then the Three Musketeers will be off into the Land of the Bones, headed for Kabul in the morning!"

He hobbled off using his cane to ease the pressure on his gout ridden feet. I told Grant that it didn't do any good to lay into him like that. What's done is done.

"Oh it ain't done, James. Unh uh. We're gonna get hit from this. Trust me. But you know what, mate? I've been in prison and I can handle it. I just wonder if you two can."

20

We blazed out of Herat on Highway 1 to Kabul. Two lanes of endless blacktop stretching out before us through an ashen, blistered moonscape. The monotony broken by eighteen-wheelers rattling by us, their mirrors just inches away from collision, rocking the Rover towards the shoulder. Like the trucks that wouldn't give an inch, the sturdy indomitable people of this hard-scrabble land would fight to the death before losing ground. And why? There were no crops, no gold or silver to be mined, no minerals, no salt, no water, not even a tree.

"The Land of the Bones. Americans and the English and the Iranians and the Pakistanis all want to control it. Why?" Jack went into professor mode and when he had an audience he could be riveting. "Why for millennia have great and powerful nations spent fortunes and thousands upon thousands of lives in failed bids to control one of the harshest and most dolorous places on Earth? Fear is my guess."

"Fear?" Grant asked as though the word was stalking him.

"Fear of someone else controlling it. I will admit I suffer the same obsession. But you're young, what do you know of it? You have no fear. You control the surf break. You carve out your territory on the prison yard, you grab any young feline you want without fear of rejection. Your body is strong. Youth gets what it desires."

"Yeah. I see," he said, looking at Jack's hunchback, maybe for the first time understanding a bit about him.

Jack went on, "The nature of man is to conquer. And we are the same, boys! We came here like Alexander to take what we want. To win."

"Fucking A. In it to win it." Grant slapped him on the curve of his back, then noticing Jack's flinch as he received the blow. "Sorry..."

"Ouch. James, my boy, are you in it to win it?"

"Yeah. Now let's see if you can avoid any more fuckups. We're going to have to deal with what happened back there. You both know that."

"What's your fear? Out with it." Jack said.

True, I had plenty of fear and it wasn't just the repercussions of Jack's loose tongue and Grant's madness. Were we making the same mistake as Alexander the Great? And the British Empire? Grandiosity aside, were we heading toward a similar fate? Watch me, Andi, on my fool's errand. My girl had warned me and she was right on. "My fear? Besides you two flipping out - a war erupts and we're in the middle of it."

"Epic events indeed, James. Tim says the U.S. and the Soviets are gearing up for a proxy war."

"What the fuck is a proxy war?" I asked.

Grant laughed, "I seen a few proxy wars. On the yard. Some chicken shit would pay another bloke to fight for him. It came back to haunt the bloke who did the hiring."

"As it may just happen here. The Soviets will prop up the present communist government. The Americans will use insurgent guerrilla fighters to foment revolution."

Grant looked at me and smiled, "Guess who told him all that? Ol' Tim's not just a newsboy, is he? And now he knows everything we're doing. Right, Professor?"

"You have a very wrong and very paranoid idea about Tim," Jack sniffed.

"You better hope you're right."

He put on a Rolling Stones tape and *Sympathy For the Devil* blew away the bad vibes. The landscape perked up for us and we rolled through a verdant little valley. We were heading north and it was getting greener, more mountainous. Jack looked at some towering cliffs in the distance, "Bamiyan."

"What's that, Professor?"

"Ancient caves. Monumental Buddhas. Magnificent history."

I thought we'd had enough of detours but there was no rush to get to Kabul and deal with Flannery. Bamyian was like a Buddhist Mount Rushmore. Two-hundred-foot statues of the Buddha, carved out of the sandstone cliffs, rose into the sky. The 6th century sculptors with rudimentary tools took decades to complete their task, their identities forever unknown. Maybe they were artistic geniuses travelling the Silk Road. Holy masters of their craft caravanning on camels with spice traders out of Arabia, heading to China. Maybe they trekked by and saw those majestic cliffs and decided to interrupt their journey and spend the next twenty years carving gigantic holy icons. Fifteen-hundred years later their work still survived (and would survive until 2001 when Osama bin Laden deemed the cliffs unholy and ordered Taliban extremists to dynamite them to rubble.)

It was ironic, I thought, that we'd found ourselves on the Silk Road, the caravan route that saw goods travelling between East and West. We were continuing the ancient practice, riding a Land Rover instead of a camel. Seeking kilos of hash from the Hindu Kush in the East to be sold in the West. Actually, Oz was south and east of what is known as the Far East, but it was the West in terms of culture.

These caves at Bamiyan had Bronze Age frescos painted on the walls that in places had been overrun with modern graffiti. We found people living in the caves. There were a few who spoke English and they told us they'd had to abandon their homes due to years of drought and famine. They had to find shelter and well springs where they could. That was one of the big reasons many Afghanis wanted the Soviets to come in. Their promises to dig wells, build reservoirs, create cities and a healthy commerce – if they materialized – might change life for these nomads.

After we'd learned all this, Jack got chummy with Grant. "You see, my handsome friend, your prison yard wisdom is spot on. Wiser minds know that Russian help will lead to a full-scale occupation. Tim says there are powerful tribal warlords who want to keep the Soviets out. So does an Islamist guerrilla organization known as the Mujahedeen. Even though they are bitter rivals, they will unite in the goal of defeating the Russians. And the Americans will use them."

"Love is blind, huh, Professor. You just can't see who Flannery really is."

They would battle about this. And why not when our entire world was looking at war. It was everywhere. Pakistan, India, Vietnam, Iran. There was no escaping it. It followed us like our shadows wherever we went. It put me into a deep funk and when I got like that I craved being in water. We were far from the ocean, far from the Black Sea and Dead Sea and the Caspian Sea. But we had heard about a place, just a short hike up the mountain. A billabong. A lake. Translucent blue, they said. There might not be surf, but it was a little bit of heaven in this bone-dry purgatory. Grant and I decided to make the climb while Jack found a place in the shade because he was so out of shape and arthritic he couldn't walk fifty yards.

When we got to the billabong, I was crushed. Maybe a foot of water left in the bottom and it was chalky brown instead of blue. "I read a book that said we all come from water. Water is the source of life," Grant said.

"Not much life out there." It was so fucking hot. I was tired, soaked with sweat. I'd lost my Ray Bans somewhere and my head was telling me bad things. Our deal was going to end up murkier than this lakebed. Grant had known me a long time and he could read me pretty well. It wasn't often I went dark and dreary, but I was there now and the Grant of old jumped to the task like a lifeguard. "We got this, mate. Give them the cash, get the hash, and get the hell back to Oz."

"What about Kabul?"

"A breeze, man. Home stretch."

"What about Jack opening his mouth to Flannery? And you stealing his film?"

"Give him the film." He took the two rolls out and handed them to me. "Done. Come on bunji, you need bit a doori. Let's get to Kabul and find you a girl."

As we climbed down, we stood on an outcropping of rock above the head of the Buddha and below on the Silk Road we saw a military convoy pass by. Was it the same one we'd seen before, the British Beefcakes? Looked like it as they towed the same long-bed tarp-covered trailers. They were certainly bringing shit with them. Missiles, guns, tools, propaganda. The caravan came closer, passing directly below us and there cruising along with the trucks and jeeps was a little red Citroen with Tim Flannery behind the wheel.

Jack had been in the shade at the massive feet of the monolith and the sight of the caravan brought him into the sun on a plateau. He waved madly. Seeing the object of his goofy crush thrust him right back into his obsession. Whether Flannery saw him or not I couldn't tell. The monuments were forgotten. "Let's take to the road, boys!" he said, eyes on the convoy disappearing into the distance along the Silk Road.

I was in such a foul mood I wanted to hogtie and gag him, throw him in the Rover and keep him there until we hit Pakistan, or at least some place Flannery wouldn't be found. I told him to get hold of himself, that he'd gone too far with this craziness.

He waved me off, "No, not far enough. Not far enough by a longshot. The heights of passion await. Onward."

Grant, amused, said, "You know, Jack, you're a really smart guy. All this knowledge you have about the past, the way the world works, and here you are, mate, blind as a bat with a schoolboy crush. You're losing yourself man."

Jack laughed, "Isn't that what it's all about? Losing oneself. And then finding oneself. That's the great mythic journey. Odysseus. Virgil! Now let's go." He hobbled off, his cane kicking up dirt as he trundled to the Rover.

Grant looked at me, shaking his head, "Well mate, the

shit is gonna hit the fan in Kabul. Maybe we just bypass it and head to Pakistan?"

21

The earth was rolling belly-up to the sun and a grim and grimy dusk settled over Peshawar. This enterprise I had worked so hard to keep together was falling apart, belching smoke like Flannery's car. A month before this when we were at Bamiyan at the feet of the giant monoliths, I didn't buy into Grant's dire prediction of getting busted in Kabul. But his prophecy came true and we were detained and questioned by Patricia. I handed over the two rolls of film, of course, and a couple days later we were surprisingly set free. Then we'd gone up over the Khyber Pass, down into Peshawar, made contact with Tariq and set up the deal. We'd paid the tobacconist, gone with Azziz to the fort, left our Rover there with the hash men. Now here I was in Peshawar, back under Patricia's thumb for the second time. Me and my partners were on a collision course with Interpol if I didn't fulfill her mandate to set up a meeting with Tariq Rahim.

After my confrontation with Flannery, I went into the Links Hotel and found it empty. This was strange because it was a luxury establishment catering to European and Asian businessmen who liked to mix golf with their meetings. If ever I needed a drink it was now. There was not a soul in the bar, not even a bartender. I was about to go behind the bar and pour myself a stiff one when the bartender entered from the kitchen and caught me. It was the same young Pakistani guy who had hooked us up before with the contraband booze on the golf course. Which was the very night Patricia corralled me and sent my partners into exile. I told him what I wanted. "Shhhhh!" he hissed, shaking his head, looking around in fear, whispering, "Don't be foolish. You saw what happened last time. It is still Ramadan."

I pulled out a $100. "Come on, mate."

He looked at the bill, then glanced around the room again. We were alone except for a girl who had just entered. She ignored us and took a seat by the window. She was maybe twenty years old, Indian or Pakistani, pretty even from a distance, sitting at a table looking out at night descending over the golf course. It was rare to see a female from the Indian subcontinent sitting alone in a bar with no hijab covering her head. She was paying no attention to us as she defied tradition. The whole mood was strange. "Where is everybody?" I said.

"Gone. Ramadan isn't much fun for you westerners."

"Come on, mate, there must be someplace to have some fun. Where can I go?" He looked at the 100 bucks again, thought about it. "Since you are not a Muslim, I am not helping you to commit a sin." He drew a little map on a cocktail napkin and a crude picture of a castle by a river.

I asked about the girl with no headscarf, "What about her? Is she Muslim?"

"Not for me to say, sir," he said. He started polishing already clean glasses, indicating he was done talking. I stood there a moment thinking about whether to approach the girl. I could only see her in profile, in dim light. She was dressed in a cream-colored pantsuit. Her hair was cut short. It could be possible – maybe a date for the evening at this castle on the river I was going to? The bartender read my thoughts and shook his head. "I would be careful, "he said. "She belongs to someone."

"She belongs to someone? Like what does that mean, she belongs to someone? Who does she belong to?"

"A powerful man. I can say no more."

I didn't need any more trouble and split. In my room all the craziness and tension suddenly hit me and I was on the fence about whether to go out and party or not. It had been a fruitless, frustrating day and I was tired. I took a long shower and as the water streamed over me I thought about just crashing for the night. I wondered if this seemingly unsolvable situation was the wakeup call I needed to abort the mission. I might have walked away from it if my two partners were not detained. I couldn't leave them behind bars, leave them to their fate and try to spirit myself somehow out of fucking Peshawar. Grant would be okay. He'd do a little time and he'd be cool, like he said. Jack might not do so well behind bars in a crazy, militarized, foreign, homophobic country. He was a survivor though. He'd had polio of the spine as a child and survived that. It left him with a hunchback and he didn't let that stop him. He had terrible gout and he still got around, almost pretending to be spry. Cripple or not, he'd developed a giant personality. He was selfish and self-centered and egotistical to the max and yet he put himself in jeopardy protesting for gay rights and aboriginal equality. Smart and funny as he was, I was sure he'd somehow survive in any dungeon they chose to throw him in. Nevertheless, the thought of leaving him in the path of sharks made me queasy. Plus, there was something else that wouldn't let me quit. Somewhere deep down, I still believed I could pull the deal off. Somehow I'd gather up all the loose springs, shove them back into the watch again and make this ragtag operation work.

Get control. In this case it was like trying to catch soap bubbles swirling down the drain. The hot water massaged me into a realization – control is an illusion. I might think I have it, but like a mirage, it's not really there. I bought the right vehicle, hooked up with the right partners, raised enough money, knew my plan, had it all set and it seemed like everything was together. But internal explosives were biding their time waiting for a fuse to be lit. Throughout our journey, potential chaos had been riding next to me. The respective craziness lurking inside my partners was waiting to blow while I gripped the wheel, guiding the car, all the while thinking I got this, I'm in control. A grand illusion. Like the time I was looking for surf in winter in New Zealand and came around a curve into a patch of black ice and began skidding out of control. Turning the wheel did nothing. For some strange reason I let go, took my hands off the steering wheel and surrendered to the four-wheel slide. I missed the guardrail and plopped into a ditch unhurt.

Maybe that was what I should do now. Take my hands off the wheel. Or maybe I should have stayed a plumber if I wanted control. Or become a bank clerk. Or a beachcomber? Maybe having nothing to lose is a form of control. Wander, eat, sleep, stand in the sun, ride a wave. The hot water was gone. There were no answers. When in doubt go party, have a few drinks, get laid and who knows, the answer might come.

The bartender found me a driver who followed the map and took me outside the city to a country road running along the

Bara River. There was nothing out there but a dark forest with owls in the trees. We came to an isolated, massive old mansion built of stone and cedar. There were cars parked on the gravel outside, lights glowed from behind curtained windows. As I approached the entrance, armed men came from the shadows. I could hear music from inside. Soft drums, slow methodical beat, the barely audible chime of cymbals, and a man singing in a plaintive high tenor, unintelligible words, but obviously calling the faithful. It was calling to me. I needed a change of head, an infusion of certainty. Something I was sure of, could count on, like music, brandy, dancing, tempting eyes I could get lost in.

I thought of my girl, Andi, back home. She was kind of a hippy but the wisest person I knew. She would say, "James, as usual you're trying to clear your mind with more drinking, drugs and girls. You talk about letting go of control, or getting more control, but you're a prisoner of doing it your own way and that keeps you blind to what you're really looking for. You're troubled and so far from what is truly good and right. Lost in your dilemma is a connection to the source of all things."

Sage advice. I took it - sort of. I said a prayer to the source of all things, but had some doubt it was heard. I paid my hundred bucks and went through the cedar doors and velvet curtains. Into a cloud of hash and tobacco smoke, a drifting, vaporous sea. The glow of burning hookahs in the hands of shadowed figures, all reclining on enormous cushions. At the center, an open dance floor except no one was dancing. The entire room was shrouded in the blue sea of smoke. It was like watching film through rheumy eyes. I could make out some faces and they were all westerners, both male and female, laughing, talking, eating, drinking, smoking. I could have been in the lounge of Club 54 in New York City. Except for the music - a low pitched, breathy flute joined the drums and cymbals and the chanting of the tenor drifted away, replaced by a girl's voice, high and crystal clear, calling the crowd into silence. Then that call became a whisper, like an angel's murmur, *I am here, come to me,* and through the smoke a woman appeared, dancing.

I didn't know they had belly dancers in Pakistan but here was one before me. All hips and bangles and finger cymbals, her predatory vibrations eclipsing whatever ethereal refuge the reclining hookah smokers were in. The crowd perked up, I joined them, kicking back on a pillow. Food was everywhere, steaming plates of shish kebab, fish, dolmas, baklava. Was this Turkey or Pakistan? From the corner shone a large silver urn, embossed in great detail and filled with apple tea that was so heavily laced it could send top fuel dragsters wheeling off the line. A hookah girl offered me a bowl with my choice of tobacco, hash or opium. I went for the trifecta, watching the dancer with her silver veil and mane of bejeweled black curls. She commanded attention, she swayed and shimmied up within inches of me, then stopped, fell to her knees, with a gleaming sword balanced across her neck. Then in a fluid move she was up and gone, swinging the sword to within an inch of some other western pleasure seeker's head.

I took a big hit off the hookah and felt a presence next to me. A girl. No mistaking it was the exotic beauty from the bar at the Links Hotel. Where was she from? Somewhere in the Indian sub-continent? Bangladesh, Kashmir, Sri Lanka... The one who defied tradition, wore no hijab, and "belonged to someone important." She was inches from my ear, whispering,

"You wish to see Tariq..."

22

The girl was very close. I was stunned by her presence and stoned from the hash, head-swirled by the sounds of the club, the music, the belly dancer, the scimitar... all had me in sort of a trance. I could feel the girl's hair next to my cheek, her jasmine fragrance rising through the scents of hash, tobacco and food as she asked me again, "Why do you want to see Tariq?"

I was mind-blown, of course, like when you search for something you lost and just when you give up - boom, there it is. "Who are you?"

"Karina."

Not her real name for sure but I was not one to judge since I was travelling under an alias myself. Then I remembered Karina had been the name of the girl who worked for Tariq and came to the hotel and told Grant where we were to meet him. Now I understood why she'd had such an effect on Grant that he was talking rhapsodically about her for days afterward. "You know Tariq?"

"He's heard you want to see him. Why?"

"Well... my car. He's having it fixed."

A whiff of a laugh met my ear. "Come on, you can do better than that."

The spotlight was on the belly dancer and we were in the

shadows where we reclined on embroidered cushions. I couldn't
see the girl at my ear with any clarity.

"It's about ...an arrangement."

"Ramadan ends tomorrow. Your car will be ready. Now
the truth – why do you wish to see Tariq?"

A wrong answer here was hard to avoid, "Better I tell him
directly. I need to talk to him now."

She laughed, "Always *now* with you people." She had an
Indian accent, but her English was flawless, like she'd studied
it in school when she was a kid. "So... who sent you on this
mission?"

"You work for him?"

She emitted a little breathy snort that carried undertones
of irony and cynicism. "We're in contact."

"So, will you please tell him I need to meet him?"

"Possibly."

"Bloody hell, can you set up a meeting or not?"

"Depends on you. With the truth, a meeting is possible."

Everything happening in the club faded into the background and I was totally focused on her. I was in a cross and
didn't know what to say. How much do I reveal to her? Here
was the only glimmer of hope I had. Her being in the hotel
bar couldn't be a coincidence. Maybe she worked for Tariq, or
maybe she worked for the police. I quickly realized here was
no telling who she might be working for. "You were there in
the hotel bar to watch me. Why?"

"Because you've made a nuisance of yourself, making
inquiries."

"About Tariq? I can explain that when I see him."

"You work for the CIA?"

"No. That's crazy."

"You are intimate with the female Kabul Station Chief." Her lips were right at my ear. "True?"

"Okay, yeah, that part is true. But..."

"She asked you to get in touch with Tariq."

"I can't say anything about that."

"Grant... your partner.... He's in CIA custody. You should help him." Her head tilted slightly. I thought I heard the whisper of her eyelashes.

"I'm trying. Can I meet with Tariq?"

"If Tariq wants to meet, I will be in touch."

And with that she was gone. The belly dancer was before me waving her sword, then she hoisted it skyward and brought it down within an inch of my forehead. The audience clapped and the hookah girl reloaded my pipe. I looked for Karina, but she had disappeared.

All great nights must end. Even one in Paradise. The cabby I had waiting outside came in and said the carriage was about to turn into a pumpkin and it was time to go. I was hopeful. I'd unexpectedly found what I'd been searching for. And who doesn't like a surprise? There was some light in the graveyard now and I'd been feeling terminal. Would Karina show up with an invite from Tariq? I somehow had a feeling she would.

I went back to my hotel room. When I opened the door ,I saw that the lights were off. I had left several lamps on. I could feel some presence there. Another *surprise*? I wondered if I'd hit the jackpot, "Tariq Rahim?" I said. I thought my search had ended.

"Hardly," a woman's voice purred. The flash and glow from her lit cigarette illuminated Patricia Adams. She blew out

the match without looking at me. I turned on a desk lamp.
"Pardon the intrusion. I just needed to get away from things
for a moment." She had a bottle of classic scotch and refilled
her glass as her eyes rose to meet mine. "Join me in a drink?"

"I guess you can get anything you want, huh?"

"Are you referring to the scotch or yourself?"

"Both."

"I was about to give up on you, James," she said, rattling the
ice cubes in her glass. The Rolex was gone again. She looked
softer around the eyes and she seemed a decade younger than
her years. It was like the artifice she'd evinced in our former
encounters was gone. I was getting the real her, if there was
a real her, after all those years playing First Woman Spook.

As incredibly hot as she looked, I had one thought and that
was to keep my distance. I felt there was a minefield around
her and maybe it was better to get the hell out. But there was
nowhere to go and not just because she was in my room. She
held the keys to my world. "Come here," she said. "Tell me
about your night." She patted the couch. "Such a warm night.
Come. Sit. Let's talk."

I stayed a few feet away, but it was like the tide pulling me
in. "Crazy thing happened tonight. Might have found a way
to Tariq. But maybe you already know that."

"I do, James. And the fact is, Tariq found you."

"Of course. And you knew that would happen, right?"

"James. It's not my first rodeo. But I'm hoping it's my last.
As I told you ,I want to go out on a win. Now sit." She held
out her hand. Like a royal hand to be kissed. How do you not
take a royal hand? The next minute I was on the couch. Her
scent hit me. Gardenia? "Let's get this out of the way. Tariq

will contact you through Karina. Probably tomorrow when Ramadan ends…"

"Wait, wait," I said, "Who is this *Karina*?"

"A young girl in a tough position. Basically, she's indentured to Tariq. She's a conduit for you, James. She's trouble. And you'd do well to advise Grant of that. If and when he's free. That's advice from a friend, okay. You get me?"

"Yeah, you're saying she can hook me up with Tariq. But don't mess around with her."

"I'd be jealous if you did."

"Right," I said. "Come on, I thought we were gonna get real."

"James, do you know how long it's been since I've been real with anyone?" She seemed lonely, vulnerable for a few seconds, then tossed her drink down like a barroom vet and was back to business.

"She'll contact you, most likely take you to a meeting with our boy. You tell him I want to see him. The sooner the better. Say… tomorrow at the Horseshoe Bar. Midnight. He's to come alone."

Why a drug and arms dealer would want to meet a CIA chief was beyond me. But what good would it do me to know any of that? I had other more pressing concerns. "And if I do this, you'll release my partners?"

"We'll see."

I took a moment to quiet my fears and gave it to her straight, "If they're not back at the hotel here by the morning, I'm not going to do what you want."

"Ummm. Backbone. I like that. Let's have a drink and pretend."

"Pretend what?"

"We're somewhere else."

She unbuttoned her blouse to reveal a turquoise lace bra. The last color I would expect but then she was full of surprises. She had perfect breasts, still beautiful, perky and round with a nipple like a little fingertip that made me want to have it in my mouth. I slid her blouse off, she leaned back against the cushions surrendering, waiting for me to keep going. I undid her bra and freed those beauties, licked them both. She sighed, going oh yes, oh yes. I was feeling crazy turned on by her. My dick was hard and pressed into her upper thigh. She pushed into it and I wanted to slide her pants off. But as much as I wanted her, I had the big picture on my mind. "You said the Pakistani cops are on us. Will we be able to make our deal and get out of Peshawar?"

"Your timing right now is very cheeky, James. Let's not talk business."

"Sorry. It's difficult to be in the moment with my partners in jail and my deal in limbo."

She brought her lips to my ear, "You could always *trust me.*"

Well, Andi did say I should trust a higher power. "Would *you* trust you?" I said.

She kissed me and it was more of a lick, really. "No. But you pretty much have to, don't you? I mean right now I am the best friend you've got."

True enough. I had it so bad for her I put my fears on hold. I undid the drawstring on her silk pants and pushed them down to her ankles while I kissed her stomach. Her skin was soft but muscled underneath. Somewhere back in the day she must have been an athlete, a swimmer or gymnast. She was sighing, saying, "It's been so long. I really need you to fuck me right now, James."

The next moment we were into it, no holds barred. We groped and sucked and fucked our way onto the bed, with stops on the couch, the floor and a rather intense vertical smash against a wall.

Once lit, her fire blazed. As she came, her hand found my ponytail and pulled it back to where my head met my spine. A good stinging slap to her butt would have been the thing to do, but I held back for the moment and grabbed her hair. We exhausted ourselves and lay on the bed. She nestled into my chest. For the first time, she seemed at peace in her head and in her world, maybe because we were so outside it.

"How come you wear the Rolex sometimes, and others you wear this little watch?"

"The Rolex is Station Chief. This one is me... from long ago."

"Before the CIA. Why'd you join?"

"Family tradition. And I married into it."

"No ring."

"We're done."

"And you're done with being Station Chief after this one? Why?"

"I don't like who I've become."

The frenzy began again. Finally, I just passed out. I woke in the morning to a banging on my door. I looked around for Patricia, but she was gone. I went to the door and there was Grant. He walked in, noticed the bottle of scotch and the glasses, one with a lipstick smudge on it. His roving eyes fell on the turquoise bra on the arm of the chair. He smiled, "So that's why she cut us loose. You took one for the team, didn't you, mate?"

23

I was inspired by the colossal Buddhist monuments at Bami-yan. If the ancient sculptors had completed their epic work of art, then so could I complete my far more prosaic task of bringing the hash home. Next stop Kabul where we'd get word from our contact about when and where to meet Tariq Rahim. I was driving, Jack riding shotgun, Grant in the back. Jack rocked back and forth like a metronome on full tilt boogie, hoping to run into the British convoy and his heartthrob Tim Flannery.

I kept it rolling steady at seventy over a steamy two-lane blacktop. It was two hours to Kabul and there would be no more side trips. In any case, we didn't see the convoy. Maybe they'd turned off, made a stop at one of the towns on the way. I was relieved, hoping we'd seen the last of Flannery and maybe he'd forgotten about the film Grant had stolen from him.

Grant passed a joint up to Jack, "You gonna rock yourself right out the window there, Professor."

"What can I say? I'm in love."

"What happens if it gets ugly?"

"Well, my rugged friend, the journey is the destination."

Grant was the genius of street smarts, and philosophy intrigued him. "I think you got that backwards, Professor."

"The prize at the destination is the journey you've just

taken. Let me put it into a context you can relate to. You find a girl, you are in *heaven*. It ends. Tragically, painfully let's say. The love you felt was the actual journey."

Grant stiffened. The memory of his dead girlfriend Tuesday clouded over him and he turned to me, pissed, "You told him?"

"No, mate."

"You fucking told him."

"No. I swear man."

"So how did he know?"

"How do I know?" Jack couldn't hide a rueful look. "You don't think I know a god like Tim would never go for a troll like me? No illusions about that. No hunchbacks for him. No clubfooted Quasimodos. No deranged motor-mouthed homos for such an epic individual. So why do I chase him? Because it makes me feel alive. With passion. Love is the journey. And no, James didn't tell me a thing."

"You just guessed? Bullshit."

Jack stopped and looked straight at him. "I recognize pain. The pain is always there. When you two hiked up to the lake. On strong legs and feet. While I, misshapen and infirm, sat in the dirt at the feet of a Buddha. Pained I couldn't join you. But then came the caravan. The heart jumps. There, the little red Citroen, my hero behind the wheel. Suddenly alive! I am full of life and strength. The endless cycle. You get it?"

I looked in the mirror at Grant, silent, thinking. It was a look I didn't recognize. He was examining the possibilities, rather than drifting into the abyss of intermittent, dark brooding. Jack knew what he was doing – engineering Grant's mind. That was Jack's way. Get a little foothold, grab a little more territory, until you willingly let him draw himself into your head. "Grant," he said, "you need to have some fun on this trip. Find yourself a girl."

It was dark when we approached Kabul. There was a pall of smoke over it, sporadic fires glowed, now and then the staccato blistering of gunfire from rooftops. Tracer rounds ripped through the night low over the city. We were dropping into another revolution, this one more explosive than Tehran. People hurried along in huddled groups, the occasional car or jeep careening around a corner, others slowly trolling through the alleys. It spooked me and all I wanted to do was get our contact info and hit the road for Peshawar, Pakistan to meet Tariq.

We pulled into the Intercontinental, our prearranged place to meet Mick, the connection Grant had found in Bombay. We parked, went to check in, and the desk clerk gave us a surprised look, "You're out after curfew." Then he did a double-take on our passports and said, "Australians. We have to give you an advisory. Everybody from your country is required to go to the Embassy and check in. If you don't, you will have problems when you make your exit. Your visas have to be updated and whereabouts recorded, so you must do that. Now."

Another surprise, but okay, something we had to do. I asked if there were messages for us and he said no. I looked at Grant. "Don't worry," he assured me, "Mick will come through."

The desk clerk had more warnings for us. "There are certain *events* happening in the city these days. Perhaps somewhat dangerous. Dangerous throughout the country, but primarily in Kabul. You'll want to avoid the Arg."

"What's the Arg?" I asked.

"The Presidential Palace. Daoud lives there." He said

Daoud like he wasn't the president's biggest fan.

Jack was immediately intrigued, "So the Arg has been the site of some public demonstrations?"

"Yes, and more to come. Hostilities."

Jack said, "Oh, yes. I've read about this. Your president came to power via a left-wing military coup. Correct?"

"I'm impressed," the desk clerk said. "He usurped the throne of our royal leader, King Zahir."

"And the Soviets? What do you think of them?" Jack asked.

For the first time the desk clerk was nervous. Finally, he smiled and changed the subject. "Your rooms are ready. Be careful. You never know who you're talking to."

Jack still wanted to engage with him, "Dangerous times, eh, my friend? The Russians backing a resistance movement, because Daoud wants to keep them out. Ironic isn't it, that Daoud, a socialist, wants to exclude the Russian communists. And you, an apparent Royalist on the right, want them in."

"My country needs help from the Soviets," the clerk said, unable to keep himself from being drawn in.

"But at what price?"

"You would have us in bed with the Americans?"

"There are other complications. You've got the Pakistanis on your southern border and the Iranians on your western border. Both fomenting their agendas. And of course, the nuclear issue between Pakistan and India." Jack's eyes were piercing and the clerk bristled.

That was enough goddamn politics. I pulled Jack away. All I wanted to do was go to the Embassy tomorrow, have our visas updated, get the fuck out of Kabul and score some hash. But first we had to get word from Mick.

We couldn't go out because of the curfew and there wasn't much action in the hotel, so we hit the hay early and the next morning went straight to the Aussie embassy. The clerk there grilled us like we were under interrogation. Imagine that. "Rug dealers," we said. "Rugs. Not drugs." She finally stamped our papers and then gave us the same advisory we'd been given by the hotel clerk, explained that there were protests with a number of political factions going at each other. Today in particular was a volatile time because President Daoud was speaking at the Arg Palace.

"I want to see this," Grant said. It wasn't any mystery why Grant wanted to go to the demonstration. Riots excited him. He'd gotten the taste in prison.

Suddenly oil and water were in solidarity? The shifting power alliance was a surprise to me, but it was easier to handle than having them at each other's throats. It just meant that our little democracy would be harder to govern. The thing that worried me most was the possibility – or probability – of running into Flannery. I knew that Jack was thinking he would be at the palace covering this scene.

I thought about moving on alone, letting them do their thing, but we were locked in together. For one thing Jack's name (or his alias anyway, Byron Rimbaud) was on the car registration and the Carnet de Passages transport documents.

Because of all the action, we had to park blocks from the Arg Palace. Grant must have felt right at home because the Palace looked more like a cinderblock prison than a royal residence. There was a moving sea of people crowding the square in front. Protesters against President Daoud on one side and supporters of him on the other. Meanwhile, a confrontation of a different kind loomed. Kabul city uniformed police, who were essentially royalists, in blue and Daoud's army troopers in brown were sizing each other up like a couple of football teams before kickoff. It was tense and simmered with the unpredictability of one side making an aggressive move toward the other – no matter who started it, this would lead to uncontrolled violence. We were watching from across the street when I saw Patricia Adams. I didn't know her name at that point or that I'd be in bed with her a few weeks later in Peshawar, but I recognized her from the hotel bar in Tabriz. She was in an alcove between some pillars talking with a British Captain - the same one who headed up the missile convoy and had been chummy with Flannery.

Jack saw them standing together and turned to Grant. "It appears you are right, my prescient friend. She is government issue." I knew what he was really thinking - if the CIA chick was here, it stood to reason Flannery was close by.

"Jack, you are not going over there. No way are you asking her about your fucking boyfriend."

"Watch and learn."

I grabbed him hard by the bicep and spun him around. "Listen to me, you bloody idiot! That is a CIA agent. We are drug smugglers. Fucking wake up to what you're about to do!"

"I'm just going to casually engage her in a bit of conversation."

Tensions were escalating in the square. A protestor with a bullhorn stood atop a U.N. jeep exhorting the crowd to protest. The U.N. corporal behind the wheel was terrified but staying at his post even when the mob surged onto the hood. Afghan soldiers moved in, subdued the men rocking the jeep.

This show of force had the crowd on high alert. Normally, Jack would be pontificating on this situation in relation to social conditions, international politics, geopolitical realignments, causes and effects and prognostications. But there was none of that now. He wrenched free from me and was off through the crowd, past the soldiers, toward Patricia Adams. She saw him coming and then she spotted Grant and me. She ended her conversation with the Captain and he elbowed through the throng back to his jeep. Out of the line of sight there was an explosion. The crowd panicked, not knowing which way to turn as tear gas engulfed us. Patricia Adams was watching all this like she'd orchestrated it herself. Above the melee, the provocateurs were yelling, "Rise up against Daoud and the Soviet presence in Afghanistan!"

Jack was a mere few yards from her when some American agents corralled him and whisked him away. He was now in CIA custody. Grant looked at me. He didn't have to say it, so I did. "I know. You told me so."

"So now what, mate?"

"Nothing we can do if we're arrested with him. So, we're out of here, bro." We made a hasty exit down a little alleyway back to another boulevard, circled round to the Rangey, and entered our hotel.

The clerk called to us. "A message was left here for you."

It was for Grant, from Mick. The note read, *Deal in progress. Bit of a hang up. Cannot meet for another three days. Stay tuned. See you in Peshawar at the Links Hotel.*

So, Jack was in custody and our deal was on hold. Now what the fuck were we going to do? Contact the embassy, try to get Jack out? Grant lit the note on fire and dropped it into an ashtray. I said, only half joking, "Are we, like, getting a little paranoid, mate?"

"We're gonna be snatched up. I'm guessing you don't want to leave Jack up shit's creek and split Kabul. Right?"

"That would be fucked."

"Right. So we just gotta hold our mud when they come for us." He thought for a moment, then said, "Look bunji, I caused this thing when I broke into Flannery's car and stole his film. I'll make it right. Give me it back."

"Why?"

"It's what the CIA lady wants. I'll turn myself in and give it to her."

"No, we're in it together mate. Now let's get the fuck out of here." I wasn't about to sit around and wait for the spooks to come. We decided to go to the Embassy and have someone of consequence there find out about Jack. We wanted to keep the Rover safe in the garage, so we got a cab. The driver spoke no English, but he understood where we wanted to go and made it clear he was not driving anywhere near the embassy because it was only blocks from the Arg Palace which was not the safest place to be. We walked the last half mile and the smell of tear gas was strong, with city police and soldiers battling as warriors had battled here for two thousand years.

We found the embassy closed. The gates were locked and not a soul around. A weird sensation made suddenly stark and personal. I felt abandoned by the country I so often took for granted. Out of options, I considered Grant's proposal to turn himself in and give back the film. I asked him to play that one out for me.

"You take off for Peshawar and meet Mick as planned at

the Links Hotel. I do a mea culpa to the CIA chick. She gets what she wants, lets the Professor and me go and we meet you in Peshawar." In a way, it was a tempting idea. But I doubted it would go as smoothly as all that. I needed time to think. We found a bar and disappeared inside it. It was packed with ex-pats, contractors, druggies, trekkers and prostitutes, all just having a marvelous time, unaware of the chaos in the streets around them. We ordered up some concoction of pomegranate juice and gin. Donna Summer, ubiquitous as ever, on the jukebox. Grant and I cringed in unison, looked at each other and he said, "We gotta fix that, mate. She's on every jukebox between here and Oz. Get some Stones on there and some Led Zep." We were just settling in for a nice run of drinks and chicks when three American spooks came in and pinned us.

24

There was no mistaking that the suits coming toward us were American agents. You could tell right away from the walk. Every American cop except Columbo walks like Wyatt Earp patrolling Main Street in Tombstone. They came up, the three of them triangulating us, and said they wanted to talk outside. A few people in the bar were watching, but most were having too much fun to notice. "I think we'll be staying in here," I said.

One of them used my real name instead of the fake name on my passport. Enjoying the intimidation game, he flashed his badge. Snapping the leather open, he flashed a shining star with the eagle embossed above *CIA, U.S. Special Agent*. The attitude was, You've seen the power, now bend over. "Gentlemen, it's not a request. Let's go."

"Uh... What's up?" I asked.

"We're going to need you to answer some questions."

Grant bristled, "We're Australians. You're Americans, gangie, and we're in a foreign country. You have no f power over us."

They spun him around, pushed him face down on the bar, handcuffed him behind his back. Blood trickled from his forehead as everyone watched.

"That all you got, gangie?" Grant said and they pulled his arms up sharply, almost separating his shoulders.

"Okay, okay," I said, waving surrender. "Fine, we'll talk to you outside."

Grant was being led out and yelling the whole way. "Fuck you, not saying shit to you fuckers!"

The agents hustled us to the sidewalk and I was going to ask for a minute to calm Grant down, but we were immediately thrown into a waiting van, its windshield dark as night, and no other windows. The van's inside was a metal box; there were no seats and we were shoved to the floor. Two different agents monitored us through a partition. Suddenly, we were the enemy of the American Empire.

"Where are we going?" I asked.

No answer. Grant was quiet now, just staring at the agents. I nodded to him like it was the best thing we could do at the moment. We drove for 10 minutes. I had no idea where we were heading or if we were about to disappear.

We stopped and I heard chains unlock, metal doors swinging open. We rolled across iron grates and those doors clanked closed behind us. The van doors opened and we climbed out and found ourselves in a completely enclosed courtyard. I had no idea where we were because I could see nothing but the grey façades of the medieval buildings surrounding us, the sky above obscured by hovering clouds. There were perimeter lights on, but they did nothing to illuminate the gloom. We passed through sliding, bolt-studded steel doors into what appeared to be a cavernous warehouse. Two lines of metal tables ran the length of the building and atop each sat banks of monitors. Dour-faced American men in white shirts and

ties sitting before the screens lifted their gaze to clock us as we
passed between them and a brick wall pasted with a mosaic of
push-pinned charts and maps.

We were led into an inner office. And there on prominent
display, like a dwarf manikin in a cheap suit shop, was Jack,
handcuffed to a metal chair. Strangely, he was subdued, didn't
even look up. I had seldom if ever seen him like that. For sure, I
thought he'd be ranting about international rights, the Geneva
Convention, his contacts in the Aussie Embassy, lawsuits.

Patricia Adams came in, silently, like a cat who wouldn't
blink. She said nothing, just looked at us, giving Grant a hawk-
eyed assessment and then the same to me. It was like we had
been abducted by aliens and were about to be inspected. Her
eyes were a cool blue. Her blond hair was up in a bun, a few
strands falling down, hints of grey at the roots. I guessed her
to be in her early forties. She had the arched cheekbones of a
model and I sensed that back in the day she was a pretty one,
though she seemed above making the effort now. She wore
no makeup and was draped in a shapeless brown pantsuit
that did nothing for the beauteous shape I would come to
know later. No rings, no bracelets, no jewelry at all except for
a man's silver Rolex.

Jack's voice surprised me. It was even, calm. "You Americans
are going to fail in Afghanistan. You know why? Because you
don't have a bloody clue about what's really happening here."

Patricia Adams was unperturbed. She seemed almost
amused. Jack was under the delusion he could back her down.
"You are in violation of international protocol. I demand to
see the Australian consul," he said.

She held his passport before his eyes. "You are travelling

under a forged passport. That makes you *persona non grata* in a target rich environment."

"What's that mean – 'target rich environment?'" Grant asked.

She ignored him, speaking to one of the men in her charge, "Put them both in D Unit."

"What did I tell you, Professor?" Grant said.

They got Jack and Grant out of there and now it was Patricia, one of her men, and me in the room. "Sit down," she said.

I had the distinct feeling that she could kick my ass. Get me in a thumb lock and have me on the floor in a hot second. But she wouldn't have to get physical to subdue me. She possessed other weapons. Her kind of smarts could slice me up like cheese.

I tried to be pleasant, "We haven't actually committed any crimes."

"Forging passports is a crime."

"Uh... I didn't forge them."

"You're the one who bought the forgeries in Sydney. Thus you *are* a forger. You are a drug smuggler. You have been engaging in espionage."

"Whoa. Espionage??"

"Yes. At this moment you have classified information on your person."

"Oh, that. Yeah, I fully intend to give that back." I took out the film.

She plucked the rolls from my hand. "Your partner in crime also stole some photographs from Mr. Flannery."

"I burned those."

"Why?"

"Trying to avoid trouble."

"But you kept the film."

"It's a long story."

"Espionage carries a long sentence."

"You don't really think we're spies. Come on."

Patricia managed a faint smile and I could tell it was just an indulgence. She gave the film to her agent. "Let's see what we have here." The agent left and then we were alone.

She walked around the table, stood in back of me for a moment. Usually a woman has a scent, but she had none. It was agonizingly quiet and that made me chatty. "Uh, wow, I didn't know there were women CIA agents."

"Now you do. I'm the first." She came around in front of me, sat on the end of the desk, her eyes trained on my forehead.

"You must be quite a brain to be the first," I said. "How did that happen?"

"We're here to talk about you, James."

"I'll be happy to. But seriously, I admire you for beating the odds. It's all guys in your world, right? So how did you get into the spy game?" I sniffed, hoping for a casual air.

She let herself be amused, lit two cigarettes and offered me one. I didn't smoke except when I was drunk, but I took it anyway. She had an elegant way of smoking, cultured and carefree. "I was a Russian Lit major. You met a connection for hash in Bombay. What is his name?" She took a long drag.

"We're here to buy rugs, that's all." I wanted to cough, but held back.

"I was hoping for a show of good faith. Now what is Mick's last name?"

"Mick?" I shrugged.

"Yes, Mick. The one who will introduce you to your dealer."

"So, you speak Russian? That's amazing."

"Interpol will be very interested in you. They love smugglers."

Her field agent came in, "We have that film ready for you, Chief."

Patricia slid easily off the edge of the desk and told him to put me in D Unit. She left without even a glance back. I yelled after her, "We're rug dealers!"

Next thing I knew, I landed in a windowless room that had nothing but a mattress on the floor. A stained toilet stood to one side. After thirty-six hours, Patricia Adams came in. This time she was wearing all black, and I couldn't decide if her severity was more born again preacher or Catwoman.

"Because Tim Flannery chooses not to make an issue of the break-in, I'm prepared to be lenient."

"Uh... so we can go?"

"Free for the moment, James. You will leave Kabul and not look back. Are we clear?"

"Totally clear." I felt my lungs relax.

"Listen closely, your freedom depends on this - any knowledge you might possess of a military nature or military materiel you will forget. If you say one single word, at any time, anywhere, I will know, and there will be serious consequences."

I was taken out and led back to the van where Jack and Grant waited. The doors closed. We looked at each other, almost afraid to say a word. Ten minutes later, we were dropped off at the hotel, then immediately got our shit together and into the Rover and we sped out of hell, away from Kabul.

25

We wasted no time burning rubber out of Kabul as dawn was breaking. I floored the Rangey toward the Khyber Pass. Behind us in the west, Kabul was emerging from the dark canopy of night, while before us in the East a somber, burnt umber, cloud-covered landscape was unfolding as the sun peeked above the mountain ridges. Jalalabad was in the distance. We were putting miles between ourselves and Kabul, but I had a twitchy feeling: could Patricia Adams still be monitoring us? I hoped it was just my paranoia, but if we were off her radar, it was only because we were, as she made clear, insignificant flies shitting on her paperwork and neither of us worth a swat.

But then why had she gone to such lengths to intimidate us? She gave the impression she was the boss, but there were probably hard liners up her food chain who wanted to turn us over to Interpol. They might want to tie up any loose ends that could unravel the U.S. mission. It was a scrape we'd skated out of and we were lucky to be on the road. Trying to share my gratitude with the boys, Grant shot back, "If you trust those spooks, you're crazy. That chick let us go for a reason."

"What reason?"

Jack smiled knowingly, "My boy, drug smuggling and

the CIA are not unfamiliar companions. The veil of separation between the respective enterprises is, on occasion, quite porous." He recounted how the CIA smuggled heroin out of Southeast Asia on its Air America planes in order to provide funding for America's secret wars in Laos and Cambodia. According to him, the CIA paid Hmong tribesmen in Laos to grow opium and then they flew it to Chiang Mai, Thailand, for processing into heroin. Then they allied with an Italian Mafia boss, Santos Trafficante, to smuggle it into Cuba. And from there shot straight into the arms of countless waiting American junkies.

I was skeptical about the CIA using gangsters in their operations.

Grant laughed like I was a knucklehead. "You don't think the cops use informants, mate? Remember ol' Detective Marx? He used us and we were criminals."

Jack nodded in agreement, "Criminals make fine assets because they're corruptible. Trafficante tried to kill Castro for the CIA."

"Why would he do that?" Grant asked.

"Because he controlled gambling in Cuba until Castro came to power and shut the casinos down."

"No shit."

"Remember the exploding cigar? That was Trafficante's work. And, some say, he had a hand in the JFK assassination."

"So how would the CIA use us?"

Grant joked, "Maybe the chick needs to get laid, James. She kept you in the room after throwing me and Jack in the hole. Did she want some hugs, some doori, mate?" He elbowed Jack and the two shared a laugh.

"The bitch is ice cold," Jack said, "She probably wanted you to slap her around. Did you do your duty, my boy?"

"No, because she said she wanted to rub her pussy up against that sexy hunchback of yours."

The ribbing continued as we flew down Highway 1 on our way to Jalalabad. I swerved around an oncoming truck, nearly hitting an oblivious herd of cattle who plodded slowly along.

Jack had a rare moment of self-reproach, "You know boys, I feel an apology is in order. I lost my head a bit chatting with Tim. Sorry about that." He looked wistfully out the windshield at a cloud of exhaust belching from the rumbling semi in front of us, "'Love is a smoke, made of a fume of sighs.'"

"Poetry?" Grant slapped him on the shoulder, "If I knew a poem about a dumbass, I would tell it to you. Because I sure was a dumbass breaking into Flannery's car."

The semi turned off into a gas station lot which jutted like a popsicle out of the flat terrain. we fell in behind a smoking Yugo and the exhaust cloud wafted over us. Oil spots flecked at our windshield. "That dude has a broken head gasket," Grant said. "Pass the fucker." I swerved around the culprit and Jack pulled out the map. "First we hit Jalalabad." And soon we could see the outlines of the city on the far horizon, at the base of charcoal tinged mountains. Jack traced our route on the map. "After Jalalabad, we begin the climb through the Khyber Pass. Then we cross the border at Torkham into Pakistan, top out at Landi Kotal and go down to Peshawar."

Five Soviet Army helicopters like great airborne sharks swooped overhead. Two of them dangled massive road graders from their underbellies. "My boys, the Russians are coming!" Jack exclaimed. "They're making roads, constructing schools, building up the infrastructure and they're doing it all in the guise of Nation Building. One day they'll try to take over not knowing they'll most likely fail, as everyone from history always has done in Afghanistan - the graveyard of Empires!"

We pulled into an outdoor market, a casbah under tenting. Local Afghans were dressed in gear that melded the East and the West. They wore western sports coats with Afghani pajama pants and big turbans. Some wore trench-coats with a turban and scarves wrapped tightly around their necks affecting the look of a Mid-Eastern Sam Spade. It wasn't a color filled scene because most everyone was dressed in white, grey or black. They were standing in front of big Hessian burlap bags full of different types of grains and lentils, beans and rice. Some locals were squatting and smoking weed, hash, tobacco, whatever, eyeing us. We went into a little stall where they were serving food, wondering, "Shall we eat in one of these places or do we risk getting some amoebic dysentery?"

Grant said, "I've eaten worse in the outback. I'm going for it."

He survived and after lunch we barreled out of that place, forging ahead on the highway which would lead us to the Khyber Pass.

I had heard stories about the Khyber Pass years earlier from Jack. It was packed with the history of all the different people who went traveled through and tried to conquer the place. Legends like Darius out of ancient Persia and Alexander the Great, Genghis Khan, the Mongol Hordes. The British tried twice in the 1800's, and now it looked like the Russians were coming. And who knew, maybe Patricia Adams and the Americans would gear up for their try, too.

"There are bones beneath us boys," Jack said as we entered the Pass. "Thousands upon thousands of intrepid adventurers over the centuries have been buried under this unforgiving rock and dirt. It's one of the dark places, the dangerous places of the earth."

The most impending danger for someone passing through in 1977 was not death by arrow, spear or bullet. The chief concern was death by traffic accident. The Khyber Pass was still a busy trade route, an ancient highway at odds with modern means of transportation. Buses, trucks, camels, oxen, horse carts, people all moving on a two lane, switch-backed strip of broken highway. The passenger buses were the biggest threats as they ferried people back and forth between Pakistan and Afghanistan. Despite their colorful and crowded attraction, these psychedelic catastrophes on wheels posed danger to passengers and pedestrians and other motorists. With men, women, children, dogs, and the occasional monkey dangling from the windows and the roof, each competed for every inch of space with battered suitcases, bags, pots and pans and even a kitchen sink tied down on top. These rolling disasters banged along, rattling, swerving out into the oncoming lane, their passengers seemingly oblivious to risk, actually getting off on the danger, even at times singing about it. It was a free-for-all, really. Just crazy mayhem in the Wild Wild East. The whole of it was mad and alive and thrilling.

Then up in the hills, we passed fortresses that had been constructed in the 1800s. "The English built them so that they could have the high ground to control and defend territory they had invaded," Jack explained.

"How do you know all this shit, Professor?" Grant asked.

"I travel and I read." Jack continued without missing a beat. "A century ago, not unlike today, it was all about the Russians. The Russians were coming to take over India, so the Brits had to take the Pass."

Jack painted a picture of an arrogant British invasion force. 15,000 soldiers padded with 38,000 servants. "In they marched with brass bands, bagpipes, foxhounds, polo ponies, 30,000 camels laden with cigars and cricket gear. Because they didn't want the Russians coming, taking over India! The English just couldn't fight without their bagpipes and cigars. Fight they did. And lost. They left 15,000 ghosts, almost every last man they had, and accomplished nothing. And in the 1870s they came back and tried it again! And lost. This time left more dead along this treacherous pass. Why? Same reason. Fear the Russians were coming."

And now a hundred years later, the Russians really were coming. And the Brits and Americans were gearing up to stop them. So this historic hard country, this strategic place of great interest and constant wars and conflicts and death, and bodies buried along the roadsides was looking at another imminent international conflict. Thousands and thousands of soldiers and fighters and invaders and contractors and trekkers and probably a few drug smugglers were coming. We were definitely not alone. Yeah, I included ourselves in that intrepid group. We were kind of like the bull in the ring, head down, ass up, keep on going and barrel in there. Our agenda - get to Peshawar, meet our contact Tariq, get the Range Rover loaded, get that thing down to Bombay, get it home, and get the hash sold, and *relax*. With the history in my head, it felt like a long road between here and there.

We rose up into leather-colored hilly terrain to Torkham, which was the border town between Afghanistan and Pakistan. We were feeling a bit nervous about this border crossing because we weren't entirely sure that the CIA hadn't dropped a dime on us. After letting us go, maybe Patricia had second thoughts or was told by her superiors to make us disappear. What better, more efficient, clean handed way to do it than to make us vanish at the border between two unfriendly countries? Even if anyone cared to ask about us being missing, fingers would point in too many directions.

We pulled up to a platoon of border guards. Standing stock still, they carried a century of tradition and history with them. Like a modern incarnation of the legendary Khyber Rifles, they guarded the Pass for the English. Though they waved most people through, when the guard came up to our window, he spoke in Pashto and indicated that we pull over into a search area. Fuck, I thought. Now what?

The first guard dragged me from behind the wheel and and directly into the guard station. I showed our passports and the Carnet de passagess. This brought some silent nods, paper checking, a phone call and finally directions in Pashto to go back outside. I hesitated to feel relief when I saw the Pakistani guards were circling the Rover. One time, two times, then they wanted to open up the hood and open up the back. They went to pull out the spare. As they searched, their Khyber rifles swung back and forth at the ready.

They grilled us again in Pashto, which none of us understood. Finally, one of their crew came over and he spoke pretty good English. I told him we were on a rug buying trip. "We're buying more in Peshawar and Lahore, then shipping them home from Bombay."

The translator said, "You need to wait."

"Wait? For what?" His look said he wasn't entertaining questions. I dreaded what further investigation might reveal, knowing full well that Patricia could have put the word out on us. If he started checking, we could get hung up in a bad way. When you're crossing the border between two foreign countries, you're at the mercy of both of them. This seemed to me to be the perfect time for a bribe. But I'd been wrong about this before. Sometimes a bribe can backfire. If you offer it to the wrong person, they resent your arrogance and see the *gift* as casting aspersions on their character. But I went for it anyway. I told the guard, "Sir. I wonder if we might make a present to you and your border guard fraternal association?" At first, he looked as if he might be interested. Then his face turned dark. He said, "What?"

I reached out with a hundred-dollar bill while looking in another direction. Somehow, eye contact seemed risky. The guards looked at each other, nodded. I heard the low whisper, "*Baksheesh...*" The first guard pocketed the cash without a word and quickly stamped our passports. He handed them back to me with a gracious smile and said, "On your way." What a relief that was to drive away. Ah, capitalism at work.

We finally made it through and entered Pakistan, where the Khyber Pass continues on to Landi Kotal, which is the summit of the Pass. We didn't know it at the time, but we'd be coming back to this scenic, seemingly innocuous, little village. Quickly on our way, we cruised right through. It looked like a sort of wild-west town. A train station right out of *High Noon* with a market, a few food stalls and what appeared to be a small brick shithouse of a jail.

Above the town, up on the highest ridge, were the ruins of a citadel the Brits had used in their second failed attempt to conquer the region in 1879. The brick and mortar parapets still stood as a reminder that hubris leads to disaster. And I took that lesson to heart. I didn't want to become one of the dead buried alongside the Pass. I didn't want to become the latest casualty on the Silk Road trade route. Picked off by snipers in the hills of Landi Kotal. Or pulled over by bandits blocking the road to rob us. Or thrown in a dungeon by border guards. We set our sights on Peshawar. A big town in western Pakistan we thought was safe. Little did we know.

26

Fear is a cancer and for me, it was growing. I tried to put our detainment by Patricia Adams and the CIA in Kabul out of my head. But all the way from Kabul through the Khyber Pass and down into Peshawar, fear nagged at me, screaming that there would be fallout.

I tried to console myself with the other close calls we had survived. Like Grant overdosing on the plane from Bombay to London. He was so fucked up they had to make an unscheduled stop in Frankfurt where paramedics put him in an ice bath. We finally got back in the air but when we got off the plane in London, the cops arrested him. Jack got him out of that one, claiming diplomatic immunity. That time Jack was the hero, but a couple days later when we hit Brussels, he disappeared for two days with a bellboy. Grant returned the favor and came to the rescue on that one by scouring the gay bars to find him. Potentially the most catastrophic mistake of all had been made by me, picking up a bar girl in an Istanbul hotel and falling asleep after sex while she snatched our money belt with a hundred grand in it. Luckily, I woke up just as she was sprinting out the door and I caught up to her in the lobby. She didn't want to give that money belt up and tried to convince some British soldiers I was the bad guy. Fortunately, Jack had been buying the whole cadre drinks and they intervened on our behalf.

The string of weird occurrences didn't end there. The thieving bar chick was followed by a group of Turkish bandits who ran us off the road to hijack the Rangey. We were saved that time by the same platoon of British soldiers who helped us with the money belt. The attempted hijacking was followed by the dog incident in which I unfortunately hit and killed an Afghan wolfhound. The owner was a Turkish cowboy and he chased us all the way to the Iranian border. I was wondering now how many more lives we cats had left.

There was some good news though when we arrived at our hotel - a note to Grant from our Bombay contact Mick that Tariq would be connecting with us asap. I had a hundred grand in American dollars in the bulging money belt around my waist. Money like that around the waist is a buzz in itself. I was amped to make the deal. It had been a crazy long road getting to Peshawar and I could feel us closing in on our score. The hash was in reach now and I could almost smell it. I was feeling the rush and the fear began to ebb. But it wasn't long before it crept in again as we waited and the appointed time came and went with no word. I told myelf that connections are always late. Just ask Lou Reed. His song about scoring played on in my head...

"He's never early. He's always late. First thing you learn is you have to wait."

I assumed Mick would be bringing Tariq to meet us. Our mysterious connection was now long overdue and soon I was left to wonder if something unexpected had happened. Mick the junky got busted? He set us up? He had burned us? The

CIA was watching us? It was hard to keep my mind from going crazy places.

We were in the bar of the Links Hotel in Peshawar. The luxury establishment was trying to combine an English Raj with its burnished mahogany and colonial opulence with New World, plate-glass, high ceilinged American expansionism. The huge windows opened to a golf course. One of those impeccably tended world-unto-itself playgrounds sparsely dotted with men of wealth and taste. On magnificent display were their luxury golf carts and turbaned caddies, hovering, waiting, happy to attend them. The bar was packed with Americans and Europeans. We were having a cold beer, curry, some sweet breads and trying to recover from the tension of our hair-raising trip down from Landi Kotal.

Jack was drunk and lively, having a high time refilling his glass from a fifth of Bushmills. At this particular bar, one could buy booze by the quart. He was into full pontification mode, grandstanding for all those within earshot about the city of Peshawar and its nickname - The City of Men. I asked how that name came about and he said, "It's obvious, my boy. Women were second-class citizens! As it should be!"

Oh, man, I thought, here we go. Of course that got some groans, especially from the ladies present, but in true Jack form, he continued on. "And to illustrate my point," he said, on a roll. He pointed to the golf course, "The fair sex is not allowed out there."

"That is blatantly false," an Englishwoman in golf togs piped up. "I played the course this morning!"

"Well then you're a rebel!" Jack said, gleefully. "And in the interests of anarchy, I shall join your foursome tomorrow!"

Yeah, sure. He'd be out there playing golf. I could see him
on the links, Quasimodo in knickers, putter in hand. His caddy
would be Grant, down on his knees on the green trying to line
up his putt for him as he nodded out cheek to turf.

Some wag winked at Jack's hunchback and asked him,
"So what's your handicap?" which drew a few uncomfortable
laughs.

"Probably the same as your I.Q." Jack shot back. "Wonderful game, golf. Churchill's line comes to mind – *Putting a
small ball into an even smaller hole with tools ill-suited to the
purpose!*"

Nobody wanted to go up against him after that. Grant was
deep in thought. I asked him what was up. He said something
about the deal didn't feel right and at that moment, I paused.
Something about him saying this made me take notice. Before
we could get into what he meant, a bellboy approached and
told Grant his presence was expected poolside. We figured this
was it and slapped five that things were happening. "Let's do
it," I said and the bellboy stopped me.

"Sorry sir, his presence is expected *alone*." Grant shrugged
as he went off with him through the hotel lobby.

Suddenly, and unexpectedly, I was feeling positive again.
The bartender came over and asked if we wanted anything else
to drink. I said no, but Jack ordered another bottle of Bushmills.
This drew a look from the bartender. "For the road," Jack said.
Having a relaxed drink in a Western oasis where drinking was
somewhat allowable was one thing, but powering down shots
out in the open in a Muslim country was dangerous. "For your
information," the barkeep said, "Ramadan starts tomorrow
and as soon as that happens, liquor is off limits for everybody,

Western or not."

"Ah, well then," Jack smiled with a sigh, "we'd better get some supplies." He ordered a case of scotch, a couple cases of beer and ten bottles of wine. Jack needed to have his wine with meals. A civilized man, as he was constantly reminding us. I pulled a hundred out and told the bartender we'd pick it all up later.

Grant was gone about an hour and I began to get restless. What the hell was going on? I went out to the lobby and looked for him, but he wasn't around. I went outside to the veranda overlooking the golf course and there he was sitting at a table fifty feet away. Next to him was a woman wearing a head shawl and sunglasses. They were talking intimately. Suddenly, he looked up and, seeing me, he ended the conversation. The girl got up and left, leaving me no wiser as to who she was. Grant came over and I asked, "Hey, man what was that?"

"A weird thing happened, man. This chick Karina came to give me a message about where to meet Tariq Rahim. And then I don't know how this came down, but we started talking. She had a black eye, man. For real. When I asked her about it, she wouldn't say much. Like she was scared underneath, you know what I mean? And we just started talking and I felt like..." He went silent for a moment. Then as quickly as he'd begun, he shook it right off. "Forget it. We're supposed to meet this fucker Tariq at the Museum. Karina said we should go there and he'll find us."

At first, I didn't know what to make of this. Weeks later I would meet this girl Karina myself in the casbah-like club, but I had no idea of that then. Instead, my mind was on getting the deal together. And if it was going to go down at a museum, then fine. Let's get to the fucking museum.

We wound our way through the bottlenecked traffic of Peshawar. It was an ancient city, one of the oldest in Asia. Alexander the Great had come through in 330 B.C. when the area was called Bactria. It had been involved in one war or another ever since. The subject of changed names over the millennia, usually at the whim of some foreign power. Now it was part of Pakistan, which Jack informed me meant, *Land of the Pure.*

Despite all the delays and calamities, we were getting closer to buying the mother lode of primo hash. And I had a buzz going. Madhouse energy swirled through me. I was so ready. Ready to meet The Man, get set up, go do the buy, get the goods stashed in the vehicle. Then we'd make our final leg down to Bombay, get the Rangey on the boat, get that boat to Sydney. In the comfort of our home city, we'd easily sell our stash, start to relax and finally reap the benefits of this long and arduous trip.

As we honked and lurched fitfully through the packed streets, Jack was playing tour guide again, competing with the cacophony of street venders and deranged taxi drivers who would slam on the brakes, leap out of their cabs to scream at a dog or a horse or a person, didn't matter who or what. The essential activity in those rabid streets was to yell and yell loudly. Jack was yelling too, as we stalled in one traffic jam after another, about how Peshawar used to be completely walled in, with fortress gates around it because it was the gateway to the tribal territories that were chock full of their enemies.

Three Muslim women in full burkas were walking together arm in arm. They looked like a trio of beekeepers. You could not see one inch of their flesh from head to toe. Same with all the women in the streets. It was the City of Men, all right. Men who walled in their women, turned them into chattel and ornaments. They were cooks and mothers, hidden behind these cloistering outfits, not allowed to drive or even to walk without an escort. They were possessions for men to do with as they pleased with impunity. Jack, misogynist that he was, thought this was perfectly as it should be. Was this because he was gay? I wondered. He didn't seem to identify with the oppression of a "weaker sex" while he championed the rights of gays, whales, aborigines and the handicapped. His prejudice against females never did make sense to me – but what can I say?

Everything Jack said indicated that he thought women were next to useless. Personally, I thought girls were angels, divine creatures who had saved my life on more than one occasion. To cover them up and subjugate them seemed to me a crime. As he was so good at doing, Jack read my thoughts, "My boy, maybe they like being covered up."

Grant was edgy the whole ride, his thoughts on the girl he'd just met. Karina. "But what if they don't like being covered up, man? Maybe they don't like it all. Maybe they have black eyes from being hit. Maybe they're hoping some day they won't have to be pushed around." Something told me Grant might be speaking from personal experience.

"Ah, my boy is sensitive about the fairer sex. Grant, come on, be truthful. Do you not exploit the ladies? Do you not fuck on and then another and then another and another, then one after the next, abandon each of the poor creatures? My, my, what a trail of tears."

"True enough. You ever shed tears, Professor?" Grant pinched Jack's neck hard, but he wouldn't cry out, took it stoically. I pushed Grant's hand away, managing to defuse that confrontation.

We arrived at the Peshawar Museum and stood in the gallery, surrounded by one of the largest collections of Buddha statues in the world. Stone, marble and terracotta bodhisattvas. Some of them two thousand years old. It's impossible not to be mesmerized in their presence, even when you're waiting for an elusive drug connection to show. I asked Grant what Karina said we should do. She had told him we were to split up, go into separate wings of the museum, and then Tariq would make contact.

We weren't sure if this was a wild goose chase or what was going to happen next. It seemed a bizarre way to meet, but we were at Tariq's mercy at that moment. As directed, we started splitting up and joining the various crowds who wandered from room to room. I strolled into a gallery full of the artifacts of the Khyber tribes. Swords, daggers, spears, flintlock rifles, silver bullets. And then suddenly there was Tariq, standing next to me.

Jack later termed him "a rather muscular and exotic gentleman." I likened him to Omar Sharif without the height. He was wearing the Armani of Pakistani pajamas, made of white silk and royally expensive. He had his prayer beads around his wrist, and but for a thin mustache, was clean-shaven. His eyes were inscrutable behind designer shades as he voiced my name, "James." The accent was Eton. "I am Tariq Rahim. You've had quite a journey."

At first, he appeared friendly, but there was also an unmistakably ominous vibe about him, like he could be the Don Corleone of Pakistan. I sensed that he had the power to deliver everything we wanted, but if he thought he was crossed, then the ax would fall. "You and your partners have gotten yourselves in some trouble along the way, no?"

We were standing in front of a glorious display of Bronze Age weaponry. He glanced at it then held me hard in his gaze, "Tell me about it."

Well, he fucking knew about our CIA run in, but he was still meeting with me. It was curious and I itched to figure him out. "You know about us being detained in Kabul?"

"That I do. And you want to know how I know."

"Uh, yeah, that crossed my mind."

"Doesn't matter. The point is why they detained you and then abruptly let you go. Just tell me what happened."

"Uh... both my partners got a little crazy in their own way. It's over. No big deal."

"You gave them the film your friend Grant stole from the photographer?"

"Yeah," I said and the possibility that I was walking into a trap rose in my throat like bile.

"Missiles and other weapons in the pictures, true?"

"Yeah."

"You kept copies of the pictures, true?"

"No."

"No copies?" He looked at me a long moment, lips set in a line. He was taking his time to decide if I was lying or not. "Patricia Adams let you go knowing you are drug smugglers?"

"Tariq, you think we owe her a favor and we're going to set you up?"

He laughed, never losing his urbanity and cool. "You're not that stupid."

"I'd be stupid if I didn't get an answer about how you knew what happened in Kabul."

"I'm CIA," he said with a chilling seriousness.

I was speechless. He laughed again. He lifted his dark shades and I could see his eyes. They were cobalt blue. Icy but mirthful. "A joke, James. A joke. I make it my business to watch and know what the CIA, the KGB, the Paki police, the Afghan army, UN soldiers... all of them, are up to. They don't see me. I see them. This is my land. I observe them from inside and outside. You understand?"

"Yeah, I do. So is our deal on?" Suddenly I was hoping it was off as this guy really spooked me.

"Did Grant keep copies of the pictures?"

"No."

The eyes of my inquisitor bored into me. I figured silence is golden in such a moment. Finally, he said, "I believe you. I like your honesty. Our deal is on."

I sighed, recalling how he had taken his time to decide whether I was telling him the truth. I wanted to do the same in weighing getting involved with him. My reticence seemed to assure him. "If you decide to proceed, this evening you will deliver half the money to a certain tobacconist in the bazaar. From there you will go back up to Landi Kotal, where a guide will meet you and take you to the tribal areas. Once there, you will contact the hash suppliers at their fort. You will make the buy, then return to Peshawar and deliver the other half of the money. If you fuck up in any way. Any way at all..." he left it hanging, as he glanced at the weapons near us. He pointed to a curved scimitar with a gleaming blade and gold and pearl hilt. "Beautiful artifact, isn't it? This design has survived to the present day."

"Point taken," I said. We shook hands, and he moved off with the crowd. I wandered around looking for Jack and Grant, but couldn't find them. I was thinking maybe they'd been corralled by Tariq when Grant showed up. I asked him where he'd been and he said Karina had come up to him, taken him aside and asked him questions about what happened in Kabul.

"You told her?"

"Sure. I had a feeling she already knew. She knew about the film, asked if I had prints. I said no, my buddy James burned them!" He laughed. "Something about that chick. With her black eye that she won't talk about." He looked at me, back in the moment of where we were. "So what happened with you?"

"Met Tariq. The deal is on. But there's something that feels really sketchy. Can't put a finger on it."

Jack hurried in from some other wing of the museum, his cane tap-tap-tapping on the marble floor. He was out of breath and pissed. "Two god damn thugs took me into an alcove and searched me! At gunpoint!" Suddenly all the anger left him and was replaced by a wicked smile, "I must say it was rather exciting. Few can say they were held in the breech by hash dealers in the Peshawar Museum of Antiquities!"

The question then became whether or not to go forward with the deal. I had qualms. Grant and Jack voted to go on with the plan. There was never any real doubt that we would, so we did. We put the fifty grand down with the tobacconist, drove the Rover to the Fort and left it, then came back to Peshawar to wait out Ramadan. So now the past and the present converge.

27

Seeing Grant at my hotel door in Peshawar was a relief. He didn't look any worse for wear after being locked up for almost a week. "Where's Jack?" I asked.

"In his room. Sick as a bleeding dog."

We went down the hall to Jack's suite and found him in the bathroom moaning. "Goddamn rat-infested jail food. Not even fit for the rodents." He was cutting loose from both ends and I had to get to a more fragrant place. Grant and I went down to the bar and he filled in the blanks about what had happened to them in the week since we'd been together. I'd last seen them when our elevator ride carrying contraband booze up to our rooms was interrupted by Pakistani police. While I was in Patricia Adams's limo, Grant and Jack had been blindfolded and taken to a holding cell. They'd spent the week there until this morning when they were blindfolded again and dropped back at the Links Hotel.

There was cause for celebration. Alcohol was suddenly no problem because it was finally the end of Ramadan. That had been about the longest three weeks of my life. We toasted the prospect of going to the hash dealers and retrieving our Land Rover. I explained to Grant that there was a wrinkle with Patricia Adams that had to be straightened out before we could be on our way.

"Yeah, I know, she wants a meeting with Tariq Rahim. She tried to twist my arm about that, too. And you went for it?"

"I had to do it to get you and Jack out."

"Thanks, mate. At least you got laid in the process. That viper bit you, didn't she? The Professor called it – she set us up to be her tools."

"We set ourselves up, mate."

"You're right bunji. I got a little crazy there with Flannery. So, where do we stand now?"

"I'll put the CIA offer to Tariq."

"She actually thinks Tariq would go for this?" Suddenly he looked like he might have been hit with a flash of prison paranoia. "How did you get hold of Tariq?"

I told him the story of my search ending with the surprise visit from Karina in the belly dancing club. He went dark on me, "Karina? My Karina?"

"What do you mean – your Karina?"

He ignored that one. "She contacted you?"

"For Tariq. I guess we're being watched by both sides."

He gave it some thought, then, "It's a sign."

"A sign of what?"

"Meant to be."

"You talking about you and her?"

"Yeah. Funny how Jack said get a girlfriend and then Karina popped into my life."

"Grant, that's fucking crazy. You don't know this girl."

"I know Karina."

"That's not even her real name."

"How do you know?"

"A feeling. The point is there are a million girls. Don't you see how insane it would be to go after Tariq's chick?"

"You don't know what went down between us. He gave her that black eye."

"Not your business. Not *our* business. Here, listen to me - she's going to show up and take me to a meeting with him. And you are not going to fuck this up by coming on to our connection's chick. We're on the thinnest ice possible. Our whole deal depends on me finessing this fucked up situation. And your freedom depends on it, too. Don't forget, you're on the run, man. They want you back in Oz. You didn't tell me that."

"Relax, bunji, it's just a bit of sorry business."

"*Sorry business?* Doesn't that mean *death* in Abo? Look, you fuck around with Karina and that sorry business might come."

"I don't give a fuck. You don't know what happened to her."

"Fuck, you're off the rails again. We have one chance to stay free and on the road. Patricia Adams could snatch you up and ship you back to prison in a hot second."

The conversation was so intense people in the bar were looking at us. He was in mad man mode and I couldn't reason with him. "Okay, you handle it then."

I went out to the pool for a swim. When in doubt, in times of frustration or trouble, get baptized. I was thinking about my options. Get on a plane and go home? That was just too depressing to even consider. Carry on alone up to the tribal territory and make the deal? Way too problematic. Somehow I had to make it work between Tariq and Patricia. I was doing all this thinking Underwater, holding my breath, my thoughts were illuminated as I looked up from the bottom of the pool to the shimmering sun above. Then there was a face looming there, blurred. I rose to the surface and Karina came into focus. "Let's go," she said.

"Can I jump into my clothes first?"

"Do it fast."

"What's the hurry?"

She was edgy and looking around, even at the windows and balconies above. Suddenly I understood her concern. Grant was striding over to us. "You have to keep him out of this. He will get hurt."

Grant smiled at her. "Your eye's better."

"All better." All of a sudden our wagon had three wheels. I had that sinking feeling a love connection had already happened between these two. He wanted to know if she was still with Tariq. She didn't want to talk about it. I knew there was no way she'd be free of him. I had a feeling Tariq had sent her because he knew what was going on. He was playing a game with Grant, challenging him. Karina knew this and was powerless. It was easy to see she had fallen in love. Tariq was too powerful. It was playing right into Grant's dark side and in that moment, I feared for his life. He wanted to tag along with us, but she told him it was impossible.

He took her hand, maybe a bit too roughly. "Look, I'm going."

She said if he insisted there would be no meeting. I took him aside, wanting to throw cold water in his face to wake him up. I had only begun to talk some sense into him when he said, "Gimme a minute with her."

I gave him his minute, hoping it would be the last time

they'd see each other. In the drive at the front of the hotel a black Mercedes waited. A Pakistani suit held the rear passenger door open and Karina and I climbed inside. Soon we were zipping through the streets, skidding around corners into alleys and back into a maze so narrow there was room for only one car. Karina was silent, stoic, and I'm a talker but she was not into a chat. I asked her where we were going.

"Only the driver knows." And that was it for the next ten minutes as the Mercedes careened around like a roller coaster. We finally stopped in a street teeming with people. We were in the Old City at the Qissa Bazaar. The muscle riding shotgun let us out and we followed him into a labyrinth of passageways lined with merchants standing outside their brightly lit stores. He was walking fast and abruptly ducked into a jewelry store, hurrying through to the back, out a rear entrance into a walkway lined with more stores. Bicycles and motorbikes were parked all over the place and we had to dodge them to try and keep up. He went into a coin shop and disappeared behind a curtain. We did the same and found ourselves in a back room. Standing to face us was Tariq Rahim. This time, he was dressed in western clothes that were tight fitting and I was surprised at how muscular he was. The suit and Karina took seats against the wall. As they settled in the shadows, I was once again face-to-face with the bloke who could make or break our whole enterprise.

"You've been having quite a dance with Patricia Adams."

"True. I figured you'd know that. You probably know more than I do."

"Tell me what you know."

"She wants a meeting with you. I told her it was a crazy

idea. All I want to do is stay out of it."

"But they are leveraging you and you are inextricably compromised. Which could be interpreted as me being compromised."

"I never admitted I knew you."

"And yet here we are. Do what she asked. Set up a meeting."

"You want to meet with her?" I said, surprised.

"I'm sure she told you that already. Think of it as a high stakes game. So, game on."

"Okay, I'll go back and tell her it's on. And then I'm going to go get my Rover up in the tribal areas. Cool?"

"It depends on how my meeting goes with her."

"What does that mean? I don't have any control over what's going down with you two."

"You have no control over anything in your situation. Now I want you to go back to her. You'll set up a meeting. But not in the time and place that she dictated. It will be at the time and place I say. And you will tell her that I need certain things in writing. Logistical analysis and a list of materiel, the arms she would supply."

"I'm out of my league here. I'm a plumber...a surfer..."

"Don't sell yourself short, James. You're in the international drug trade. And now you're involved in politics as well. You'll do this for me because I'm responsible for making sure that you get the things you want. Think of ours as a symbiotic relationship. I'm responsible for your very expensive vehicle. The cargo it will be carrying. In fact, I'm responsible for your safety and freedom right now. Right here in Peshawar."

"So, what are you saying?"

"It means look on the bright side – you're alive." He let that point settle and then spoke to Karina in a language I didn't recognize. She went to his side and he gave her a note and some instructions about what to do with it. I could see she was ill at ease, like a star walking the red carpet with toilet paper on her shoe. He took her hand, the hand with the note and squeezed it. It hurt her. Her jaw muscles tensed, but she kept cool. "She's beautiful, no?" he said, eyes on me. She winced.

"So how do I get my Rover?" I refused to look at Karina.

"If all goes well, you will find Azziz at the same café in Landi Kotal and he will guide you."

I said, "Well, okay, let's do this." He let her hand go and we left. When we were back in the Mercedes and driving away, she gave me the note. It read, *Patricia Adams – we will meet at the north entrance of the Mohabat Khan Mosque at dusk, tomorrow. I don't need to say that this will be one-on-one.*

I said, "I'll tell you something funny. I don't even know how to get in touch with her."

"She'll probably be waiting for you at the hotel."

"How is it everybody knows what everybody is doing except me?"

"Pawns don't know when they're about to be moved."

"Well, that stings. But it's true. Are you going to make my life easier and keep away from Grant?"

"I promised to speak with him. I have enough bad karma without adding another lie to it."

"You? Bad karma? Come on, what could you have done that's so bad?"

The muscle riding shotgun turned around and censored her with a look, then did the same to me. Karina said, "Don't worry, he doesn't speak English."

"Then what's his problem?"

"Me being so *familiar* with you."

"How did you get involved with these people?"

"Fate."

"So you're a pawn?"

"To Shiva, all are pawns."

"Not me."

"That's what you think. Now, *shhhh*," she patted my hand and that was the end of the conversation until we arrived back at the hotel. Hawkeye riding shotgun opened the door and let me out. Karina got out, too. He said something about getting back in the car, but she backed him off and led me into the lobby.

Grant and Jack sat near a window. Grant was up and moving to her while Jack slumped in his chair looking like a wreck. Karina took Grant aside. They said a few words and then she gave him something, then left. As Grant walked toward us, he held up a small figurine of an elephant. "What's up?" I asked.

"Nothing," he said.

"She just gave you that. An elephant?"

Jack hobbled over, leaning heavily on his cane. He smelled bad and looked pale, like a slab of cheese. He saw the elephant, carved of beige marble. It stood in mid dance, leg and trunk raised. "Ganesh," he said reverently.

"Ganesh?" Grant asked.

"Son of Shiva. The remover of obstacles." Jack held it up to the light, "Beautiful. But beware of Hindu sluts bearing gifts."

Grant seized him by the arm and pulled him close, "Don't talk like that about her, Jack. Gimme that." He swiped the small gift and held it in both hands.

I wondered if by giving the elephant to Grant, Karina was

saying she would remove obstacles for him. Or was the message that he would remove obstacles for her? I saw problems ahead if there was any association at all between them. "Listen up, you guys," I said. "We are good to go here. I set up the meeting between Tariq and Patricia. She's gonna get the details from me tonight or tomorrow and then I'm heading up to the fort to fetch the Rover. Everything is set. I'll be back the following night. Then the day after tomorrow at noon, we are out of here. You two understand? Wednesday at noon. We hit the road. No more delays, no more sidetracks. You both know what I'm talking about. Nothing gets in the way. In the lobby ready to split forty-eight hours from now."

28

It was a new dawn and a new day and I was feeling good. That Nina Simone song played in my head and the birds and the butterflies were flying out on the golf course. The sun was shining, there was a little breeze and I had a note in my pocket that Patricia Adams wanted. My native boy caddy was looking to the southern sky, his mind elsewhere. I asked him for a putter and he pulled it out of the bag, but his mind was on the sky. I asked him what was up and he said a storm was coming. Impossible, I thought since the sky was a crystal blue billabong, not a cloud to be seen. And this would be a day to remember. Patricia Adams would come for her note. We'd hop in the sack for one last hot root. Then I would grab a cab up the Khyber Pass to Landi Kotal, meet Azziz, make my way to the fort, get the Rover loaded with hash and we'd be on our way to Bombay.

I played a few holes and then a bellboy came rolling up in a golf cart with a message that someone was waiting for me in the drive. I rode back with him and found Patricia Adams sitting behind the wheel of an ice blue Mercedes.

Her hair was in a bun, the Rolex was back on her wrist and she wore the black pantsuit. Funny how her getup was like reading a barometer. I told her Tariq had agreed to meet.

She wanted to know word for word what went down. I started talking, but she stopped me time and again making me go back and remember his exact words. It wasn't enough to paraphrase our exchange.

"Something about a list of materials."

"Materials? Or materiel?" she said with the accent on the last syllable.

"List of arms. And something about logistical analysis. In writing."

"The note from Tariq, please." She held out her hand and I gave it to her.

"How did you know there's a note?" I asked, frustrated and tired of being the pawn.

"It doesn't matter." I gave it to her with a more than slight puff of frustration. "What else did he say?"

"That I was now involved in politics. And that the police were watching me. The three of us getting out of Peshawar depended on how this goes." I shrugged, partly because of that frustration, but also because I was getting tired of being the pawn.

"True." She pulled over under a half-completed freeway viaduct. The sky seemed darker all of a sudden. There were no clouds, but rather a deep gray haze in the distance and I wondered if my caddy had been right about a coming storm. She read the note again, thinking, saying nothing.

"Everything will go ok, right?" I asked. "We'll all get what we want?"

"It's shaping up that way. Well done, James."

"Could we go somewhere and celebrate? My place or yours?"

She looked at me and in that moment her face softened and she looked young and so pretty. "Just go get in our little bubble..." But the look turned to stone as quickly as it had come. "Don't worry, James, I've got your back. You're not going to fuck me, literally or figuratively."

She was right that I looked at our intimacy as an insurance policy. It even surprised me that I really did want her. And maybe it was only later that I realized there was another reason for my desire – above everything else, Patricia Adams had the intelligence and self-assurance that I wanted to soak up.

The sky was a dark sea now, a giant gray wave heading our way being blown in by twenty knot winds. It was a typhoon of dust approaching.

She pulled back onto the road. We could barely see oncoming traffic unless the vehicle had its headlights on. We passed a tree bent over by the wind, branches and leaves whipping. Sand blasted into our windshield, limiting visibility to a few yards. I was startled to see a motorcycle beside us, the driver hunkered over his handlebars, his female passenger wearing a full burka, riding sidesaddle and clinging to his back. They passed us without effort and almost ran head on into a bus without headlights.

"Look, we should get out of this. Let's go to a hotel and talk," I said.

"No more hotel rooms, James. That part has to be over."

"Guess I should have known by the Rolex."

"My little milkmaid heirloom broke."

"I could get you one if I knew how to find you."

She looked at me and for a moment was again that sweet young girl. Or was she suddenly years older? "Now why would you want to find me, James?"

"Have some fun."

"And what about your girl back home? What about Andi?"

"Buzz kill," I said. I immediately heard the hollow and disingenuous me. Here stood the lowlifel, solely interested in what he wanted at that moment.

The CIA Station Chief was back. "What else did Tariq say?"

"Basically that if I fucked up, he'd kill me."

"Oh really?"

"Serious business, as Grant would say."

"Oh, but you're a survivor, James. If I know anything about you, and I know a lot, I know that."

"I might need a guardian angel to make it home." The suggestion made her smile, like a half-hearted sphinx.

"You'll make it home and be sitting out in the waves with your surf buddies telling them how you fucked a spook."

"Maybe you'll be telling your buds how you took one for the team."

"Then we both got what we wanted, didn't we? Let's leave it at that."

A big blast of sand and wind rocked the Mercedes. With just a few feet of visibility, we were driving at ten miles an hour. It would only get worse heading into the heart of the storm so Pattricia hung a u-turn and returned in the direction we'd come from.

By the time we got back to my hotel, trash-strewn sand traps lined the driveway and the entrance. The sand was blowing so hard it dulled the windshield.

"Surfer boy, you're out of your element here. It's amazing

you got this far. I'm impressed. You know how you did it? You're lucky. Incredibly lucky. But luck runs out and you're not cut out for prison. Go home and get a real job."

I leaned in to her, close. "Why do I get the feeling you don't really want to say goodbye?"

She really did want to go to the room. I could feel it as we sat there in silence with the storm rocking the car like a cradle, so I kissed her. She pushed me back. "No. Go on now. And when you leave Peshawar, do not go back through Iran. Iran is not a safe place to be and it'll get even worse. And as for Peshawar, Tariq was right about the police watching you. He should know. He's well connected with them."

"To the police?"

"See what I mean about you being lucky? Now go!"

I got out and hurried into the hotel. Sand had found its way into the lobby and the staff was cleaning it up. I wanted to get on the road to Landi Kotal right then, but I knew no cab driver would make the trip until the dust settled. There would be no swimming, no golfing or restless jogs around the course. I looked for my partners, but neither was in the hotel. So nothing to do but settle in at the bar and watch the wind blow.

Two beers and some Bushmills later Jack hurried in. His skin was gray, covered in a coating of sand, he had a pile of newspapers and a few books under his arm, and a manic look as he tapped the bar with his cane to get the bartender's attention. I'd seen that wild look before. It usually meant he was about to go freaky on me, lock himself in a bedroom or a bathroom, stay there for a couple of days on a speed run. Sometimes it was porno jag and others it was some issue he had to get his head around. That looked like what was happening now with the newspapers and books. I asked him what was up.

"A puzzle, James. A magnificent, political, world chang-ing puzzle." He called to the bartender, "You sir! A bottle of Jameson's. Make that two bottles. You saw the CIA bitch and it's all set?" he said.

"Yeah. It's on. Why?"

"Why? Because it's fucking historic! I'm going to do some research."

"Research?"

"These are world shaking events, my boy! Political upheaval. Coups here in Pakistan and Iran. Another brewing in Afghanistan. Worldwide nuclear détente threatened. Proxy wars between the U.S. and the Soviets. Fabulous times, James. And we're in the middle of it!"

"Look, I just want to pick up our Rover, get our hash and get the fuck out of here."

"Sit tight for a couple of days. Meanwhile, I'm going to disappear for a bit." He managed to tuck the bottles of whisky in with the newspapers and books.

"Disappear where? What the fuck are you talking about?"

"I need to figure out how we play this."

"When I'm ready to go you'd better be fucking ready, too. Where's Grant?"

"A wild guess would be he's off with that Hindu hooker." He split and I knew the door to his room would be locked. If history was any guide, he'd be in there with an ounce of crystal Meth and buried in his research. He might be glimpsed sneaking out into the hallway at midnight in his long white robe, ungodly stains running up and down, a sweaty, gaunt specter you'd want no part of.

Meanwhile Grant was with Karina? Doing what? Nothing but stirring up trouble. The last thing I needed was a pissed off Tariq Rahim. Patricia was right. It was an outright miracle we'd gotten this far in our endeavor. How long would my luck last? Long enough to get us out of Pakistan, I hoped. First things first – get the Rover. An hour later, the storm had abated enough for me to go in search of a cab to take me up to Landi Kotal.

29

Despite the calming skies, no cab driver was willing to make the drive to Landi Kotal so I'd have to travel on the Khyber Pass Railway. The historic forty-mile trip over shaky trestles around treacherous mountain curves took about two hours. Longer than normal because the train was halted at the top of the pass and the Khyber Rifles came on board and scrutinized every passenger. Something had obviously happened up ahead and there were whispers about a bombing. The soldiers stayed with us and when we finally rolled up to the Landi Kotal Railway Station, the army was out in full force.

I saw a hippy couple watching the action from the shade of a tree and asked them what was going on. "The trains are all shut down," the girl said. Her casual ease told me she was American: smart and intelligent, a valedictorian turned fatalist earth mama.

"There was a bombing," her boyfriend added, cupping his hands together and then exploding them apart in a dramatic display of force. You could see beneath all the road dust and hair he was a good-looking guy and lean in a macrobiotic sort of way.

"Bomb?"

"They bombed the tracks. *They* being Pakistani separatists

or Afghanistan insurgents, depending on who you talk to." She rolled her eyes as if to say, what's the difference? "Spare change?" the girl added.

"God will provide," the boy said.

I gave them a few bucks, shook my head and moved on. Wandering over to the café where I was to meet Azziz, all was quiet and I could see he wasn't there. Hours later, still no Azziz. I was considering my options when a familiar face walked in. It was Mick, the connection Grant had found in Bombay who hooked us up with Tariq. He saw me and came over to sit down. The British ex-pat spoke fluently in Urdu to the waiter, ordering something for both of us. I remembered in Bombay he said he'd married a local girl. "Long time no see since Bombay. You blokes have had quite a trip. Not exactly low profile like you originally planned, eh?"

"Plans change," I said, mildly, trying to suss his meaning. "That they do, mate."

"So you're here? The plan was that I'd meet Azziz."

"As you say, plans change. I'm taking you to the fort."

Mick didn't appear to be loaded, not even mildly like when we first met him in Bombay. He still sported the upscale hippy garb with his hand-tooled leather satchel and madras scarf, sort of a cross between the High Plains Drifter and Lawrence of Arabia. He was throwing me a curveball – or Tariq was – but I'd come to expect those. I could have walked out, but somehow didn't feel like it was a setup. I asked him about the railway bombing.

Turns out it was all about The Bomb. The big one. What India called "The Smiling Buddha." India had made Pakistan extremely nervous when they'd conducted a nuclear test.

Pakistan's Prime Minister at the time, Ali Bhutto, expressed his concern to NATO. NATO, controlled by the U.S., declined to sanction India, so Bhutto went directly to the White House. Secretary of State Kissinger told him that Pakistan had to "live with it." Now there were loyalists to Bhutto voicing dissatisfaction with the new military regime.

"The Khyber Pass is high profile and gets a lot of press," Mick explained, "and they're making a *statement*. Locals aren't very happy with the Americans right now. Good thing you're Australian." He winked like the Artful Dodger, "Don't worry, I won't tell them you're in bed with the CIA. Which was very smart of you by the way, James."

We finished off the lunch and beers he'd ordered and then hit the road, Mick astride his BMW motorcycle and me in the sidecar. It was brand new under all the dust so I figured Mick was doing pretty well for himself. "Did you bring the other half of the money you owe Tariq?" he asked.

I said no, that wasn't the deal. "I know," he said, "just making sure you're not vulnerable."

"Oh, you're looking out for me?"

"You betcha, mate. That's why I'm here."

We took the same precarious road up into the mountains, bumping our way through the same small villages, saw the same cows, goats and rambunctious kids. And then finally arrived at the fort.

Two medieval gates creaked open and sitting there in the dusty courtyard ready to go was our Range Rover. The Chief was very proud of his team's work and patted the roof rack. "Fifty kilos in here. Undetectable. Look." I checked the wood out. No evidence at all that it was now a hollowed-out shell with hash in the middle like a 4' x 8' Oreo cookie. The Chief slapped the rear fender, "The gas tank is perfect."

I looked underneath the car, tapped the tank a few times. The compartment with fifty kilos of hash inside it that had been secreted inside the gas tank was, as he said, undetectable. I fired the Rangey up, it rumbled like the beast it was. The Chief asked me, "Would you like tea and a bowlful of our best?"

"No thanks," I said, "I've got to hit the frog and toad."

"You from the west... always in a hurry."

Mick came over to my ear and whispered, "It's bad manners to refuse a bowl."

Well, what could it hurt? I took the pipe and huffed off a huge hit of pure hash. The cloud of blue smoke as I blew it rose up toward the gods and I hoped that what I was about to do next wouldn't get me shot.

"I'll need to take a look," I blew a long, blue line into the sun, "before we take off."

Mick rushed to my elbow and said in a low voice, "Look man, that's an insult."

Okay, fuck, you might call it bad manners. But there was no denying things had gone a bit sour It was like that awkward moment in a looming beach fight when you're not sure who's going to throw the first punch. I wanted to get moving, but I had too much time and money invested to head out without knowing for certain. It might look like a lack of trust, but I'd have bet The Chief would do the same if the tables had been turned. The Chief was staring at me. All his bandolier boys in their turbans cradling AK 47s and Kalashnikovs had me pinned. The whole fucking world now depended on the next word. It was a tense and scary moment, but it's funny how you can get used to scary things. Politics, the art of the possible, as Jack would say. I think he attributed the quote to some genius Prussian General who was a master of diplomacy. The idea is you do what's possible, not necessarily what's right or ideal. Perfect advice in problematic, and even in dangerous, situations like the one I was in with the Guru of Hash at his Fort could go sideways in a flash. But there was no finessing this. I would be out of my mind with worry until we got back to Oz if I didn't know for sure the load was there. "Sorry, but I have to see the hash. There's a hundred thousand on the line here."

The Chief looked to Mick as the shot caller because he was Tariq's rep. Mick wasn't happy about it, but he acquiesced. Mechanics brought the tools out and drilled a small hole in the plywood rack. I could see the hash on the drill bit. They did that in a few other spots with the same result and I was satisfied. Then they had to deal with the gas tank. This was an involved operation. They had to jack the car up, pull the tank out, break the weld, then take the inner tank out and break the weld on that to show me the bricks of hash stashed inside. Then they put the whole enchilada back together. It took a few hours and everybody was grumbling. I felt pretty chagrined, but what the fuck. Better to be safe than sorry.

After that moment and everyone calmed down, I felt I deserved an eye-watering, billowy bowl of the best blonde the fort had to offer, then climbed in my Rangey and motored out of there. Following Mick through the Hindu Kush, I thought about two other dicey situations facing me in Peshawar. Grant stirring up trouble with Karina and Jack in his methamphetamine psychosis. And then I wondered how the meeting between Tariq and Patricia had gone. Was I off the hook there? I said a little prayer. I don't know why, nor did I know to whom I was praying, but the hope it gave birth to was enough. Hope and faith, there you have the difference.

I couldn't help smiling as I thought of my beautiful Andi and that gorgeous piece of land on the knoll above Lennox Head where we'd build our dream house. The dream seemed within reach now. Our long sought after load of primo hash was finally in the Rover and we were a step closer to pulling off the operation. *Exhilarating.*

I followed Mick through the tribal territories into Landi Kotal, past army trucks and a big crowd that had converged on the tiny railroad office. A roadblock had been set up and I suddenly had soldiers detaining me. The first test. I had the jitters as guards circled the car. The jitters are a dead giveaway and I lit a cigarette to cool down. Opening a soda, I casually tossed the ring pull and took some deep breaths, picturing a waterfall and tranquil pool in Lennox Head. The tall one looked me over, had me get out and show my passport. Meanwhile, two others like snub-nosed dogs sniffed around the Rover and I held my smoke, staring at the cig's reassuring coal. Again, I said a silent prayer. To the smuggling gods, to Andi, to some angel I hoped might be listening. They had me open up the rear doors and the back and on they searched. Thankfully this time, I had no drugs or booze in the car. Just as I thought it was over, in came the dogs. These hounds stuck their noses inside and under the car. I puffed on that cigarette, which ordinarily I wouldn't have smoked without a whisky or a nose full of blow. I coughed and it made the guards laugh which I guess was better than seeing them scowl. The dogs wagged their tails at me and that must have been a sign because finally they seemed satisfied that I wasn't a terrorist. They sent me on my way, rolling on down the Khyber Pass to Peshawar.

Back in the land of the midnight golfers, I climbed up to Jack's room, hoping on hope that he'd come out of his meth-induced psychosis. I pounded on his door relentlessly until he finally opened up. A noxious smell hit me, like egg salad or sour milk, and his look was deranged, an acid head with his eyes rolling skyward to the clouds. The maniac said nothing, but went back into his bathroom, a skin crawling stink hole with paper strewn all over the floor, political journals mixed in with gay porn and glossy magazines. A god-awful rat's nest of stuff lined every surface. Jack's glasses were broken, he was filthy and his hunched back was coiled up like a spring, his spine threatening to pop out through his translucent skin. "I've figured it all out, my boy," he croaked and swept his hand over the mess of papers on the floor, "I know what's happening!"

Here would come the routine – listen to his wild rambling, the convoluted conspiracy theories and then after he'd showered and coffeed himself up, I could get him to make some sense, and occasionally a theme would emerge.

Stomach turning as the task was, I helped him peel off his soiled pajamas. A crust of dried bodily fluid – was it pus, dried feces, or blood? - fell from his splotched and sore-riddled body. I shooed him into the shower as he ranted, "There's going to be a Communist takeover in Afghanistan! A coup by the People's Democratic Party! The Americans don't want that. The C.I.A. was outfoxed! They are right at this moment fomenting a counter-revolution! Establishing an insurgency with the Mujahedeen. They're enlisting Tariq. You get it?"

Like we didn't know that. "Yeah, yeah, he's the key," I said gritting my teeth and helping him into the shower. The water hit him and turned brown on the tiles.

"No, he's the lock! He's the son of Ahmad Khan for Christ sakes! The brother of the nuclear scientist heading up the Paki nuke project. Pakistan's going to have the bomb soon. Does the West want that? No! A military dictatorship with a nuke? Do we want that? No!"

"Jack, come on, get into the cracks there," I said pointing to some gnarly scale-like substance around his groin. "And your hair. Wash your fucking hair. Twice!" I poured liquid soap into his flailing hand.

"They want a stable government for the Pakis so the nuke's not in the hands of the military. They're going to bring the former Prime Minister Ali Bhutto back and get RID of General Al Haq."

I was skeptical. "The CIA helped General Al Haq engineer a military coup against Bhutto and now they're using Tariq to create insurgency against the very dictator they had backed?"

"Divide and conquer. That's the way it works."

"Okay, that's good, Jack. I'm glad you figured all that out. But what does any of that matter to us? I don't give a shit. Just clean up! And then help me figure out how to find fucking Grant."

"Fucking GRANT! Now, there's a fine idea," He cackled lewdly, then lit up with an idea, "Ah, my boy, I know what we can do. We'll get hold of Tim Flannery!"

"No, we don't want to see him. Bad idea. But maybe the Station Chief would know."

"The CIA bitch doesn't want to see you, don't you get it yet? She doesn't give a shit about you, James. She fucked you because she knew you'd do her bidding. That wench totally manipulated you, used her feminine charms and hung you out to dry."

"Got your ass out of jail, didn't she?"

"Tim is the answer!"

It made no sense. His brain was still sideways from the drugs and part of me wondered how long his body would take the beating. Sex was a powerful motivator for him, but politics could sweep him up as well. I told him, "You are thrust into the middle of world shaking geo-political events and you want to fuck that up chasing some guy who wouldn't give you the time of day?"

He heard that and sighed because he knew I was right. "Pffft," he sputtered spit and soap. I concede – and defer to your better judgment."

"More soap, Jack, more soap."

It took the world's longest shower and three scrubbings, but finally he was clean. Once dressed, we had lunch and a couple of espressos, which seemed to help. Jack was silent for most of it, even when I tried to get him to talk. "So where's Grant?" I asked.

He waved me off and said, "I'm thinking."

"Look, we don't have a world of time here, Jack. We have a Rover in the garage with one hundred kilos of hash stashed in it. We've got the Pakistani police possibly watching us. We need to get out of Peshawar now."

"No soldier left behind, James. Now go take a walk or something and give me some space to think. And another espresso. Double."

When he got like this, I found it best to let him take the

bit in his teeth so I wandered off down to the garage to check on the car. I put a Steely Dan tape on and sat behind the wheel deciding how much time I was going to give Grant to show up. I couldn't really leave him behind, so I'd have to search Peshawar for him. I went back to find Jack at the bar table. He'd had a phone brought to him and was on it, listening, making notes. He hung up and nodded. "All good. Grant is a naughty boy."

"You found him?"

"Close. Here's what I think – he's trying to get a fake passport made."

"Why? He's already got one."

"It's not for him. Do the math."

30

The time to leave Peshawar was at hand. I'd given Jack and Grant a noon deadline. Jack was in the lobby ready to go. Grant was still MIA. Jack was unconcerned and suggested I go play a round of golf and relax. It was all I could do not to unleash my frustration on him. Not knowing how the meeting between Patricia Adams and Tariq went left me aggravated, but I assumed no news was good news. I desperately wanted to split while we could and if what Patricia told me about the Pakistani police watching us and Tariq having influence with them was true, I knew the sooner we did, the better. Now Grant was messing around with Tariq's concubine? That was just too many guns aiming at us. I told Jack to help me find Grant or else we were hitting the road without him.

"You wouldn't do that, my boy. I know you wouldn't."

"I'm giving him an hour. Then I'm driving out of here."

"No soldier left behind, son."

"Unless they're a deserter."

He knew I was making threats just to blow off steam. No way I could leave without Grant. We had to find him. I was frustrated with Jack's dismissal of the danger we were in, but at the same time I admired his loyalty to a guy who had a habit of giving him a blistering bad time. For all his faults and eccentricities, Jack had a noble streak. If he had been born six-foot-two with features chiseled like Rock Hudson, he would have been a charismatic leader of men. "Grant wouldn't bail on a mate in trouble," Jack said, and I had to agree it was true. One of the really cool things about the whole adventure had been the indefatigable solidarity in the crunch we three had experienced. Despite the upheavals caused by their wild-ass personalities, we really had stuck together through thick and thin. I knew brotherhood like that to be rare.

A couple hours later Grant finally showed up. I kept my cool and didn't ask any questions. I told him to get down to the garage as I already had his stuff in the Rangey. He knew I was pissed and offered an apology. "I just had to take care of something, mate." But he wouldn't look at me.

I glanced at Jack sitting in the backseat. He raised one eyebrow, saying nothing, just waiting for what he knew was to come. I stayed silent, kept driving, which kind of surprised Grant as he must have expected a hailstorm of questions. I drove on because of course I already knew the answers. We pulled out onto the main street and Grant gave me a brotherly slap on the back. "Hey man, we're doing it! We're on the road with our hash."

"Yeah. It's a good thing you remembered your priorities. Even with that girl in your sites."

"Karina?" Still, he couldn't look me in the eye.

"Well, you said your fond farewells," Jack said. "Next stop Bombay!"

"Actually..." Grant said, "we need to make a quick stop."

"That's not happening," I said, foot to the floor.

"No, wait. You gotta turn here."

"No turns, no stops. We are heading to the border."

"Look, man, here's what's happening..."

"No, Grant. This is what's happening. Nonstop to the border."

"James, we're taking Karina with us. I gotta pick her up now. She's waiting for us. I've got her stashed in an opium den and I can't leave her hanging."

"Not my problem, Grant."

"Well it's *my* fucking problem, bunji, and we're going to pick her up!"

Jack watched, loving every minute. Conflict put him right in his element. "Never fear, Grant, my love, your Hindu whore is a survivor. Before you're halfway to the coast, she'll have found herself a *benefactor.*"

Grant whipped around and grabbed Jack's shirt. Swinging his fist back as if to land a full punch, I snagged his arm and yelled, "Listen, mate, I know you want to save her. I know you want us to go and get her and take her with us and free her. I get it and I know why, but it's an insane idea, man. You've gotta let her go. You know it and I know it." From the back corner, Jack twittered, only enraging Grant more. "This is nothing but sorry business! We are not going to be shot by Tariq in the eleventh hour after waiting out Ramadan, being blackmailed by the fucking CIA, and dealing with the insanity both you guys have caused. We are finally heading out of this place with what we came for. You wanna save someone, you'll do it back in Oz."

"No. I can't leave her here. Get me across the border with her and we'll split off on our own."

Jack tipped his panama hat to him, "I admire your heroics,

Grant, a true knight of the first order. But even St. George had to exercise caution when he faced the dragon."

"Shut the fuck up. Turn here, bunji." He tried to grab the wheel causing me to almost swerve into oncoming traffic. I knocked his arm away.

"Fuck it then! Just let me out here!"

"Don't tempt me, man!"

Jack leaned forward and patted each of us on the shoulder, "Now, now, boys. Pause a moment to appreciate the inherent beauty in this situation..."

"What??" I said.

"The passion of it. The great passion. And it is said that passion is the very fact of God in man."

"What the fuck does that have to do with us picking up Karina?" Grant said.

"My boy, your passion for her makes you both divine. And the Divine is worth saving because '*The greatest gift you'll ever learn is how to love and be loved in return.*' So you, my good sir, have my support. I vote we pick the strumpet up."

I spun my head to look toward him, unable to believe my ears, "What? No way."

Grant didn't know whether to thank him or slug him, "What do you mean *strumpet*?"

"A figure of speech. The lady. We shall pick the damsel up. You say she's in an opium den? Which is where you no doubt obtained her fake passport. Let's hope you're doing business with honorable men."

At that moment, a wave of calm washed over me. All I had to do was keep my mouth shut because after all, I was the one behind the wheel and I was driving us to the border.

"James, much as I love you son, it is time for you to concede."

The fact was that at the start of the enterprise we had all agreed that we would function like a democracy. But time and again they both had acted so irrationally that more than once I had had to make an executive decision.

"We are an egalitarian society, James. A representative democracy, to which you agreed. Most of all, you are a man of your word."

The calm evaporated as quickly as it had come and I was left with the tension that snapped like a hamstring blowing. Finally, I said fuck it and let go. I knew that forcing the issue would cause more problems than going with our agreement. Every cross word was costing us time and it would simply be faster to ride the current. I had to flow with it. If I didn't, Grant would do something crazy, get in a fight with a border guard, raise a dust storm of bad vibes over the rest of the trip. We'd be going through borders, dealing with all kinds of sketchy situations and things were precarious enough without adding his misery to the mix. And I wasn't up for his grumbling and dolorous mood all the way to Bombay either. "Fine. You wanna screw this whole thing up, ok. You want me to turn, I'll turn." I careened around the next corner. "Where's this fucking opium den?"

"Now you're talking," Jack said. "Grant, direct us to the den of inequity and to the arms of the beloved."

Grant's directions to a derelict shantytown on the outskirts of Peshawar were strikingly accurate and I wondered how many times he had visited this place. We stopped on a rutted trash littered road outside a candle shop. Paraffin mixed with the odors of garbage drifted in on a hot wind. I said, "Okay, let's get this taken care of, so we can get the fuck out."

Walking into the candle shop, we were hit with a yellow haze and the deepening smell of roasting opium. There were small groups in circles passing a pipe and then at the sides and back of the room heads reclined in wooden bunks, smoking, drifting. Two men blocked our way, "U.S. dollars. Twenty each."

"No, wait a minute, that wasn't the deal," Grant said.

I said, "No sweat about the money, but where's Karina?"

"You pay and then you see her."

Grant was going to argue, but we didn't have time for that. I handed over the bills and we passed through. We found Karina on a bunk in back. Her eyes were dark and hooded, not yet recovered from earlier beatings, I guessed. She might have been rethinking the decision she'd made to run away from Tariq. The reach of his power was long – but not longer than the odds of Grant spiriting her away to safety. Grant told her everything was cool, we were taking her out of there and his certainty reassured her. But the next minute the men who guarded the entrance stood to block our way. They weren't going to let her leave without a hefty sum.

I'd known Grant to go volcanic in the face of a power play. Diplomacy was an alien concept. "Fuck you gammon yowie," he said. "I'm walking her out."

Suddenly he had a .45 at his temple. Any normal guy would have frozen, but Grant is not that guy. He just kept marching to the door with Karina. From the opposite direction some other guy had a gun on him and everyone started yelling for him to stop. Karina screamed, "Don't kill him! Don't kill him!" She pulled her hand away from his and turned to face them - and it was only then that he stopped. With two guns to his head, it was only then that he seemed to realize how insane the situation was. I raised my hands slowly and said to the leader, "Relax. Of course, we'll pay you want you want." I gave him the hundred, counting out five twenties like they were pure gold. This seemed to satisfy him and he nodded to the others who lowered their weapons. Grant glared at one guy, then slapped the gun out of his hand. We all walked out holding our breath. Karina stumbled and seemed to hesitate – what was wrong now? She was looking at Grant, then back at the den and I wondered if she thought Grant might be just as dangerous as Tariq. Grant took her hand decisively and finally she acquiesced. He led her away from the place. Once out in the street, we all got in the Rover. I powered out of there thinking, Hallelujah, we've done it - we're finally leaving this godforsaken city.

We were barely out of Peshawar before I heard a siren and in the rearview mirror saw the flashing lights of Pakistani police. They were pulling us over. Two more Pakistani police cars raced up from behind. One swerved in front of us, while the other crowded our tail. The cop in front was half out his window waving, ordering us to the curb. Patricia had told me the truth - they'd been watching us. They were going to take the dope, take the car, and we'd end up in prison. I looked at Jack and said, "Baksheesh, baksheesh. Get some cash ready to pay these guys off." We pulled out a few hundred-dollar bills each. But somehow I knew a few hundred wasn't going to do it this time.

Karina had her head in her hands. She knew what was coming. I looked at Jack as if to say, *So much for your fucking democracy* and pulled to the curb. They were on us in seconds ordering everyone out of the car. We stood on the sidewalk and it about broke my heart to see Grant and Karina shoulder to shoulder holding hands. Her face was grief-stricken, his was stony and the message was clear: each was screaming, *I love you and I'll probably never see you again.* Grant was always defiant in the face of authority. Standup street guy that he was, he hadn't yet given up and his wheels churned away, trying to figure some way out of this. But there were six heavily armed cops who looked nervous enough to send us to the promised land. One of them ordered Karina to step away from Grant, but he held her hand tightly. Another cop came up from behind and slammed him in the head with his rifle butt. He pulled Karina away, dragging her over to an SUV. He threw her in the back seat and I saw Mick was already there. Mick, the emissary of Tariq, looked on with resigned defeat. He knew which side of his toast had the butter on it. To him it was an admirable but foolhardy move on Grant's part. Tariq would have his girl back. Grant was on the pavement and saw Karina being kidnapped by the cops for Tariq. He moved to get up and the cops pushed him back down. Jack yelled at him to stay down. If ever a man was brokenhearted it was Grant in that moment. I had could see tears in his eyes and failure, just as when he told me the story of the girl, Tuesday, jumping out the hospital window. There was nothing he could do then to save her and here he was again, powerless to save Karina.

From somewhere I could hear Jack yelling, but it was like it came from a distant tunnel, "I am with the Australian consulate! This is an outrage! I demand…" it was like a torn mainsail flapping in a headwind. We were rudderless and going

down. In that moment I lost all ideas and all hope. Karina was
going back to Tariq and we were going to prison.

31

We were handcuffed in the street, herded into a tight little threesome, encircled by puffed up Paki cops, who seemed all too keen on busting westerners. The head cop looked on as his confederates tore apart the Rover. They knew we had drugs, they just didn't know where the stash was hidden. The dogs arrived and sniffed around. One of these dogs had a better nose than the last one I'd encountered back at the Landi Kotal roadblock. This beast was a humongous black shepherd and as he circled the Rover, his head suddenly cocked toward the rack on top. The moist tip of his hungry nose began twitching. He stopped dead in his tracks almost pulling his handler's arm out of joint. He zeroed in on that rack, took a step forward, then back, his massive head like a compass needle landing on North. His nose was an arrow pointing at the place in the plywood rack where the hole had been drilled back at the Fort. The very hole I asked to be drilled so I could make sure there was hash between the veneers was now emitting hash vapors. He was quick to pick up on it and quickly jumped up. He sailed over the rack and had it now. This was a dog who loved success. He was absolutely ecstatic. His handler began a close inspection of the plywood. He ordered the luggage and spare tire pulled off the rack. I saw a dark cell in my future.

A vocal crowd had gathered, shouting and jeering. The street was entirely blocked, but the people began moving, making way for a vehicle to slowly arrive on scene. A long, black Mercedes with government flags on the fenders pulled up. Behind it were several Pakistani army vehicles.

Even the cops were mystified by this turn of events. The police car with Mick and Karina drove off. Karina's hands pressed in vain at the window, her face foggy behind the glass. Grant yelled, "I'll find you! I swear to God I'll find you!" The cop whacked him in the ribs and Grant cursed him, then another cop sent him to his knees. Karina was gone. The drug sniffing shepherd was barking and trying to jump up on the rack which was now half unloaded. The cops had slashed the spare tire and torn apart our luggage, one of them was holding Jack's funky white robe. Jack yelled at him not to touch it. The cop took one sniff and threw it into the gutter.

The flagship government car stopped and an army general and a cloaked official stepped out. Both approached the lead cop and said they were establishing jurisdiction over the prisoners. The glory of a huge drug bust was being handed to the Army. The cop argued with the general, but it was obvious who held the power. We were now prisoners of the Pakistan government. The grumbling cops pulled their dogs away. The beast did not want to leave and had to be yanked to the vehicle.

As the grumbling cops split, we were still handcuffed and eventually shoved into one of the waiting military vehicles. The crowd shouted at us thinking we were Americans who needed hanging. I looked at our lonely Range Rover sitting there, doors open, ransacked, all our shit in the street. A sad end to our noble ride. And to our great enterprise. As we were driven away, the soldiers threw our stuff back in the Rover. One of them got behind the wheel and pulled out to fall in line with the military vehicles.

The three of us were crowded into the back seat, Jack in the middle. Grant was bleeding from the rifle butt he'd taken to the side of his head. A crimson trail ran. over his ear and smeared onto his neck, creeping into a muddy Rorschach blot on his grey T-shirt. He had a deep scrape on his cheek where his head had been ground into the pavement by a cop's boot. His worst injury was not physical, not even his broken heart, but what seemed like a shattered soul. Jack was not what you'd call a sympathetic individual, but he was moved to raise his cuffed hands and pat Grant on the shoulder. "More than one human being can take," he said, with a note of genuine compassion.

Grant said nothing, just looked straight ahead at the helmeted soldiers who sat in front. He was going hard. I had seen it a few times over our long friendship, like that time I visited him in prison. There was no goodness in the world that he could see. No help from man or God or angels. Just him against the fucked up and empty, cold universe. Even his father had been his adversary. I couldn't imagine what it was like to be brought into this world by a hostile dad and an absentee mum.

Jack could feel where he was at. "My boy..." he had never called him my boy before... "We shall be okay. I guarantee it. I have connections at the highest level."

I looked at Jack and said, "I hope you're right." But I have to admit that my normally optimistic outlook was bleak. As we drove on through the streets of Peshawar, a certain resignation set in. Whatever had happened to this point, I felt like I could handle it. Even now, if the worst happened, a cell ala

Midnight Express, we would somehow be okay, like Jack said.

Grant's hand went to the door handle like he was going to jump out. But it was locked. There was no telling what craziness was going through his head as we motored along to whatever fate awaited us. I prayed he wouldn't try a stealth attack on the soldiers in the front seat. Knowing him as I did, I could feel he was in that nothing-to-lose state. I leaned over Jack and told Grant, "Let's just ride this out and see what happens."

He looked at me with a strange grin, "Bunji, I shouldn't have dragged you into this. Sorry, mate."

We arrived at a warehouse and were driven in with our Rover following behind, while the other cars peeled away into the streets of Peshawar. It was a cavernous place, windowless and dark except for a few fluorescent lights strung from a wire above. The soldiers got us out of the vehicle and we stood there handcuffed, wondering if we were going to get shot. Maybe that's the way they dealt with drug smugglers in Pakistan's new military regime. A figure walked through the shadows up to me. It was one of the American CIA agents who had busted us in the bar in Kabul. "You, come with me," he said. He led me over to a couple of black Lincoln Continentals parked against the wall, their luscious chrome and nervy fenders glowing at the edge of the light from the fluorescence above. He uncuffed me and put me in the back seat of one of the Lincolns. I found myself sitting next to Patricia Adams. "Wow, am I glad to see you," I said.

"I'm not glad to see you, James." The soft interior light did nothing to dim how sharp and harsh she looked. She wore the Rolex, the black pantsuit, hair in the tight bun, chiseled cheekbones throwing shadows, her eyes hooded and opaque like a shark.

"Yeah. Guess we fucked up."

"You could have seriously compromised my position. And you could be dead right now. Tariq controls the police. They would have taken the three of you somewhere and shot you."

I knew it was true that she had saved us. I remembered her in the softness of the moment in my hotel room when she had the other watch from her youth on and her hair was down and she looked so young and I wondered if she had saved us because she felt something for me. Or was it just all business from the first to the last? I had to ask, "So why did you save our asses?"

"Because you delivered on your end of the bargain. You gave me what I wanted. I gave you my word and despite all the lies we tell in my business, sometimes we actually mean what we say. But the real reason I saved you is..." She stopped and just looked at me.

"The real reason is...?"

"Because I didn't want three dead fuck-ups on my conscience." This hit me harder than expected.

"Okay."

"Besides that, I'm running an operation involving ten countries." I suddenly saw the power she wielded. The operation she was running. Our tiny but pivotal role in it. "Ten countries. Nuclear bombs, revolutions, invasions, the fate of the world at stake here, James. Three dead Australians would be a little screw in the gears. You understand?"

I did. Jack had been right all along. We were in the middle of world-shaking events as he had said. "I get it," I told her.

"Now here's what you're going to do if you want to get out of Pakistan alive. You're going to keep your crazy friend in your car when he tries to go back for Karina."

"He won't."

"It's sweet that you think the best about everyone, James. But that quality will get you killed."

"So you're giving us our Rangey back?"

"I'm sure it's temporary."

"Temporary?"

"Yes. I would make a bet you lose it somewhere along your journey. And don't worry, it won't be us doing you in. You'll take care of that yourselves. Do try not to fuck up again, James. You're a charming boy, but have no business in the smuggling trade." This was when I began to see that Patricia Adams had always been light years beyond my orbit, beyond the orbit of anyone I'd ever known.

"Do I have to worry about Tariq coming after us?"

"Who knows? He got his girl back, so maybe not. He's got other fish to fry for us. I'll be able to protect you as far as the border. A car will follow you and any deviations from what I've told you will shut off my support for good. And then you're on your own."

My hand went to the door handle, but my eyes stayed on her, "I'm guessing I might not get to see you again."

"Let's hope you don't." She laughed, "Now *go*."

The agent walked me back to Jack and Grant and ordered them to be uncuffed. Both were surprised. "Get in the Rangey," I said.

We all climbed in and I drove us out to freedom. Jack, sitting next to me, slapped me on the back, "My boy! God, you are a genius with women! How did you do that? She succumbed to your charms. Was it the ponytail? Or the smile? Or did you insert a magic finger into her luscious cunt?"

"Go fuck yourself, Jack."

"It was the magic finger. It writes and having written moves on."

"Pull over," Grant said.

"Pull over? What do you mean pull over?"

"I'm getting out, bunji. Going back for Karina."

"Grant, listen. Patricia told me you'd try this. The Pakistani cops and Tariq want to kill us. We have protection behind us right now. See that Lincoln back there? Those guys are making sure we get to the Indian border. You get out, you lose the protection."

"No worries."

"You've got a big share coming. Big money, Grant, when we get back to Oz. You get out and you might not get back."

"I'll be back. With Karina. Hold on to my share for me."

I had to stop for a red light and Grant bolted out of the Rangey to the street. Time stopped for a moment as his smile turned away. I saw the kid in him, the confident, funny beach master I first met on the sand when I was a grom. All our great adventures passed between us in that look. He flashed a victory sign at me, then took off running. The light turned green, a bus behind me honked. Taxi drivers swerved around us, yelling. I pulled across the intersection looking for a place to turn around and go back for him. "Let him go," Jack said.

"Let him go? We can't fucking let him go! Aren't you the one who always says no soldier left behind?"

"You can go back and look for him but he's not to be found. He doesn't want to be found. He's on a different mission. A higher calling than ours, my friend."

"A *higher calling*??"

"Love!" He paused savoring the word, then, "Though I must say the object in question is a very poor choice. Drive on to the border, my boy. We must leave our friend Grant to his fate."

32

The idea of turning around and going back to find Grant nagged at me as we drove. But I knew that was a fool's errand. Besides I didn't want to lose the protection of the CIA car following us.

Around dusk we arrived in Rawalpindi and its twin city Islamabad, the capital of Pakistan. Jack was napping, Steely Dan was playing...

Aja, when all your dime dancing is through, I run to you...

The kind of music that takes you on a trip into the past. And I kept thinking about Grant and all the adventures we'd had. All the waves we'd surfed, the girls we'd sweet-talked together, the dirt biking through the hills of Mullinbimby. The deals. The busts. Now I wondered if I would ever see my bunji again. Sorry business? Maybe. Crazy fucker. How could he get so bonkers over this doori he just met? Jack ascribed it to love, but I knew it was something else that Grant was seeking – redemption. Saving her was going to atone for not being there for Tuesday. Fix his tortured head. Or so he thought. Driving along, I felt like there was a black cloud in the Rangey. I wanted to get down to Bombay, get the car on a boat and go home.

Our next stop was Lahore, but then about twenty clicks

outside the city, the Rangey began to lose power. Even if I floored it, our trusty ride kept getting slower and slower. What the fuck was going on? I thought maybe we were out of gas. I looked at the fuel gauge and saw we had over a half a tank. To be on the safe side, I found a petrol station and fueled up, but it didn't help the problem. Gradually, the car continued to bog down until it wouldn't do over twenty mph. I couldn't figure out what had happened. By the time we entered Lahore, the Rover's max speed was down to 15 and we limped into the city with our emergency lights flashing. I wondered what our escort would make of this, but the shadow of protection was now gone from our tail.

One more time, the unexpected had reared its ugly head. After all we'd been through, car problems? I was feeling Patricia Adams was right – I should leave smuggling behind and get into real estate. Our Rangey was a bust and I had to get us off the road so I pulled into the first decent hotel I saw. Jack wanted five-star luxury, but I said, uhn-uh, this is it until we find out what the hell is wrong with the car. We parked in the garage, got our rooms, and I said fuck it, I'm going to have some dinner and a nice six pack of Taj Mahal, then go to bed. We could deal with the car problems the next morning, right enough.

I awoke to a humid daybreak that first day in Lahore. Gone was the dream about the good old days with Grant. Then I woke up clammy and cross-eyed and went down to the garage to check on the car. I wished Grant was there because he was a good mechanic. I popped the hood and inspected the fuel lines. They were semi-clear plastic and I could see black gobs inside. Sand or dust from the road? Further inspection was required. I scarfed a quick breakfast, half a pot of coffee, then borrowed what tools I could from a maintenance man – a flashlight, screwdriver and pliers. Headed back down to the garage, I took a closer look. I pulled a fuel line off the carb and it wasn't dirt inside. It was *tar*. There was fucking tar in the fuel lines. Which meant the carburetors were full of the shit and hence, the tortoise pace.

So how the hell had the gunk made its way into the fuel lines? It had to have come from the fuel tank. I crawled underneath and right away smelled gas. Inspecting the undercarriage, there was a thick pool of sludge. It looked like a membrane of chocolate syrup sliding down the sides of the tank. What the fuck? I put my hand up to the top of the tank and found it layered with the same tarry ooze that lined the carbs and fuel lines.

I realized that the mechanical geniuses back at the fort had fucked up when they installed the inner tank holding the hash. Sealing the top of the outer tank had been a half-assed job and they'd used petroleum-based sealant instead of latex which proved defective and was quickly dissolved by the gas.

The fuel system would need a complete overhaul. The gas tank, the fuel lines, carburetors, the distributor and every other place the tar had leaked into would need cleaning, flushing and reinstalling. This would all require a professional skill set and more than I could offer. Was I going to limp the Rover loaded with two hundred kilos of hash over to the local mechanic and say, Can you fix this for me? The obvious next question would surely be, Of course, but why does your fuel tank have an inner compartment? I shook my head in disbelief at this latest situation, a situation that was not going to be easy to fix. Jack couldn't screw in a light bulb. Grant and I could have maybe pulled the repair off, but my bro was MIA. It seemed so stupid of him, so pointless to head back into the lion's den. Wasn't redemption possible by some other means? Why for God's sake would he choose a girl to save who was tied to the Pakistani Mafia? My resentment kicked in fast. He should have been here with us to help us with this fucked up problem.

I was suddenly feeling sorry for myself which was unusual for me and my antidotes of choice in such moments were usually girls, booze and drugs. I had no drugs. A girl was possible, but lately the idea of cheating on Andi, the one I really cared about, was starting to feel really sleazy.That left booze. I went to the nearest watering hole and got sloshed. I was falling off my stool when I felt someone propping me up. It was Jack. "Come on my boy," he whispered as he helped me to my feet. I leaned into his arm, grateful for the support. Up in the elevator and then I was in his room crashed on the bed. The last thing I remember of that night was him saying, "Methinks the boy doth protest too much."

33

I awoke in the morning to an amyl nitrite cracking under my nose and the popper sent me bolt upright. Naked under a hotel bathrobe with Jack's hand on my dick, I shouted, "You fucking sleazebag, what the fuck?!"

"Now, now my boy. You don't recall a thing about it, do you?"

In fact, this was true. Feeling an odd mix of relief and confusion, I was glad I couldn't remember much about the night before. I got out of there as fast as I could. My mind went to the task at hand - finding a professional mechanic to repair the Rangey, but I wouldn't last long without a meal. Jack found me having breakfast. He was all jaunty and chipper, smiling like the Cheshire Cat, "You were magnificent last night. Simply spectacular!" I groaned.

"Will you shut it? Now listen up — we've got to find a mechanic who will do the work and keep his trap shut for a good price."

"Ah, somewhere out in this vast metropolis there must be a discreet automobile technician. I'm just the right one to find a young, available man. And personally inspect his equipment." Jack was a sucker for the rustic types, working class, fresh-faced boys he could easily corrupt. But he was too high profile for this mission.

"No," I said, "You've done enough inspecting. Go explore the sights of Lahore while I check around."

I asked the concierge at our hotel where the local auto shops were. There was a kind of mechanics row in Lahore and I walked past a few garages to suss things out. There were a couple of places that looked like possibilities and I went in and explained our predicament. I said that I had a Range Rover and needed to have a mechanic come to my hotel and fix it. In both instances, the owners said that wasn't possible, I'd have to bring the car in.

"Can't do it that way," I said.

"Why not? What's the problem?"

"Because I can't, that's all, and I want somebody that will work exclusively with me for a few days. This is a rare vehicle."

"Range Rover? Rare?"

"It's been specially modified. It needs expert attention and I will pay what it takes to get it."

But money wasn't assuaging their suspicions. It was the times, you know. The coup had just happened. Soldiers were in the streets everywhere. The average Joe didn't know who to trust anymore. Anybody could be a spy. Loyalists of the old ruler Bhutto were disappearing faster than goldfish down a toilet bowl. They saw me as the enemy because they figured I was American. And as we'd seen in Peshawar, there were rumors in the streets that the CIA had been helpful in ousting Bhutto because he was "a man of the people," espousing socialist programs, and playing nice with the Russians.

The shop owners were suspicious even when I assured them I was an Australian and only wanted an in-house repair because we Aussies can be kinda funny about our vehicles. I went to yet another garage and before walking in, saw a young intelligent looking guy working on a car by the side of the building. I approached him cautiously. "Do you speak English?" He said that he did and I asked if he was a mechanic. Wiping his greasy hands on a pair of dingy overalls, he eyed me up and said, "Good guess."

"Wonderful, that's great. Got a talent, have you?"

"Aye, but there's always more to learn."

"You know English cars?"

"But of course. This is Pakistan."

Sensing a prospect, I went to work chatting him up. "What else do you do?" I asked, trying to sound casual. He said he was a student and I drew him out a bit more to further assess what kind of a guy he was. I talked to him about what he was studying at University. Medicine. He wanted to be a doctor. He found similarities in fixing cars and operating on people. He likened the effectively simple 1000 c.c. engine of the British Morris Minor to the human cardio-vascular/digestive system. He asked what I was doing in Pakistan and I said I was studying art and culture in the tribal regions.

"Ah, very good, and what have you found?"

"A lot of great art and rugs and the surprising fact that most of the economy is hash based." I couldn't help myself.

"People have to make a living," he said.

Good answer. I told him that I liked to surf and occasionally smoke hash.

"Ah, well," he said glancing around, "Who doesn't?"

He was young and cool and I was picking up a vibe from him that he could be our guy. I got to the heart of the matter.

"I need some special help fixing my Range Rover."

"Of course. Bring it in."

"Actually, I would like you to come to the hotel garage and fix it there," I explained.

He looked at me putting two and two together. He was a very smart young man. His name was Haroon. "I see," he said.

"It'll probably take three days, I don't know, maybe more. You'll need tools to take my gas tank apart and all my fuel lines because they're dirty and I need to get them cleaned out. The same with the gas tank. Most importantly this must remain between us. You think you could do that, Haroon, and not tell anyone?"

He thought it over a bit, "I will come and see the situation and tell you then."

"Cool," I pulled out a hundred. "Here's a down payment." I said, "Come to my hotel tomorrow morning and let's start the work," and as a precaution I gave him the name of the hotel across the street from the one I was actually in. Haroon said, "Okay," and went back to work and I cruised to our hotel and told Jack I had found our boy.

He was immediately skeptical. "What if he arrives with the army?" I told him my vetting plan. "Ever vigilant! Good thinking, my boy."

I moved the car to a back area of the garage by some storage lockers. Then I went to the concierge and explained I'd be fixing the car while it was there. I gave him a bill and he was happy. The next day, Haroon arrived at the hotel across the street promptly at seven. I walked across and suggested we have a coffee and a little chat beforehand. I wanted to make sure he didn't have anybody floating around watching us. When I was sure he'd come alone, I said, "Okay, let's do it. I have the Rover parked at the hotel across the street."

Haroon was surprised, "Ah. There's a trust issue. I understand."

My look leveled us. "Cool." So we headed across the street into the garage. We jacked the car up and put it on blocks. After crawling under, I showed him the problem. We unbolted the tank and thought it was difficult to get that fucker out with just the two of us, we managed to do it. With its two hundred pounds of hash, the weight was immense and at one point I wondered whether we might be crushed in the process. Haroon saw the inner tank that housed the bricks. "Ok. It is as I thought. A large operation, your smuggling?" he asked.

There I was, totally busted. Which of course I knew would happen. The moment of truth. Now I had to trust that he was a capitalist at heart. I pulled out a hundred and extended it to him. But he didn't take it. Just stood there looking at me. After our initial root around, we both had the oozy tar all over us, running down from head to feet, seeping out across the concrete floor. And there was that hundred dollar bill, sticky and wet in my hand like a dead fish. It was the ticket for foreign interlopers to pry what we needed from the locals. It was like his eyes were saying I was yet another in the long line of exploiters. That bill felt like a cannon ball weighing down my hand.

"What drug is in the tank?" he asked.

I said, "Nothing. It's a special tank. Don't ask questions. Here's another hundred."

"If there is heroin, opium or cocaine, I won't work for you."

"Okay. What if it was hash?"

He nodded, smiled, everything relaxed. "Hash, I will do the work."

As I suspected, the tank was awash in tar and it took a half a day to clean that mess up. We then repaired the tank, doing it the way it should have been done in the first place. Over the next few days, we pulled all the fuel lines apart and flushed them out. Then we did the same with the carburetor and the distributor and the spark plugs and everything else we could reach. On the fourth day, we bought a couple extra floor jacks so we could lift the tank back up into place. We hooked up the fuel lines and the carburetor and took it for a test drive. Our Rangey ran beautifully - we were back in business. A little uneasily, I asked Haroon what it would to take to keep him from opening his mouth. "James, you have been very generous. You have nothing to worry about from me." And with that I actually believed, and paid him triple what we'd agreed.

Somehow things were working out. I couldn't help but say a little prayer of thanks that once again we'd sailed through the storm. Time and again we'd ridden straight into the thick of it and somehow managed to avert disaster. It made me wonder about Grant. Where was he? What had happened to him? Was he even alive? But right then I had other things to worry about – like crossing a border between two countries who were on the precipice of all-out war.

34

Within an hour of the big fix, Jack and I were on the road out of Lahore. Jack tried to regale me with details about my drunken night in his room. I was edgy and my mind was on Grant so I shut him up quick. "There's someone missing in the car," I said, grimly. "And your antics aren't helping."

"Our good friend is a survivor," Jack said, lighting up a joint. "And we do have free will, do we not? Look deep into our motives and we usually do what we want to do." It was a double entendre that I let pass. I set some music blasting and was feeling confident with the Rangey back to its perky self, cruising at 70 down the blacktop on the way to the Indian border. It was a free-spirited drive with Johnny Nash singing "I Can See Clearly Now." That reggae beat rocked the car with good vibes and the feeling that this long journey with all its trials and unexpected tribulations was now going smoothly. "...*Gone are the dark clouds that made me blue, It's gonna be a bright, bright sunshiny day...*"

But then, as often happens, the end of the song was a prelude to reality. Under those clear blue skies of the Indian subcontinent we saw a shit storm raging at the border. The crossing looked like a refugee camp in a war zone. Battle lines were forming with the Pakistani army on one side and the

Indian army on the other. There was a trail of cars half a mile
long, waiting to cross in both directions. Hundreds of foot
travelers trudged through the heat toward guard stations.
Hundreds more formed a line along the roadside while yet
another throng, waving papers and passports, converged on
a guard kiosk near the checkpoint.

Pakistani border guards were on hyper alert, pulling cars
over to an inspection area. Vehicles were being searched, pedestrians pulled out of line and questioned. A team of dogs sniffed
the undercarriage of vehicles. I suspected they were searching
more for bombs than for drugs. All this tension had my wheels
turning as I remembered the last time a dog sniffed his way
over our Rangey and was leaping eight feet in the air trying
to gnaw through the plywood roof rack to get to the hash.
There was no wolfhound beast here at the Indian border like
the one in Peshawar, but a well-trained Pekingese could be just
as effective. If we were found out by any of them, we could
easily disappear without a trace as we were out on our own in
this remote territory. I decided the best thing to do was for
one of us to drive through the checkpoint and the other to
walk through. In this way, if there was a bust, one of us would
be free to get help.

"Jack," I said, "you or me? You want to drive the car across
the border?"

Despite his gross handicap, Jack loved to drive even though
his feet could barely reach the pedals. "Thought you'd never
ask!" he said. We got all the car's paperwork and passports
in order, ready for inspection, I got out, threw a backpack
over my shoulder and suddenly became a trekker on foot.
Jack immediately found a Billy Holiday tape and was singing

along with "I'm a Fool to Want You" as he inched forward
along the line of cars.

Crossing a border is always ripe with tension. A steamy
cauldron of problematic uncertainty even in the most innocuous conditions. There at the mercy of persons and situations
beyond your control. Maybe the border guard has had a bad
lunch, his stomach is gnarly, he doesn't like your haircut, or
he envies your sunglasses, or his politics conflict with the
West. In the event you have some drugs in the car and you're
nervous, the tension escalates and you're a bust waiting to
happen. Border guards have a sixth sense when it comes to
spotting a case of nerves. One little eye flick, one glistening
bead of sweat on your lip and you're being ordered out of the
line and escorted to the Search and Detain Area, an isolated
containment compound where the contraband sniffing dogs,
handcuffs, and detention cells await.

All this was going through my head as Jack drove and I
walked toward the station. My paranoia was ratcheted up a few
more notches because of the looming conflict. Nuclear war.
The armies of both India and Pakistan were tense at attention,
tanks looming, helicopters circling on full alert, patrolling,
scrutinizing both travelers and border guards alike. No guard
wanted to fuck up and let artillery or spies slip through.

I joined the line of pedestrians. Jack, in the Range Rover,
slowly moved forward in the long line of vehicles. There was a
rope separating the cars from foot travelers and I could almost
reach out and touch the Rangey as we both moved along. I was
being asphyxiated by dust and exhaust from trucks, buses and
cars with defective mufflers. It was an eclectic mix of vehicles.
Buses overloaded with people, packages, furniture and bicycles

hanging on like Christmas tree ornaments. Trucks loaded with junk, car parts, dead washing machines, other carts with animals braying and shitting. Then, navigating around the dented vans, motor scooters and people, was an occasional black-windowed Mercedes sporting government flags or Red Cross insignias.

Despite all the danger and craziness around me, my natural optimism had me feeling pretty good as I watched German, Swiss, South American and even some Australian travelers intermixed with Pakistanis and Indians going and coming from one country to the other. And then there were the trekkers who had been up in the hills of Srinagar or Kashmir or Nepal and hippy adventurers who'd come down through the Kush and the Khyber Pass like the two hippies from San Francisco I'd talked to back in Landi Kotal. Thoughts of Grant hit me and I wondered how he was doing. Meanwhile, Jack was having a high old time in the Rover singing along with Billy Holiday...

"I'm like an oven, That's crying for heat, He treats me awful, Each time we meet, It's just unlawful, How that boy can cheat, But I must have that man..."

Jack was looking over at me and wiggling his eyebrows like he was singing it to me. He was loud and flamboyant enough to where he was drawing looks from the soldiers and the border guards. This was not the plan. The plan was to stay as low key as possible but "low key" was not in his vocabulary. Oh, was he ever enjoying himself, singing at full volume, *"He's hot as Hades, A lady's not safe in his arms, When she's kissed, But I'm afraid that he's cooled off, And maybe I'm ruled off his list, I'll never be missed..."* He had the car swaying and caught the attention of the guards.

They approached his window and began questioning him.

One reached in the passenger side and turned the tape player off. Jack pulled out the carte du passage and his passport and smiled as the guard inspected them. It seemed to be going well even though the process was agonizingly slow. I kept hoping they'd be waved through and I'd breeze past the inspection as well, have my passport stamped, hop back in the car and continue on into India.

This was the last border crossing we would have to make and we were so close to being home free. I forced myself into a positive state of mind, not wanting to inject any bad vibes into the situation. My hopes were clouded when I saw the border guard point Jack toward the detention bay for inspection. I hung back in the foot traffic line watching, trying to be casual as people edged past me, bumping the backpack, chattering in languages I didn't understand. Jack, frozen behind the wheel, glanced at me, his head barely visible above the window, like he was an adolescent who'd been busted trying to commandeer daddy's car. The guards slapped the hood of the car trying to get his attention so he'd follow their orders. He looked to me for direction. There was no choice but to obey. A guard stuck his rifle in the window, tapped the wheel with the barrel, shouting and pointing. Jack finally did as they said and steered over to the detention area.

Soldiers made him get out of the car. Soon he was surrounded and pushed over to the front of the vehicle where they ordered him to open the hood. Jack was all thumbs when it came to even the simplest mechanical tasks. He didn't know how to open the hood. The guards didn't believe he was that much of a dunce and they thought he was trying to stall or con them. Their suspicions escalated as Jack fumbled, searching

for the latch. A guard was at his ear yelling, "Open this. Open
this. You are hiding something!" Jack was lost.

35

Four soldiers converged around Jack, shouting, "You have guns? You have bombs? You are American?" He got agitated when a soldier tried to frisk him and he blasted them with his usual "I am an Australian diplomat!" routine. The success of our entire endeavor suddenly depended on his ability to unlatch the hood. In truth, that Rangey hood was difficult to open because you had to finesse it, take two fingers underneath the grill and push one lever while sliding another. Then you had to pop it and actually push the hood down a little bit before you lifted. Jack glanced at me and there wasn't fear or "Help me!" in his eyes but rather almost a delighted excitement.

More soldiers came over to the fracas, and they were really tense so I knew I had to do something. I was standing by a restraining rope not ten feet away and I yelled over to them, "Hi! Is that the Range Rover HSC with the 350 Hemi in it? Or is that just the regular 300?" I ducked under the rope and put a big smile on my face and went over to them.

The guards were pissed, "What are you doing? Crazy American! Get back in line."

I said, "I'm Australian. And I love these Range Rovers. Hell of a machine." I was just so happy and positive they were all stunned. "Yeah, these Rovers are so cool." I said, "But the hood latch is tricky. Check this out."

I put my hand under it and just manipulated the latch, pushed it down, popped it up, looked inside. I said, "The 350 Hemi! Now that's a beautiful motor! Finest engine on the planet. I'll bet this beauty drives like a million bucks." The guards were livid at me for being out of the pedestrian line, but at least they now had the hood open.

"Wow," I said bending over the engine, "Those fuel lines are beautiful. They're clean too. Nice job there. Well-maintained vehicle."

Jack patted me on the back, "Yes, my boy, glad you like that motor. You're a fine young man. Look me up at the Australian embassy."

One of the guards pulled me away from the car and pushed me toward the foot traffic line. "Get back behind the rope. Stay in line."

"No problem," I said. I looked at Jack, "Have fun on your trip." I jumped back in line. The guards were looking in the engine compartment. They didn't know what the fuck they were looking for. Jack was all smiles now, rambling on to the soldiers, "Marvelous piece of equipment. Yes, a great motor. You want to take a picture of it?"

The guards checked the VIN numbers on the engine block and found they matched up with the carte du passage and the registration, both of which were in Jack's alias – Byron Rimbaud. They were dying to find something wrong and under scrutiny from the soldiers were pulling out all the stops. They took the air cleaner off and inspected the spare tire and the tool kit. They started tapping around the fenders. They tapped in the firewalls and the trunk. They tapped the wheel wells and then one got down on the ground and tapped the fuel tank. It pinged just like it was supposed to. Then they looked at the bumpers. Eventually, they started searching inside the car, pushing on the seats and door panels to see if they were stuffed with contraband.

Then one looked up on the roof and said, "What's up there?" We had a couple of suitcases strapped on the rack. They pulled them down and searched them.

"Be my guest," Jack frowned, shaking his head as if his disapproval would deter them.

Then they tapped the rack. Uh-oh, I thought. They were getting too damn close. All they needed was a simple little drill. If they drilled into the plywood, it would be all over, baby. Because that drill bit would have exited the wood along with the pungent smell of hash. Fortunately, that didn't happen.

Finally, the border guards and the soldiers were satisfied the Rover was clean. The head guard was certain that the Rangey carried drugs, but he had to admit he couldn't find them. Time was wasting. Cars were backing up. They had other business to attend to. They helped Jack pile everything back up on the roof and tie it down. Jack handed out gifts of T-shirts and baseball caps from our stash of border guard bribes. "Thank you for your help. Have a nice day."

Jack got in the car and drove through the checkpoint. He pulled up to me about two-hundred yards down the road where I was waiting for him. He smiled like nothing had happened and said, "Hey, good looking, you want a ride?"

"Yeah." I said, "Nice motor. Let me tell you how to open the hood one day. It might be good to know, just in case I'm not around."

"Ah but you *will* be around. I'm already planning our next trip!" In truth, I seriously doubted I'd ever repeat this mad jaunt again. But I was feeling happy and lucky and I had just the song to play as we were now in India on the last leg of our journey headed toward Bombay. I searched through the cassettes, found the Allen Price tape and stuck it in the player...

"If you have a friend on whom you think you can rely, you are a lucky man, If you've found the reason to live and not to die, you are a lucky man..."

I was lucky, and I was happy, but I was also sick at heart that Grant wasn't with us. Nothing good could possibly come of him on the run in Peshawar searching for Karina. He was a survivor and all, but he was reckless. I was worried I'd never see him again. Our friendship had been tested through all the unexpected fuck ups and disasters, through all the crazy risks we'd taken together and the dangers we'd faced. The places we'd been and the things we'd seen. Temples and caves and ancient ruins, palaces and beggars and lepers in the most sordid and exalted places on earth and our bond had stayed strong. Until now. I was pissed at him because him going his own way had left me to finish the trip alone with Jack. I felt abandoned.

"Preachers and poets and scholars don't know it, Temples and statues and steeples won't show it, If you've got a secret just try not to blow it, Stay a lucky man! A lucky man!"

Jack put his hand on my knee as I drove. He smiled, "Just you and me now, kid." He squeezed my thigh. And there was no Grant around to run interference for me. I blew. "You motherfucker! Just fucking STOP!" I was screaming so loud my head was throbbing. The gloves were off and I went for the jugular. "I'm not a fucking faggot and if I was, I wouldn't be interested in your old, fat, sorry fuck of a body coming onto me. What are you thinking, old man?"

I was off the rails in my anger, weary from this adrenaline-fused adventure that had almost cost me my life and my livelihood time and again. All I wanted was to finish this and get home and see my Andi. If I was the rock star I fancied myself to be, this must be similar to when the band has been on tour too long and everyone just wants to go home, detox, rest and not talk to each other for a year. Sometimes they come back together and create even better music and hit the road again for more. Sometimes they break up. This band of three was breaking up.

Trips, adventures, journeys, whatever you want to call them, always have a beginning, middle and end. This one was no different. In the beginning, my excitement was fueled with expectations about our drug safari along with a fervor and appreciation for my traveling mates, maybe a false sense of knowing how their uniqueness could really carry this expedition through to the end. I believed in our plan. Then, the middle – the challenges that all journeys with a team have in common - personality conflicts, sickness or injury, logistical fuck-ups, homesickness, power struggles. Ours had been chock-full of all of that and more. It was harrowing at times but so cool to witness and power through all that with my mates.

Then, as journeys go, an issue arises that becomes a tipping point in the relationship. This was our watershed. Jack and I on the brink. On the outside, what had just occurred may not have looked like a big deal. I had been in Jack's presence for countless hours at this point. I knew his personality. I had tried to be the good-time guy, the fixer and keep my cool so we could all fucking survive. But in that moment, when his hand touched my leg, I exploded. I had had enough, not just of him, but of the whole fucking business.

There was a heavy silence. For the first time, Jack did not quip back with some joking remark. He only stared out the window, his hand under his chin. In the silence I drove on, my breathing calmed and my release in finally getting through to him settled into me. As we continued, I thought about the end for us - would the emotional brutality that I bludgeoned him with have a lasting effect? Had I caused too much damage to find a common ground where we could carry on and wrap this up? The fact was that we needed each other if we were going to finish.

36

I sat in the bar of the Taj Mahal Palace Hotel in Bombay looking out a window at a giant mural of Ganesh. The remover of obstacles. I remembered the little elephant Karina had given Grant that he'd latched onto and seen as a symbol that Ganesh would help him get her away from Tariq. But the figurine seemed to have brought obstacles rather than removed them. And where was Grant now? Dead or in jail? Hiding out somewhere alone or with Karina? There was no way to find out and I had to try to be cool with the uncertainty. But it was like losing a brother because I had the feeling it might be the end of him. Finding Grant. Good title for a movie, but a pretty hopeless scenario from where I was sitting.

I had to put that all aside and turn my attention to the task at hand - finding the right cargo ship to carry the Rangey back to Oz. Time was running out on us and our money was, too. We were almost broke. We weren't staying in the Taj Mahal Presidential Suite like we had when we first arrived, but some little dump of a single room. And as I was sitting at the bar paying a ridiculous price for a beer, I wondered if we should move our asses to a motel.

I was drinking Kalyani Black Label Beer because it not only tastes great, but one bottle gets you blitzed. The fans were whirling and there was a bustle of business people and international travelers sitting around. Donna Summer was singing about bad girls. I'd heard this song and cringed at it every time a jukebox or bar speaker played it from London to Landi Kotal. But this time it soothed me. I was thinking to myself, "Man, I have hit the wall here. But there's a door and through the door is home." I was so glad we were near the end of our journey. I found it miraculous we'd actually made it this far. How the hell did we pull this off? It was amazing. Me, apprentice plumber turned successful international smuggler? Soon to be rich.

I wondered if this smuggling adventure would be my last. Even if the enterprise was successful it had been so hairball out of control, I couldn't imagine ever taking the risk a second time. But on the other hand, I was thinking now I know how it works, and I can avoid the pitfalls. Of course, there's always the element of the unexpected. Even if it's all working, it's just a fly-by-the-seat-of-your-pants kind of business. Another possibility was bankrolling the next operation. Hire people, AKA mules, to do it while I stay home out of the firing line? But then I'd have to worry about getting burnt or finked on, face the possibility of living like a criminal on the run, hiding and looking over my shoulder, constantly worried. I'd have to have a safe house I could escape to, money stashed. Plans for contingencies. Where are you going to go? What are you going to do? Better to take Patricia's advice and go legit. Land speculation with my profits, that was the ticket.

I didn't want to get greedy, or worse, cocky. I remembered my original plan was to make one big score and use the money to bankroll my real estate development biz. Starting with the house on the headlands at Lennox Head. With Andi. And possibly some kids. Smuggling and family life don't go so well together.

But I was future tripping because nothing could go forward until I booked the Range Rover onto a cargo ship. Which was no easy thing to do. Things move slowly in India. I went to three shipping agencies trying get our vehicle on a freighter as soon as possible. *Soon* is not in the Indian vocabulary. The Indians are probably more mañana than Mexico. They can be very sweet, quite charming in their assurances, "Ooh, let me tell you. We can handle that. Yes, we can help you. Just wait a few days, please." You wait and nothing happens and you get, "Oh, a problem? We will solve it quickly." But when it comes to actually doing something, it's always somebody else's job. I'd go to one dispatcher and they'd say to check with this other dispatcher, and I'd go to the other and they would pass me on to someone else. I checked and rechecked only to find nothing happened, and they'd say, "We're waiting for an answer." I ended up running around in circles like that for days. It was all on me because there was tension with Jack that he wouldn't let go of. He hadn't spoken to me since the car blowup.

A week of this and then he found me at the bar and suddenly wanted to continue the conversation that had produced the rift between us.

"James, you must admit that there have been times in the past you were a willing participant to my advances."

He was right that there had been a few romps when I was curious. I got seduced, let's say, with the cool, avant-garde scene around his world. And the drugs and booze released my inhibitions. "I let my guard down after you got me stoned to the max. In other words, *non compos mentis*. Get it? Date rape, Jack." It was a feeble argument and he took it harshly.

"Date rape? Bullshit. You were fully conscious, in your glory, basking in all the love and attention. Think of it in the classical sense – erotic male bonding."

"You know how I think of it, Jack? I missed out on having a dad. Occasionally, I'd put you in the role."

"Boys don't usually sleep with their fathers, James. Come on, you were a bit enamored of me as well. What I brought to your life. Right. Fatherly advice. Lessons about politics... history... philosophy, food, fashion... and of course, sex."

"Okay, you've been a teacher to me. But I am not gay. So, stop trying to fucking convert me."

"Don't have to. It's a fact of nature. Look at the Greeks, the Romans, all were swinging both ways."

"I'm not into it. Which is why I should have found you a boy toy somewhere along this trip. Or better yet brought someone along that you could play with."

"But instead you brought Grant. Who I would have no interest in sexually. Ergo maybe you did that because you wanted all my attention."

"Mate, you've lost it. I brought him because he needed a win. This was about business, remember? And because I thought he would keep you so busy analyzing him you'd be too busy to lech after me."

"My, my, well that worked brilliantly, didn't it? Even though he practically blew up the whole operation."

"And you didn't?"

"Fine. We'll go our separate ways then."

He walked off. I let him go because I knew he wasn't really

going anywhere, and besides, I had to turn to the business at hand – finding a boat to get our hash back home. I finally found a shipper that could handle the Rover, but they said it was going to take another three to five days. I figured I'd just trip around and check out the Dharavi slums. Not your usual tourist trip, but fascinating, nonetheless. This is one of the biggest, gnarliest, most heart-breaking shanty-towns in the world and it sits right in the middle of a vast district of million dollar real estate. While I explored the garbage-strewn walkways, the mountainous pyramids of refuse reeking of human hell, kids played everywhere, oblivious to the death surrounding them. But who could be oblivious to the high-rise city half a mile away? Looming with the inescapable message that the peasants were forgotten worthless little pieces of shit. But they were making do in the devastation, living with dignity amid the ruins.

I came across this homey restaurant, it seemed clean, the people were lovely and I had a nice lunch. Little did I know the food was only fit for those that had a well-acccustomed stomach. Which I didn't. I contracted a kickass case of Delhi Belly. With Delhi Belly it starts out bad and gets progressively worse. Vomit and diarrhea spewing until you have nothing left inside. Finally, I was down to the bile of my stomach. It looked like my next place of residence was the hospital, but I was fighting that idea. I spent a few days in bed sweating and puking, passing in and out of consciousness. In my delirium I was hearing the Doors doing "Riders on the Storm" and I was cruising through deep powder in Utah, snow falling, surrounding me like some divine cocoon. That hypnotic beat pulling me along, Manzarek's keyboard so light and feathery, born aloft by the pulsing base and glide of Densmore's snare and cymbals... *"Riders on the storm, Riders on the storm, Into this house we're born, into this world we're thrown, Like a dog without a bone, An actor out on loan..."*

And then snow and freedom were gone and I was back in my hotel in the disgusting smell of my own bed, the sickening heat of Bombay suffocating me. I was drifting toward death, all thanks to a samosa! Done in by a fucking deep-fried pastry I was dumb enough to eat. Man, you never know where or how the Grim Reaper will grab you. But never in my wildest fears did I think it would happen this way, felled by the vile grease from a meal in Bombay.

I remember squinting through crusty eyes at a huge orange sun streaked and vaporized by clouds of pollution and there in the distance the golden arches of the "Gateway to India." And then I was gone again. I thought it was the end. I said my goodbyes to my mum and to Andi. And then I began to hear "The End" by the Doors... the tambourine shaking, those trippy hypnotic reverb guitar notes beckoning and Morrison, the Priest of High, the shaman, the brave soul taking the journey to the underworld for us all, incanting, transporting...

"This is the end, beautiful friend, This is the end, my only friend, the end, Of our elaborate plans, the end, Of everything that stands, the end, No safety or surprise, the end..."

I was going with Morrison, it didn't matter where. It felt like a happy ending. To a fun life. I'd come so far, not just on this smuggling trip but from that little kid way back in Texas who lost his father. I was thinking about my dad who I realized at that moment I missed so terribly and I wondered if maybe Morrison was taking me to see him. Tears came to my eyes, happy tears...

"Can you picture what will be, So limitless and free, Desperately in need, of some stranger's hand, in a desperate land..."

I was out past the Gateway of India, above and beyond, floating into the great orange Elysian Fields, going, going, gone baby, the sticky, suffocating heat replaced by a cool breeze smelling of frangipani and lotus blossoms kissing my face... and then I heard my name... "James... James..." a whispering voice calling me, from where, from where? Above me, "James... James..." a girl's voice... I opened my gummy eyes a crack and saw a young nurse bending over me. Then I heard Jack's voice, "My boy, my boy... thought we lost you there."

The hotel doctor stood over me with turban-topped medics pushing a gurney to take me to the hospital. I didn't want to go and told Jack to get rid of the doc and the medics. Then I passed out, and a day later I woke up. Sure enough, I was in the hospital. Into both arms, the pale tubes of IVs, the monitors blinked and I didn't even know what had happened.

By the time I was able to walk out of the hospital a week later, the Rangey was ready to get loaded onto the cargo ship. We watched it go through the process, being driven onto the freighter, the Gateway to India across the water. Man, that Rover had been through a lot. How many countries did it roll through – England, Belgium, Germany, Switzerland, Italy, Croatia, Turkey, Greece, Iran, Iraq, Pakistan, Afghanistan and some other Stans... a fucking lot of terrain. That ride had served us well. I felt a great affection for that car. Now finally, after all these months and all those miles, there she was on the huge barge going home to Sydney harbor. The Rangey disappeared into a container. All was well. Final leg in progress.

The ship would be in transit for ten days moving south over the Arabian Sea, then east through the Indian Ocean across the Equator and Tropic of Capricorn, curving down under the bottom of Australia to finally arrive in Sydney harbor. Slow boat, fast plane. We'd be back home waiting for her when she pulled into port.

It may have been intuition, but I decided that it was best if I was on a separate plane from Jack so I stayed in Bombay a few more days to gain my strength back. I was lounging by the pool when someone eased into a deck chair next to me. It was Mick, our connection to Tariq. I couldn't hide my look of disgust. Even though Grant had brought the calamity on himself, somehow I wanted someone else to blame.

"Guess you know what I'm going to ask you huh, mate?" he said.

"I haven't heard from Grant and if I had, I wouldn't tell you."

"So, the fact that I'm here asking tells you something, right?"

"What? That he's still alive?"

"I'll tell you what I know. Your partner will never get to Karina. And Karina will never get away from Tariq. Until he's done with her."

"Go fuck yourself. And that nice guy you work for, too."

"Nice guys don't make it in the drug and gun trade. You should know that, James. You're turning out to be a bit naive for an international smuggler."

"Guess I'm not used to dealing with killers." An admission I was happy to make.

"Grant fucked up and you know that. You don't go into the

big dog's yard and steal his bone. Now if you tell me where he is, maybe we can work something out. A reprieve, let's call it."

"Grant does a mea culpa and then Tariq forgets all about it?"

"Exactly. So, where is he?"

If I had known, I wouldn't have told him. Mick was lying and Tariq would kill Grant. I shrugged. Let him think I just didn't give a shit.

"So be it. Sayonara, mate." He walked off and that night I jumped on a plane back to Sydney.

37

Exhausted, relieved and ready for a nice restful trip home, I made it through customs in Bombay and boarded the big bird to fly back to Sydney. It was like seeing your longshot horse ten lengths ahead in the last quarter mile. I got a good buzz on and for the first time in a long while I could finally relax. The hash was on its way home. I'd be back there when it arrived to pick it up and would then begin the distribution process. I was feeling totally confident. The dangerous part was over.

I had a meal, watched Burt Reynolds grin his way through "Smokey and the Bandit," and mesmerizing as that flick was, passed out. I woke up as the plane touched down in Sydney to the early morning rain, breezed through customs, picked up my bags and walked out as the clouds parted and the sun began pouring through. Damn, but it felt good to be back in the land of Oz. Where everything is normal and you can see unpredictable things from a long way off. Not like the worlds I'd been moving through for the last three months.

The first thing I wanted to do was see Andi. Turned out she was with her girlfriends at the beach, enjoying her life – maybe in the way she'd been doing ever since I'd left. She rolled in later looking tanned and luscious in a yellow bikini. When she saw me, she was stunned. We *immediately* grabbed each other and drifted in each other's arms for a while. "You're okay, you're okay," she kept saying with relief.

"Sure, I'm okay. Why wouldn't I be?"

"Don't try to avoid this, James. I've heard stories about how dangerous what you're doing is from my brother-in-law."

My mentor, the mega dealer Mr. Big, had the smuggling business down to a science. "Look at him, I said assuring her, "he's been doing it for years without a bust or even a rip off."

"You're not going to do another trip like that again, are you?"

"Probably not," I said and pretty much meant it.

"Good. Because a weird thing happened yesterday. Some guy came around. I couldn't tell if he was a gangster or an undercover cop. He said he was an old mate of Grant's and he was asking questions about you guys." She'd had a bad vibe about this stranger and told him nothing. Now she was scared.

"Probably just some friend of Grant's from prison. Everything is okay, Andi. Are you okay?"

"No. Not okay. Who is this guy? And he wasn't alone. He and another person sat in a car outside our house for a couple hours."

"What kind of car?"

"A black pickup truck."

I fixed her a drink, we smoked a bowl and she calmed down. The next thing I knew we were in the sack and everything was beautiful despite the ominous foreboding of a stalker. It felt so good to be back in my Palm Beach house overlooking the ocean with my girl. We lazed around in bed for a few hours and finally she leaned over to me and said, "So, how many girls were you with on your little three-month sojourn?"

"I was way too busy to be concerned with that."

"Come on, James, I know you. You would have been okay for a couple of weeks and then..."

"I had Jack chasing me around half the time. Fortunately, Grant was there to distract him."

"James, tell the truth." She looked at me with such sweetness I couldn't bring myself to lie. Bad move you might say, but she would know if I bullshitted her. Although her look was innocent, she was no dummy when it came to reading people. She had it all: looks, brains, sex appeal. So why was I fucking around on her? Why does any guy do what he does? I was young, we were far apart, and it was the Seventies. A good enough excuse, or so it seemed, nevertheless I was feeling pangs of conscience. She looked at me, waiting for an answer, so open, so vulnerable and I was having trouble finding the words. "Well... in Istanbul I was being one of the boys, hanging with a platoon of Brit Special Forces ..."

She looked at me skeptically, "Soldiers? Not your usual choice of companions, James."

"We were selling them hash, hanging out, pounding drinks with them..."

"There were girls around?"

I shrugged, "Yeah."

"And you fucked one."

"To be honest with you I can't remember. I was too drunk."

"Who was she?"

"Don't even remember."

"Was it good?"

"Let it go, Andi."

"How many times?"

"Once."

"So you do remember. Did you do that thing to her that you do to me?"

"No baby."

"I want you checked, I want you totally checked, and I'm going to go and have sex with somebody now, to even the score. Was there anybody else?"

"Well..."

"Who else?"

"Actually..."

"Oh my God. Who?"

"This CIA chick."

She shook her head. I had gone too far. I tried to explain. "There was a gal who was involved with kind of an Interpol situation and you don't really need to know about it because I don't want you to have to..."

"What do you mean Interpol?

"They somehow got wind of what we were doing."

"You had to fuck her to keep from getting busted? Is that what you're telling me?"

"Yeah. I could be sitting in a jail in Kabul now."

"How many times did you do it?"

"Only twice."

"Was it good? Better than what we have?"

"Nothing could compare to what we have."

"Were these girls prettier than me?"

"No, they weren't as hot as you baby, never."

"James. I'm evening the score."

She was kidding. Sort of. It was the era of free love and we did have an "arrangement" whereby we could, ahem, engage with the occasional "other." I could see she was hurt. I wanted to take her out and paint the town with her. She pushed me away with a dry smile and said, "It's hard to be with you knowing you were with other girls."

Thinking I'd get her mind off the subject, I told her what had happened to Grant. Bad idea. Her jealousy took a back seat to fear. "So that scary guy who came here looking for him means he's in trouble and we're in the line of fire?"

I told her to forget about it, but she couldn't. She looked at me a long moment and her eyes filled with tears. "He was that much in love with Karina? How beautiful. I wonder if you would do that for me."

"You know I would," I said. And in truth, I probably would have.

Andi and I both figured that the scary guy who'd come round asking about Grant was in fact no prison buddy. He was working for Tariq and he'd be back looking for answers. I told her that if he came round to play dumb and leave a phone number and I'd call him. She was freaked out enough that I knew I had to find the bloke and somehow back him off. But I had other business to take care of first.

How do you tell a father his son is missing, or possibly even dead? I found Grant's dad out at his ranch sitting on his back porch sipping whiskey from the bottle. He was glassy-eyed even though it was still lunchtime. Three mangy hounds howled and barked as I walked up. The old man's eyes were more bloodshot than his dogs, squinting from a face that looked like shriveled cowhide. Off in the distance, a young broad-shouldered ranch hand mended a fence.

Grant's dad fired a missile of spit into the dirt, "Just so you know – you ain't foolin' nobody."

"Uh..."

"There's two kinds a young men, fair dinkim. There's Skip over there – honest..." He looked out at his ranch hand. As if on cue, the Outback's very own Gary Cooper stood up tall, removed his cowboy hat, and rubbed sweat from his face with his forearm. "And then there's your kind. You and Grant. I know what you been doing and now you can get on off this ranch."

The hero out at the fence was back at work hammering away. "Uh look, Mr. Flynn, no disrespect intended, but I need to tell you something about Grant." He seemed to know what was up and just looked at me. "Grant... well the fact is..."

"He done something bad, probably headed back to prison."

"We kinda lost track of each other in Pakistan..."

"He didn't come back with you and that pufter you went with, did he?"

"No, sir." He snorted derisively, spit, emphasizing his disinterest. I tried for bright and cheery, "I didn't know you met Jack."

"Haven't. Don't want to. People been around. Talking, asking questions..."

"What do you mean? What people? What questions?"

"Some slick-talking guttersnipe who crawled out from under a rock. Prison friend of Grant's. No good to the bone. Wants to know where he is. Don't know, I said. Don't want to know. He left saying he'd be back. I told him better he didn't. I'd show him the business end of my shotgun."

"What did he look like?"

"Like trouble. Like all of you. That boy been trouble since

the beginning, just like his mother. You can get on now."

"Was he driving a black pickup?"

"Yeah. Had someone with him. Couldn't see who. They parked up the road off the property. Which is where you should be. Now get!" He uncoiled himself from his chair and limped on bowed legs off in the direction of the good boy mending his fence. The dogs decided to stay in the shade. I left that happy place and driving away across scorched outback and wondered if maybe Grant had somehow escaped Tariq's net. Maybe he'd even spirited Karina away. I wondered about a dad who wouldn't give a shit about his son. Trouble from day one? I thought maybe it's better to have been without a father than to have one like that old man.

38

Where the hell was Jack? That was a nagging question. Crazy thoughts raced through my mind that Tariq's thug had kidnapped him. Maybe Tariq knew Jack would be the one who had to retrieve our load of hash from customs because all the paperwork was in his alias, Byron Rimbaud. The thug was going to hold onto Jack until we coughed up whatever we knew about Grant. Jack had a couple of Dobermans he loved. He'd left them at my mother's house before our trip. I went over to Mum's to see if he'd been by. And besides I needed to assure her I was alive and well. I gave her a big hug and she said, "Oh, how lovely to see you, James. You've been gone for months! Where have you been all this time?"

I said, "Well you know, I went up to the Northern Territory on a long road trip. No phones up there. Then went through the Outback and no phones there either. Then I went over to Western Australia. Then surf in the Seychelles. I've missed you, Mum."

How did I feel about lying to my Mum? I was used to that because I'd been living a lie with her for a long time, presenting myself as a plumber. Even though I was a plumber, the cover this provided hid the real truth. A plumber/dope dealer. Then I'd become a smuggler, so I'd moved right up the food chain.

Admirable in my circle, but probably not to Mum.

Lying to her was shitty, but the alternative would have been worse, "Yeah mum, I just got back from Afghanistan and Pakistan with 200 kilos of hash." Probably the lesser of two evils. She said, "Oh my, you went all the way over to the Seychelles Islands. I would have loved to get a post card from there. Always thought that was such a lovely place to visit."

"Yeah, it was a last minute decision and we decided to stay so we were there for a month. Mail service was really sketchy."

I had gone to elaborate lengths in my travel ruse, pre-addressing postcards that I had friends send her from Northern Territory and Western Australia. I had my buds send mum a card every two or three weeks to keep her from worrying. But Afghanistan was another story altogether and not one I wanted to share. Changing the subject to the dogs, "How're those Dobie pups doing, Mum?"

"They're in the backyard," she said forcing a smile.

"Great - bet they've been having a good time out there."

She rolled her eyes and said, "Oh they certainly have. Come see."

My mother took pride in her beautifully tended backyard with a gorgeous lawn and verdant bushes, flowers and trees. I went back there and from fence to fence it was ravaged like a swarm of locusts had devoured every shrub in sight and then a herd of wildebeests had rampaged over what was left. The culprits came bounding over, jumping up with their big paws and claws.

"Hey, Ruby and Basil." They looked dangerous but they were just goofy, lovey dogs. Taking in all the damage they'd caused, I said, "Oh mom, your poor garden is done."

"Well, yes, I suppose it has seen better days."

"I've got to fix this for you," I said. "Don't worry, I'll get the best gardeners in Sydney in here to make it beautiful again," because I knew as soon as my stash was sold, I could spend a couple of grand and restore her yard. As I was leaving, she said that a man had come by looking for Grant. "He said that I should tell you he'd be back. I hope he's not one of your companions, James, because he looked a bit unsavory."

"How's that, mum? What did he look like?"

"Hair all slicked back with oil on it. Dressed like he was a fancy pants. He smiled, but only with his teeth." She told me he was driving a black pickup and had someone with him. A dark-skinned person. Maybe a woman.

"Some old mate of Grant's," I said trying to assure her. I took the rambunctious pups over to Jack's house to drop them off. He wasn't there and his mother didn't want me to leave them. She was afraid they were so unruly they would jump on her and knock her down. Which, in fact, they probably would have. But I already had enough fires to put out so I stuck them in the garage and told her not to go in there until Jack came home. She didn't know where he was and he hadn't been home in days. Well, Jack would have a nice mess to clean up when he walked in. I had a pretty distasteful task facing me as well. How to deal with this guy looking for Grant?

I went back to the house and found Andi sitting quietly on the couch staring at the phone. I wondered if maybe she was thinking of moving out, breaking up with me over my transgressions. I didn't want to lose her. I was kicking myself for being unfaithful and then being stupid enough to tell her about it. She was so pretty, especially when she was happy, and now there she was like a sad little girl. I told her how sorry I was and it would never happen again. "I knew what I was getting into with you, James. And I don't expect you to change. I just don't know if I can handle it."

"It's a thing of the past."

"What about dealing drugs? Is that really a thing of the past?"

"Well... I do have 200 kilos of hash coming in, but after that..."

"It's too much! I can't take it. Look what happened to Grant. He might be dead. And Garret could go to prison!"

"Mr. Big? No way."

"My sis just called and she's hysterical. The police are looking for him. He could get fifty years."

"Why? What happened?"

"He got set up by someone."

This was news to me. My mentor was one of the biggest dealers in Australia and hardly ever got his hands dirty. He had connections and protectors in the police force. He was the guy I admired and wanted to emulate. The guy who made no mistakes, who taught me to "expect the unexpected." I asked her if she was sure about this.

He had called her sister and told her he might have to leave the country abruptly because some deal of his had gone bad. Andi didn't know anything else about it. I hugged her and assured her everything was going to be okay. Both with her brother-in-law and with us. She wanted to believe it too, so she clung to me for a bit, and begged me to look out for her brother-in-law. I said I would, but the truth was he was in another league from me. Complications were dragging me down like the chains of Jacob Marley.

In the middle of the night I got a call from Jack. He went on drunkenly about all the dog shit in the garage. I finally stopped him and got it into his head that we had to meet up. The next day I drove over to the Eastern suburbs and pulled into Double Bay, also known as "Double Pay" because of the ridiculous prices there. I was meeting Jack at the most expensive restaurant in Oz. He was sitting out front in a luxurious, vintage 1936 Hillman Hawk. These old English cars were very rare and distinctive. This one had classic lines like a Bentley Mark IV and wore a two-tone paint job of cream and magenta. The interior was burnished wood paneling with fine leather. There were probably two of these classics in the entire country. Drive down the street in one and you'd draw more looks than Lady Godiva.

"So much for keeping a low profile, Jack. Looks like you're living quite the high life here," I said, letting him know that wasn't the plan we'd agreed on.

"We have to present ourselves as successful entrepreneurs," he said brushing past me into the restaurant. He picked a table in the center of things. Over shrimp scampi and champagne he told me how he had been entertaining prospective buyers for our load and what an endless supply we would have for them.

"You didn't tell anyone it's on the cargo ship, I hope."

"Just that we're going to have some magnificent hash for them post-haste."

"You've got to keep this on the down low. Don't be broadcasting it until we've got it in hand."

"Well I'm priming the pump, getting the market ready." He left a ridiculously ostentatious tip and we walked out front.

I told him, "We have to be careful. The cops are all over the drug trade right now. Even Mr. Big is under investigation."

"Mr. Big? In a jam? Good."

"Good?"

"If he's off the scene it means we are the kingpins now."

I told him about the bloke looking for Grant. "So what?" he fobbed me off and then drove away in the most conspicuous car in Sydney. Delusions of grandeur. So now I had more trouble to deal with.

That night Andi and I were in our Palm Beach house with a sweet jasmine breeze drifting in off the moon sparkling sea. I was in that proverbial eye of deceptive calm, but I could feel the tempest about to hit. We clinked flutes of bubbly and smoked some of the finest hash on the planet as we listened to Leonard Cohen, who was Andi's favorite. I was beginning to get his message...

"Like a bird on a wire, like a drunk in the midnight choir, I have tried in my way to be free..."

I could see myself settling down with Andi, buying that beautiful bluff above Lennox Head. I was even picturing a couple of nippers trouncing around the jungle gym in the back yard, the dogs romping about, a Volvo station wagon with child seats in the expansive brick driveway.

"Like a worm on a hook. Like a knight from some old-fashioned book, I have saved all my ribbons for thee..."

We were, despite the circumstances, trying to be happy. And then we got the call from Andi's sister Maggie, who told us Mr. Big's troubles had worsened. "Some *things* are happening," she said and though she was distraught, managed to convey that she needed to see us right away, but not at her house.

Andi's paranoia was high. "Things are *wrong*, a major problem...What the hell is going on?" She abruptly hung up. All the romance in the world was not going to overcome Andi's concerns about her family. Hardly the happy homecoming I'd expected. And what's more, I knew we all had reason to worry.

39

Maggie lived in the eastern suburbs while we were up on the northern beaches, so we arranged to meet together the next day at a place in Mossman, halfway between us. When we met for lunch, Maggie was frazzled. Not looking her usual foxy self, she was covered head to foot in a burka-like outfit. Her manner was stiff and she seemed certain she was being followed. She said that her husband Mr. Big was doing a huge deal. Something on the order of *two tons*. Two tons of Afghani hash. Nobody had ever brought in such a massive load before. This was the World Series Game Seven of drug smuggling. Worth somewhere in the region of twelve million dollars, which in those days was a gargantuan amount of money. To my mind, the stuff of legend.

Mr. Big had never had a problem before, but somehow on this load the shit had hit the fan. Somewhere in the chain of command during the importing there was a weak link that caused a security breach. Now the van he had shipped from Bombay carrying the two tons was being watched by narcs agents. Ever since its arrival in Sydney, Mr. Big had been sweating it out. He wasn't the only one who stood to lose everything. At that very moment, the Rangey loaded with hash was on a cargo ship plying the same route.

The two mules Mr. Big had employed to pick the van up from customs were under surveillance. These were an unlikely pair - Mr. Big's flamboyant aunt and her lesbian lover. Two middle aged dykes who'd been busted and threatened with a life sentence unless they gave up Mr. Big. Both had gone for the deal, of course, and were now cooperating with the cops. Mr. Big had a spy inside the police department so he knew from the inside out everything they were doing to corner him. Not willing to go down easily, Mr. Big was taking evasive action and went on the run. Maggie said that he needed his passports and some things delivered to him - clothes, food, and money, so that he could hide out for a little while before skipping the country. She was afraid she was being watched, too, and didn't know who to trust. Since she saw me as part of the family, she asked if I would get him what he needed.

I thought about it and sketchy as the whole deal was, I said I'd help. Maggie told us her man was hiding out at a safe house in Rose Bay, an affluent little coastal burb in New South Wales. The next day, Andi went over to visit Maggie at her mansion and picked up Mr. Big's passports, some clothes and a few bags of food. Then she met me at Lennox Head and handed it all off along with ten grand in cash.

Andi wore a Borsalino hat with a flowing yellow scarf. She looked like Faye Dunaway in "Bonnie and Clyde." She had this wild look about her, like she was really digging the intrigue and even though she was scared, she stayed calm. It turned me on she could be so cool, even fun, in such a dangerous situation. I had the same kind of buzz. Sure, I was apprehensive about helping a fugitive from justice, but then I thought, wait a minute, this is my mentor. This is The Guy. This is the man who taught me everything I knew about smuggling and helped me pull off my operation. So, if the worst happened and he was busted, I could say I tried to help him escape. Then, for one delirious moment, the dealer in me was embracing Jack's selfish idea that if Mr. Big went down in flames, we'd be the ones on top. That prospect was exciting.

Then I came to my senses and remembered all the craziness I'd just come through on my trip. Mr. Big's famous words rang in my ears - "Expect the unexpected. You never know what's going to come around the corner. Be ready at all times." Those words were driven home by the fact that Mr. Big was now running for his life.

Maggie had told me I should go to the King's Head Pub in Rose Bay and wait by the payphones for a call from him. The King's Head was also a bookie joint so there was a frenzy of betting going on, much of it on the two payphones. I had to wait in line for a turn to use a phone and then when I was up, I stood there hoping to get the call while anxious rugby bettors gave me the evil eye to get moving. Third time through the line was the charm and I got the call from Mr. Big who told me where to meet him. "Hey, James, thanks man," he said in his American accent. He had been the soap opera equivalent of Dirty Harry and could be very dramatic when he wanted to be. "Cover your tail and make sure you're not being watched, because I know I'm on their radar. I know they're looking, they want me bad. And if the heat is tracking you, it won't be good for either of us."

"Roger that," I said, and went down to an area near where he was in Bronte Beach. I parked a few blocks from a store, walked a circuitous route to it, went in and then out the back door to the alley, hopped a few hedges and returned to the car. Then I drove to a high-rise office building, parked on the rooftop deck, looked all around down in the streets for anything suspicious, anybody surveilling me. I had a good nose for narcs. I knew their cars, I knew how they dressed, what they were like and how they operated. Some were sharp but most were meatheads.

A creeping suspicion made me turn through a few roundabouts to see if anybody was on my tail. Finally, I was one-hundred percent certain that I wasn't being watched but who knew about Mr. Big? Hey, no guts no glory, I thought so taking a few more precautions, I kept the meeting.

I arrived at the address he gave me, got out of the car, went across the street to an empty house, knocked on the door, and then turned around and watched. Nobody seemed to be checking me out. I couldn't see anyone on the street on either side, up or down. There was a back alleyway. I walked back around there, didn't see a soul. It felt cool. Finally, I grabbed the suitcase and the bag of groceries, and went to the house he was in. The door opened and there he was. Mr. Big.

His TV star good looks were obscured by mangy stubble. He appeared hollow-eyed and distraught. Where there once was a supremely confident character, that cool was shaky now as he nervously checked out the street. "You took precautions?" he said. I told him I used more stealth than James Bond.

He took the clothes and bag of food, rooting through it, "Thanks mate, thanks for bringing all this over here." I laid the money on him and his passports and he sat me down and explained the situation. "It's my biggest load ever, James. More than two tons. Welded into the body of a big Mercedes van.

My people bought it in Germany then drove it across Europe and Asia to Afghanistan." I thought, Wow, this sure sounds familiar. Mr. Big went on, "They loaded it up, got it to Bombay, onto the freighter, made it to Sydney."

"You were doing the same operation as we were, at the same time?"

"Yeah. Bit bigger, though. I hope you don't run into problems like I did."

This was really bad news. "The same thing could happen to me, right?"

"Possibly. Never should have trusted my aunt. Family above all, right? But never hire the desperate – and I'm not saying (but I'm saying) you know, *lesbians*." He raised his eyebrows. "Expect the unexpected, mate."

I joked, "Well, I don't have a gay aunt as a mule, but I do have a pretty queer partner."

We both had a good laugh. Sometimes in dire straits you just have to find the humor. But I sobered up quick with his next request. "My van with the two tons is now at a submarine station down in the Mossman area. I am going to pay my pal James to drive down there, have a look and give me a report. Tell me how thick the surveillance is."

"Uh..." I definitely didn't want to go down there.

"All you have to do is cruise by and check it out, see if it's actually sitting there on the road."

Just drive by? That seemed doable. Anyway, I was glad to get out of that house. It was so fucking claustrophobic and depressing. My role model, my mentor, Mr. Big, reduced to a mere shell of himself. The van was in an area close by, so I borrowed a bicycle from a friend and rode down there, like a nice little local dude on his way to a workout. I had my gym clothes on and a gym bag strapped on the rack, cruised the area, and sure enough the van was there and I could smell the narcs before I saw them. They were sitting around in their cars, staking out the van. I knew right then Mr. Big's great deal-of-the-century was toast.

I kept on riding, took a meandering route over parks and beaches, borrowed a board, went for a surf, and then finally doubled my way back to his safe house in the middle of the night. The report was simple. "Dude, it is so dirty you don't want to know." At that point, there wasn't much more I could do. He had money, he had clothes, he had some food. The next choice was his to make. Somehow or other he was going to have to get out of the country. I think he was going to try to take a slow boat to the Maldives.

All I could think was, shit, what does this mean about my load? Was it now on the radar? Or was it going to be safe because all the attention was on his big load. And big it was. Newspapers in the following days would run front page stories reporting how the lesbian grannies were tricked by this "unscrupulous, charming, super dealer." They ran a photo of Mr. Big from his soap opera days alongside a picture of the vulnerable eccentric aunt and her lover.

A week went by and the drama was still front-page news. The narcs were using the media to play a game of cat and mouse. They planted news reports and stories of how the van had slipped through their net. They moved the van around, parking it here and there, as they waited for Mr. Big to make his move to try to grab it. But of course he wasn't falling for that shit. Then the Daily Mirror ran a story taking up the whole front page. A huge headline reading: "Grannies, tricked by this man. Vow to catch the nephew!" Mr. Big's real life soap opera was just beginning. And it would have dire consequences. The public was rooting for the grannies.

Of course, they weren't really grannies. And they weren't tricked at all, but were totally in on the deal. But now they were "seeking justice" and the public's help, pleading to catch Mr. Big and "put him behind bars where he belongs." The Attorney General knowing the truth, gave them a slap on the wrist in exchange for ratting out Mr. Big who engineered the "largest haul in Australian history." It was weird to see this giant in my industry done in by a couple of little old ladies. But then, it was Mr. Big's choice – he was an equal opportunity employer – and he'd used them as mules. A decision that backfired worse than a three-cylinder Ford Pinto.

With nothing more I could do for Mr. Big, I turned my attention to my own shipment. Jack and I had a contact in the customs department, and we were getting updates. I heard that the Rangey had arrived safely and on time and was now in line to be inspected. The word was the load was cool and we could pick it up soon. I had some trepidation about this because of all the scrutiny caused by Mr. Big's bust. Jack was saying, "Oh, I can help him. I have people in high places that can fix this situation."

But I knew that was a fool's errand because no one was going to stick their neck out returning a favor in a lost cause. The case was so notorious that Mr. Big couldn't even buy his way out of it. Jack stubbornly thought he could make it happen, though. And like always he went forth doing his own thing, no matter how crazy or precarious it might be. It was odd he was trying to help Mr. Big while he imagined himself in the vacated kingpin role. But that was Jack, a study in contrasts. I would never really understand him.

He was endlessly on the phone talking to his connects in the political world, and the police and military. I told him he was jeopardizing our mission. He responded arrogantly, "Our fabulous cargo is going to make it into our well-deserved hands, and we're going to be on top of the heap. No need to trade your kingdom for a horse, my lad." I was thinking that his Richard the Third reference was more apt than he knew. Defeat seemed more possible than not. The heat was ratcheting up. We'd spent time and money and a number of cat lives to get as far as we had, but to me that was not worth the price of a prison term. I had plans and dreams. There would always be another deal.

But I had another voice inside my head saying don't walk away from your endeavor just yet. Get your load in. If you pull it off, do one or two more smuggling trips. Learn from your experience. Then I had to check myself. I wasn't about to do another deal with Jack as a partner. He was actually scaring me now. His arrogance was astounding and he just didn't know how to be discreet. He was driving around Sydney in that Hillman Mark 6. I pulled him up about it, but no matter the spin I put on it, he didn't listen.

"Don't worry my boy, I bought it because this is the kind of automobile that any mega dealer worth his salt should be driving."

"Why not a VW Bug? So you have half a chance of surviving your success."

"Nonsense, my boy. Let's live grandly in the style we're

accustomed to."

I knew he was a disaster waiting to happen.

40

"Young hearts be free tonight, Time is on your side..."

I heard the music coming from the van. Andi and I walked across the church parking lot with two bottles of fine champagne. We were going to get buzzed and then christen a boat later that evening. Hopefully. If all went well and we weren't in the slammer. We were in Port Macquarie, a sweet little town on the coast south of Brisbane. It had been a penal colony back in the old days. We were outside the St. Thomas Anglican Church, built in 1824 by convicts. It was an ironic place to be at the moment because I was there to help Andi's sister Maggie and her husband, Garrett Jones, aka Mr. Big, escape a police dragnet. If Big was caught, he'd be doing at least several decades in prison. I was meeting with a buddy of mine who was selling his boat. A 32-foot teak-hulled shallow-draft sloop that Garrett and Maggie could buy and then sail to Hawaii.

Big was really feeling the heat and needed to get out of the country, so the plan was to buy the boat and escape from Oz in the dark of night, journey 4,750 nautical miles across hopefully calm seas and pull into some small harbor on the Big Island of Hawaii. Since he was American and had several fake IDs, no one would be asking any questions once he was there. That was his plan, anyway. I had my doubts because just a few years prior he'd been a soap star. As if that wasn't enough notoriety, he was now a recognizable international fugitive. He'd have to figure out some masterful disguise. He was convinced the tumult would all die down and he could be stateside without crossing any international borders, hiding out for a year or two and starting a new life.

Garrett, Maggie, Andi and I waited in the van for my friend to arrive. We were listening to gimlet-eyed bad boy Rod Stewart singing about us – the Young Turks...

"Billy left his home with a dollar in his pocket and a head full of dreams. He said somehow, some way, it's gotta be better than this. Patti packed her bags, left a note for her momma, she was just seventeen, there were tears in her eyes when she kissed her little sister goodbye..."

After paying cash for the boat, Garrett and Maggie, alias Billy and Patti, would have about a grand between them, the rest of Big's fortune being frozen by the cops. The four of us would soon go our separate ways, on to our different lives on different islands, still surfing and hopefully living large and being in charge of whatever would come next. Garrett and Maggie in Hawaii, me and Andi... well, who knew where we'd be? A lot depended on whether we got Big and Maggie safely off on their journey.

My friend from Port Macquarie showed up and we followed him down to the harbor. His boat was a beauty. Garrett was a very competent sailor and Maggie knew how to hoist a sail. We said our goodbyes and the sisters hugged and cried. We all vowed to meet up stateside within a year or two. I told Garrett, "Sorry it came down this way, man."

But he seemed, after all this, as if a huge weight had been lifted. He laughed, "All part of the game, James. Expect the unexpected."

We shattered a bottle of bubbly against the hull and Garrett and his beautiful wife - the fortunate two who once had everything - sailed off under a cloudless sky.

And Rod kept singing... *"Young hearts be free tonight, time is on your side... we got just one shot at life, let's take it while we're still not afraid. Because life is so brief and time is a thief when you're undecided..."*

I sat down on the dock to look out at the horizon. Thousands of miles to the northwest was Pakistan. And where was Grant in that wild country? Had he found Karina? Was he on his way back with her? Was he alive? Andi sat next to me, trying to hold her tears back. She lost the battle and cried quietly. I felt like doing the same.

On the ride back to Sydney, I marveled at how our lives had all taken such unexpected turns. Grant god knows where, Garrett and Maggie on the run. They had been living the complete high life, had everything they wanted, whenever they wanted it. Travel, the best of foods and clothes and houses and cars. Living like royalty. But it went too far, got too big, until finally it all collapsed on itself. From riches to rags. Well not exactly, since a 32-foot teak-hulled sloop isn't exactly the gutter. But the most precious thing – freedom – was in a perilous state. They'd gone from having all the freedom one could imagine to being on the lam in a state of constant vigilance. A change in lifestyle that I felt I might be looking at, too.

It made me want to get out of the dealing game. Fast. But first I had to try to retrieve our load, which was waiting peacefully in the Sydney customs house. I'd sell it, then take Patricia Adams' advice and go legit.

Andi was quiet on the ride back down the coast, subdued, missing her sister, her Bonnie and Clyde buzz left back on the dock, shattered with the champagne bottle. I could feel her looking at me. "What?" I said.

"Who knows when I'll see Maggie again..." and her small voice trailed off.

"We'll take a trip to Hawaii real soon," I said.

"What if we get arrested?"

She hadn't shown any fear up til then. Matter of fact she had enjoyed all the drama. Guess now it was getting too close to home. "We're not going to get busted," I assured her.

"You don't know that. They could be watching us right now."

"We'll get our load. We'll lay low for a while. Everything will be fine."

"Until the next time."

I told her there wouldn't be a next time. This was it for me. I was going legit from now on and then start my real estate development business.

"Jack will talk you into doing another scam. He has nothing to lose."

True. Jack was thinking he was going to be the next Mr. Big, and that he had everybody under control. In the past he'd bought off cops and politicians and was so self-aggrandizing and arrogant he thought he could do whatever he wanted. We were inextricably tied via the load so I had to deal with him. Unless I wanted to walk away from the enterprise, and I wasn't ready to do that.

As I pulled up to our house, I saw the black pickup sitting in front. "That's him!" Andi said. "Oh shit, now what? Keep driving, James."

I told her I was going to take care of this and sent her inside. I walked over to the truck, which was a sleek, lowered stealth machine. The darkened driver's window floated down and the guy behind the wheel stared at me. He said something to his passenger who I couldn't see. "I've got someone here who wants to talk to you," he said.

"Tell Tariq I don't know where he is, haven't heard a thing from him. He probably knows more than I do."

The guy spoke to the passenger again and then said, "Who's Tariq?"

"Who are you?" I said, wondering if I had it all wrong. Maybe the guy was, after all, a friend of Grant's from prison. But then who was the passenger? A woman got out of the truck and one look at her and I knew who she was. Grant's mum.

"Is he...? Is Grant...?"

"He's probably okay. I wish I knew more but I don't."

She lowered her eyes and her long black curls hid her tears. "He stayed because he was trying to help somebody."

The guy got out of the truck, and I saw he was around fifty but trying to look younger. "Help some chick, right," he said with nowhere near the arrogance I had figured him for.

"You heard something?"

"She knew. She has... intuitions sometimes. Visions."

I didn't know what to say and neither did they. We stood together bound by our mutual concern. My friend, her son. Finally, I asked if her intuitions had told her anything else about Grant. "That you could find him," she said.

"I could find him?"

"Will you?"

My instinct was immediately to hit reverse. I was definitely not ready to be tapped like this. "I can't right now. I'm sorry. I have to deal with..."

"Your shipment, we know," the guy said. Looking at his passenger, he added, "He's got to deal with what they went over there for. Right now. But he could help when that's done, right?" He turned square to face me.

She nodded soberly. I knew what she was thinking – that it could be too late. They got in the truck. The guy handed me a business card that said *Jasmine Escort Service.* "Call when you're ready," he said, and with that they drove off.

When in doubt about something, when life gets too crazy or complicated, go surfing. Being out in the waves was the real world for me. I spent the day at Bondi Beach, escaping if only for a few hours, into a great surf session. I was walking up to my car when a dark van pulled up. Two suits got out, opened the back doors to the van and told me to get in. They were Aussies and I figured them for narcs. I hesitated. One moved around in back making it clear there was nowhere to run. I asked if I was being arrested. "Just get in, James, or we can help you."

"I'd like to call a lawyer."

"Get in the van now."

"My board."

"A nice one, mate. Now leave it." This hurt.

I got in the van, the doors slammed and they dove off. As I looked out the back window at my board lying in the parking lot, I figured this is it, I'm busted. I'm going away for a long stretch. We drove through Sydney and finally stopped in an industrial area near the harbor. The doors opened and they had me get out. I stood there blinking in the bright sunlight, dockworkers and deliverymen and me in my surf trunks. One of the suits told me to go across the street and go into the phone booth. What the fuck? What did they mean? But I went over and stood in the booth while my abductors drove off. My confusion grew as the minutes ticked off. Then the phone rang and I answered. "Hello, James." It was Patricia Adams.

"Patricia!" Without so much as a conscious thought, the bad boy in me began scheming how I would lie to Andi and then spend a steamy afternoon in a hotel room with her. Just the sound of her voice made me want to feel that again. "You're in Sydney?" I asked.

"No."

"Well, where are you?"

"It doesn't matter. Listen carefully. Your van arrived."

I had a sinking feeling I was getting a warning. "Uh...ok."

"No, not ok. Do not pick up the van." I stood there silent for a moment as the bubble burst. "James... you understand me? Do you hear what I'm saying?"

"Yeah."

"Tell no one about this call, especially not your loudmouth partner. He's being closely monitored. The police are waiting for him to go for your Rover."

"I've told him and he's not listening. How did they get onto us?"

"There's a hyper alert in customs now due to the discovery of a huge cache. I'm sure you know about it... Garrett Jones."

There was a humming in my ears and some gut instinct reached for salvage. Maybe, just maybe..."Fuck, bad timing. I want to see you again, Patricia."

"That can't happen. Let me emphasize – if you divulge to anyone that I warned you, there will be consequences. You really do not want to take that chance."

"Don't worry. Does customs have my name?"

"Let's hope not. They have the name on the carnet du passage. But it's not safe for you in Sydney now. If I were you, I'd make myself scarce. Take a trip somewhere, James. You need to disappear."

"How about to where you are?" *What was I saying?*

"You have a nice girl, James. Stick with her."

"What about Grant? Have you heard anything?"

"He's M.I.A. Karina is with Tariq, and that's where it ends."

She hung up. I took a cab back to Bondi and of course my board had been stolen.

I finally got hold of Jack and we made a plan to meet at the King's Head Pub that evening. He was an hour late. I went outside to look around for him and he drove up in that ostentatious ride. At first sight, I knew something had happened because he was frazzled. I asked him what was up and he said, "I hit a dog in the road." He pointed to the front fender, which was dented and had blood on it.

"You killed a dog?"

"I don't know."

"What do you mean you don't know?"

"I didn't stop."

"Oh fuck, that sucks. Hit and run on a dog."

"It happens. As I recall, my boy, you hit a dog on the road through Turkey. And then we ran."

"The point is you're already on the police's radar. Our van

is under surveillance in customs. If they tie you to your fake name on the Carnet du Passage, we're fucked."

"You sure about this? How do you know?"

"I got a tip from a friend who works in customs," I lied.

He thought for a moment, "I'll figure it out. We'll get our van."

"Forget it. They're waiting for you to go pick it up and when you do, they're going to bust you. So that's it. It's over."

"No, my boy, not over by a long shot," he announced with that mad gleam he had when some crazy plan was percolating in his fevered brain.

"No, Jack. Don't even think about it. We are not retrieving that load." I wasn't going to walk into a trap and I wasn't going to let him do it either, because if he got busted, there was a good chance that I'd go next.

"You're ready to take a loss of a million dollars?"

"Yeah. And thank God I found out the load was being surveilled before we went in to get it. We're going to consider ourselves lucky and write this off, Jack."

"Well, not necessarily, my boy," he said, "I have connections with all kinds of people. I think we can get it out."

"How?"

"Pay off the customs people is one possibility."

"Too risky."

"I can pull it off."

"You that sure, huh?"

"Even if I can't, there are other ways to get the hash."

I knew where he was going with this and shook my head, but he was hell bent on his plans, "I don't think they guard the holding area too heavily, and I know some people that can get the job done," he said, his excitement rising. "Or we can go ahead and bust it out ourselves!"

I had a sinking feeling that this was going from bad to worse. "Bust it out? What the fuck do you mean, Jack? Go in there with guns and hold the place up?"

"Just like Bonnie and Clyde."

"No, that is insane. We go that route and we'll be up for armed robbery next, and that gets you life, Jack. Life. And maybe a murder charge? Say somebody gets killed?"

He said, "Oh, that won't happen, and if it does, they'll never catch us."

"You have lost your fucking mind. There's no way. We are not doing that. I am not doing that."

Short of tying Jack up in my basement there was really no way to stop him if he actually decided to go through with his crazy idea. I thought it best to distance myself from him and think about my own future, but the problem was I was tied to Jack.

The next day, Andi and I went to my bank and pulled all the cash out of my safety deposit box. I felt like I was being watched so I gave the money to Andi and told her to take it to my brother for safe-keeping. After she did that she called me at our house from a payphone. She said, "I'm being watched. I'm sure of it."

I told her to come home and that it was all going to be okay. I had a plan. I was worried, though. I knew I could play it safe and cool, but Jack could not. I had to somehow get him to stop being so fucking ostentatious and crazy. I had him meet me at the Lord Dudley Hotel, a pub in Woollahra. I ordered a 1970 Laffite Rothschild Bordeaux and Chateaubriand to keep him happy. "Look," I said, "things have really escalated here. I'm being tailed and so is Andi. This is no game anymore. We're looking at a lot of jail time if we get busted."

"We've faced that possibility from the beginning and come through unscathed every time. Not to worry, my boy."

"Jack, you, particularly, are looking at time. The Carnet de passages are held in your name."

"Byron Rimbaud, I believe is the holder of said document."

"It's got your fucking address on it! So does your car registration. You bought the Hawk using the name Byron Rimbaud, remember?"

"I know people that can help me out with our situation. I'm not worried."

"Well, I'm worried. We're probably being watched right now. Let's forget the hash."

"That is not only the coward's way out, but also insane," Jack said.

"This is the fucking feds, mate! You're not dealing with the locals anymore. Do you seriously think you have the feds in your pocket?"

"Nonsense." Jack raised his voice loud enough for everyone in the place to hear, "Are there any feds here?"

That caused a little uproar and after it died down, I said, "We need to disappear. One of us goes to Perth, one goes to Adelaide. Take your pick."

"No, my friend, no, thank you." And his look turned serious. "I'm not abandoning what we worked so hard for."

"Listen to me! We have to lay low. We want to be like lizards in the desert. We need to get under some rocks, let this pass over for a while. Take a month or two if we have to. Whatever, and then reconvene and see where things stand. Come on back to my place and we'll smoke some hash and hash things out."

He laughed. There was nothing I could do. It was going to be every man for himself. The problem was if he went down, I would be busted, too, unless I was long gone.

I got up to leave and my leg was throbbing so bad I could hardly stand. I had an ulcerated laceration on my calf that was erupting. I'd cut myself on some rocks surfing and it was now an ugly painful mess. It never really healed properly and I needed to have it lanced and stitched. I gave Jack one last chance to get on board, but he was arrogant and hardheaded as ever. "Okay. Cool," I said. "Do it your way."

I hobbled out of there and went straight to my doctor in Sydney. Turned out it was a good thing I did. If I'd gone straight home or to Jack's house, I would have gotten busted.

After our meeting at the pub, Jack had gone back to where he lived at his mother's mansion in Double Bay and lo and behold, there were six federal narcotics agents waiting for "Byron Rimbaud." I found this out when I called after I left the doc. Jack's mother answered, "Yes, hello?"

"Hi, Edna, is Jack there?"

"Well, he was, but..." I could hear her stifling a few tears.

"What happened, Edna?"

"Some government men just came by and took Jack away. They say he was using a fake name. And that he hit a dog. And that he has a car with drugs in it in customs." She knew what was going on. Over the years she'd seen the big bricks of hash under the bed and the bundles of money and fake passports. And she had turned a blind eye to the elephant in the room because she was in her own world. She loved her crazy ass son, thought him a genius who could do whatever he wanted and get away with it.

I said to her, "This is very, very serious, Edna. I'll see what I can do for Jack. Meanwhile you need to do two things for me. One, if the feds ask you about Jack's associates, you don't even remember my name. And two, if there's anything that Jack left in the house, anything the feds didn't find, just burn it. You're not going to see me for a very, very long time. Do we understand each other?"

She said, "I think so," in her Aussie mom voice.

I called Andi and she said the feds had been there looking for me and also at my Mum's place. I told her I loved her and that I'd be in touch again soon as I could. I hung up the phone and said out loud, "This is fucking it. I'm gone." I needed a safe house to buy a little time and make a plan. I had a friend with a cabin in the hills behind Sydney in a place called French's Forest. I went up there and called my brother, "I need to meet you. Bring me some clothes and some cash. One other thing I've got to do is talk to Mum. Go over to her work and say you're taking her out for lunch. And then I want you to bring her up here."

Later that day my brother arrived with Mum and I came clean, "Mum, you know that trip I went on? Well, I didn't go to Perth and Darwin and the Seychelles." Her look told me she had had a feeling about that. "I ended up in the Middle East and I ended up smuggling hashish, and it didn't go well, and now I need to get out of the country. Fast." I could see her go a little weak in the knees. But Mum had tons of pluck. "Son, I had a notion there was something going on. Well, don't you worry. You just take care of yourself and get to where you'll be safe." She was so supportive that I lost it and hugged her a while. After Mum drove away with my brother, I called Andi and told her I didn't know where I was going exactly but I'd call in a month and arrange for her to meet me. "Everything is coming down. But we'll figure it out, Andi." Between the tears we vowed love for each other and that was it.

Next thing I knew I was at the airport. I got to the ticket counter and still wasn't sure where I was going. Hawaii or L.A. or Texas or New York...

"Young hearts be free tonight. Time is on your side. We got just one shot at life, let's take it while we're still not afraid. Because life is so brief and time is a thief when you're undecided..."

EPILOGUE

I hadn't left Sydney, but was already feeling nostalgic for my city, my family and my girl. I didn't really know where I was going. In those days you could turn up at the airport and make a last-minute decision. As I approached the ticket counter, I considered whether or not I'd go back to Texas where I was born. I liked Texas, but I always thought it was a good place to be *from*. I wasn't sure whether I wanted to go back there to live. Just a little too... *Texas*. New York sounded really exciting, but it was a big concrete jungle, and not a lot of surf. Hawaii had lots of surf, but not much else going on. So, it really narrowed down to L.A., which had a little bit of everything. I bought a ticket to the City of the Angels.

I strolled onto the plane feeling a sense of relief. We started taxiing out and were about three minutes down the runway when the pilot came on and said, "Sorry, ladies and gentlemen but we're going to head back to the terminal."

I thought they'd run my name and the cops wanted me back there. This was it. Busted. "Oh shit!" I said out loud. I was in the aisle seat and the guy next to me saw how agitated I was and asked, "What's wrong mate?"

I said, "I just got a bad feeling about things."

He said, "Don't worry about this. I fly all the time. Seen

this situation before. Probably one of those landing lights out on the wing."

Little did he know. I said, "Oh man, I hope you're right."

We taxied back to the terminal and no cops boarded the plane. The pilot and co-pilot didn't yank me out of my seat. My helpful neighbor nudged me with his elbow as he glanced out the window, "Yeah, just a light," he said. Sure enough, some maintenance guys were in a cherry picker rising up to the wing. They walked out to the tip and began replacing that bulb. Ten minutes later the ground crew had the light glowing and they floated away in their cherry picker. We taxied back onto the tarmac for takeoff. With a sigh of relief and as soon as we were sky high, I ordered a couple of stiff drinks. Twelve hours later we landed in L.A. and my new life began.

I got through customs just fine, walked out into a warm Lotus Land night, struck by the traffic noise and smell of fossil fuels. I really was perplexed as to what to do. I had limited bucks and no idea where to go. I knew one person in L.A. One of my old smuggling contacts, and he said, "James, the Chateau Marmont Hotel is *the* cool place to stay."

The Chateau Marmont was a hip gothic castle of a place built in the 1920's, with vaulted ceilings and cavernous lobbies. I would have been right at home there, but I only had a couple grand in my pocket. I called my friend back and told him I needed a beer budget kind of joint.

He suggested a downscale infamous fleabag on Santa Monica Boulevard called the Tropicana Motel. I pulled my rental car into the parking lot of a funky sprawling old flop-house with a legendary greasy-spoon out front called Duke's Diner. Classic. A drug and sex Mecca if there ever was one, a kind of halfway house for wannabe rock and rollers who were descending on Los Angeles in droves. And then you had the usual fringe crowd of hippies, hookers and pimps. And in the shadowed recesses of the dank hallways lay the heroin junkies. Occasionally they'd venture out into the light and you'd see them nodding out by the pool, drooling on themselves. Or waiting at one of the payphones for their connect to call them back, or they were hitting you up for bus fare and hot dog money.

After I stayed three weeks in the Tropicana, I found an inexpensive apartment down in the slums of east Hollywood on Kingsley Drive in an old, ravaged, once elegant apartment building. I thought it was going to be quieter than the Tropicana, but every night there were helicopters buzzing the neighborhood looking for bad guys.

Once I got situated, Andi came over to live with me. At first, she was excited to try something new and was stoked about all the wild shit going on and the night life. Which was great except I didn't have the big fat rolls of cash that I used to have, and we were living in a landlocked, noisy, dangerous relic instead of a beach house on the Gold Coast. But Andi hung in there and I got a job in construction. Then who showed up in town but Garrett, Mr. Big himself. He'd grown up in Hollywood and was home now after he broke up with Maggie back in Hawaii. Not much of a surprise she couldn't handle life on the run. It was just too much stress because Garrett had a big target on his back and had to roll super low key, change his identity, change his hair color, grow a beard. It was a whole new life and image he'd had to create for himself, and so Maggie went back to Sydney to live with her family.

The irony was her sister was in Hollywood with me.

Andi was excited at the prospect of starting a new life. I thought, "Maybe I could do a little dealing here. And get us back to the style of living to which we were accustomed. I explored the idea but abandoned it quickly. Partly because I just didn't know anybody in the biz except for my one buddy who had steered me to the Chateau Marmont and he was dealing smack. I wasn't going down that road for sure. I had definitely learned my lesson. I could have gone into the coke and pot trade, but you need resources to set up shop and, too, I felt very exposed. The whole L.A. dealing scene was different from what it was in Sydney. There's much more of a gun presence in America and especially in the L.A. drug underworld, and all of it was getting under my skin. I decided that phase of my life had run its course and was ready to take Patricia Adams' advice. I was going to do something different. But what? I did some construction work, a little plumbing, which I hated. Then one day I looked in the newspaper and saw, "Make a Hundred-Thousand Dollars a Year! Red Carpet Realty, Century 21." I thought, That's it. I love real estate and I love mansions. And I can sell, sell, sell.

I fell into a job in a curious way. Andi was waiting tables and it was hard because she didn't have a green card, so we went down to the courthouse and got married. Bureaucratic shotgun. We did that and went down to the Santa Monica Pier and celebrated with a bottle of champagne.

We were hanging out by the Merry-Go-Round and we met an energetic, smooth talking real estate agent working out of an office in Pacific Palisades. After I got my real estate license, he gave me a job and I launched my real estate career.

I soon found out that to make it in the legit sales world, you had to work dawn to dusk and beyond. You had to think, live, and breathe *deals*. I was constantly on the phone or running all over the Westside at a moment's notice to show a house. I was forever schmoozing and boozing because that was what it took. Andi hated it. What was worse, she couldn't find a job she liked. She decided she was going to learn how to be a belly dancer. I was struggling selling houses and we were drifting into our separate worlds. Finally, we parted ways and she went back to Sydney to pursue her belly dancing dreams.

My real estate career gradually started to take off and by the mid-eighties, I was not only successful, I was *known*.

Mr. Big was always trying to put some kind of deal together even while keeping himself under the radar. He got popped for selling heroin, skipped bail, went on the run again.

Jack ended up getting five years in the slammer. I think he had a secret desire to get busted. It was the *romantic* thing to do. Like him wanting to be a drug smuggler because his hero Rimbaud ran guns to the natives in Africa. What's the next best thing to being a drug smuggler? In Jack's mind, it was being a convict walking the Big Yard.

A few years later I read in the paper that Tim Flannery went missing in Cambodia. He'd gone up there on a story about the Khmer Rouge and never came back.

Patricia Adams stayed in the CIA and became the first woman Associate Director. I tried to get hold of her numerous times to no avail. I was hoping she could tell me something about what happened to Grant. There was no denying that I also just wanted to see her. Something had clicked with us – call it magnetism, or whatever. I still had the fantasy, especially after Andi and I broke up, that one day a black limo would pull up. A stone-faced agent would get out, open the rear door and there Patricia would be – with her Rolex off and her hair down.

Grant... what happened to him? It took me a while, but finally I went to Pakistan to search for him. And that's another story.

ABOUT THE AUTHOR

Randy Holland is an Emmy Award winning writer and filmmaker. His work has been seen on HBO, Showtime, and PBS networks. His film on the Los Angeles riots, "The Fire This Time", premiered at the Sundance Film Festival and was nominated for the Grand Jury Prize. The film was also nominated for a Writers Guild of America award and during its TV run was an L.A. *Times* "Pick of the Week" twice. Holland has written extensively for episodic television and film, and as a journalist been nominated for the Sidney Hillman Award and George Polk Award.